TRINITY

PUGLIA'S SON

Liminal Books

TRINITY

PUGLIA'S SON

Steven Zizza

For Grace, a daughter of Puglia

War Wounds

Guilt can crush a person's soul, leaving its rotting corpse exposed to the harsh realities of a cruel and unforgiving world. A decaying pile of dust is often its final gift to the tormented. It can destroy the essence of the strongest individual and drive him to the darkest regions of despair and torment. Left unchecked, guilt is a spiritual squatter and dominatrix, an unwanted houseguest whose power flourishes when flogging its victims' souls to a drum's constant beat of anguish and hopelessness. It will tie you down, twisting and turning your life into knots before making you, its servant.

War provides a clear and horrifying example of the fatal power of guilt, whose influence reigns supreme over life and death. *What if* is a common lament for the inflicted and resonates as an uninterrupted nightmare 24 hours a day seven days a week. For one young man, guilt's enormity would be life changing. Its damaging effect would be revealed to all the residents and staff of a military hospital during the Second World War.

Our story begins on a beautiful and warm June morning. The hospital's energy, normally a frenzied pace that was comparable to worker bees performing their seemingly choreographed tasks in the operation of a well-functioning hive, manifested a different level of vitality that day. For a brief moment, nurses were no longer running feverishly from patient to patient, skillfully attending to each soldier's wounds and pain. A young orderly had just burst into the ward with his arms raised and screamed for all to hear that the Allies had landed in Normandy and Rome had been captured without a fight. "Our guys landed in France and they're kicking ass! Rome is ours too!" None of the hospital medical staff would chide the young man for his salty language that day. The end of the war was in sight and that's all that mattered.

Everyone in the ward reacted with unrestrained joy at the announcement and shared the same thought as each person looked toward heaven, praying to a merciful God to protect friends and family members who were still fighting at the front. "The war will be over soon! Please God!" The news had provided the nurses with a welcomed respite from changing bandages that covered festering wounds, holding a crying soldier reliving the horrors of war or reading heart-breaking letters from their loved ones. Several of the men would lie still and emotionless as they listened to nurses reading letters from mothers, wives, and girlfriends. The love expressed in the letters was not something they understood or could accept. It wasn't that war made them unfeeling or cold-hearted. Rather, these men believed they were undeserving recipients of any love, internally or externally. Their attention was primarily focused on the dead brothers whom they left behind. It was a massive guilt that consumed them. Why were they saved and not their buddies who paid the ultimate price for family and country? This was a familiar refrain that would play in their minds daily, and it would take time and patience for these young men to recover mentally, physically, and spiritually.

A chorus of claps and cheers continued to echo throughout the ward for several minutes. Nurses, recovering from the initial shock of the news, scurried from bed to bed in a vain attempt to calm patients who had tried to stand upright and celebrate. "Boys, please lie back down. You'll tear your stitches." But it was no use; these young men could not be restrained that day. For a moment, they set aside their pain. It had been nearly three years since Pearl Harbor, and everyone wanted the war to end soon. The nurses had no choice but to let this burst of emotion run its course and to hope no one got seriously hurt. Nurses received an extra allotment of hugs from their patients that day.

Everyone working at the hospital had been touched by the war in one way or another. Some of the hospital staff had seen the results of combat firsthand at triage stations near the front, while others had family members who were sent overseas to fight. Often, nurses could be heard simultaneously whispering in contemplative prayer when not comforting the wounded. It didn't matter whether they were old or young, married or unmarried; each had a maternal side that was visible to all. Their most common appeals to Heaven were, "God, please protect my baby," and "Bring our boys home safe and sound." After all, they still thought of these warriors as boys. That opinion never changed.

The barracks-style hospital at Camp Edwards on Cape Cod had been built several years earlier to house convalescing soldiers. It was for those men who were injured defending their country and battling an enemy that refused to surrender — the ravages of war clearly evident on their faces, bodies, and minds. For some hospital staff, it was difficult emotionally to handle the stress of seeing the casualties of war up close. It was a common sight for nurses and doctors to shed a tear when admitting a new patient. The sight of a 20-year-old boy with a leg blown off by a land mine wreaked havoc on the psyche of even the most hardened soul.

Wounded doctors and nurses were also here; they were remarkable individuals who put themselves in harm's way to save lives at numerous frontline field and evacuation hospitals. War was a dirty business. No one was safe or immune from its effects.

The news about Rome was notably heartwarming for a son of Italy. Rocco Farfalla had recently been sent back to the States to recuperate from his wounds, which were both mental and physical. His division had recently fought in the advance up the coast from Naples to Rome. The battle over rocky terrain was a long and brutal one for an army of young men and boys. Multiple bullet holes and lacerations to his arm and leg were considered million-dollar wounds that bought him a ticket home. While these wounds got Rocco a second Purple Heart to go with the various other medals for bravery he received during the war, they carried a heavy toll for a young man with a heart of gold.

Americans had become familiar with far-off places like North Africa, Sicily, and mainland Italy, not as tourist destinations but as battle zones, where humanity inflicted immeasurable cruelty on itself. Two years before arriving at Camp Edwards, Rocco had volunteered to fight for his adopted country and to save his family from the ravages of war and a life of desperation. He saw family as the most precious thing in life. Losing them wasn't an option. Thoughts of surviving the war and bringing his family to the US armed him with a personal mission, while still trying to save the world from the horrors of fascism. While Rocco had immigrated to the US prior to the start of the war, his family had stayed behind, biding their time until they could join him. War interrupted that dream in 1939 when Poland was invaded and defeated in less than six weeks. The Polish army was steamrolled by Nazi Germany and Soviet Russia, two political systems at opposite ends of the political landscape but allies for the purpose of regaining territory lost twenty years earlier at the conclusion of the Great War. That arrangement would change in 1940 when Russia was invaded by the Wehrmacht juggernaut.

Rocco's story was the most gut-wrenching tale the hospital staff had ever heard. Army Command sent him home in May to recuperate; he had done enough in service for his adopted country. It was time to heal. Rocco was a hero, damaged by war and the monstrous actions of others, but he survived. The hospital staff was amazed at how his gentle soul could endure the horrors and pain of an unimaginable ordeal.

As the celebration began to settle down and the ward returned to a more normal state, Rocco sat in his wheelchair peering out a window that was next to his bed. He had a different focus. He was expecting his family's arrival at the hospital for their daily visit, and he wanted to be ready. Libby Endicott, a recent graduate of a local nursing school, was providing the young hero a good deal of extra attention, as she normally did. Everyone could see that she had a bit of a crush on Rocco. She sat with Rocco during the entire celebration, fixated on the health of her patient. Turning her head to view the festivities continuing throughout the ward, Libby smiled as she surveyed the celebration and took note of the unbridled sounds of joy filling the room, "Wow, what a great day! I hope we get more good news tomorrow."

While still peering out the window, Rocco's manner was cold and dismissive. "I doubt it. People are animals. The war will only stop when they're put down."

Rocco's reaction frightened her. She had never seen someone look so unsympathetic or detached from the world. Needing a moment to regain her senses, Libby decided that it was best to change the subject quickly. The young nurse gently leaned over and touched his hand.

"Rocco, would you like to go outside to the courtyard? It looks like it's going to be a beautiful day."

Rocco smiled softly at his lovely nurse and looked at the happy faces throughout the ward. "In more ways than one it seems."

"Good point. Let's go, Ranger." Always the proper young lady, Libby rose slowly from her seat and gently fixed her uniform. She smiled from ear to ear as she took hold of the handles on Rocco's wheelchair. The young man had a way about him that made others feel at ease. Everyone was his friend. Libby couldn't envision any person being his enemy.

Some of the patients who knew his story wished him a nice visit with his family. "Hey, Rocco, it's gonna be a nice day. Say hi to your family for us." It was the only way they could show compassion for their battered, but not defeated, brother.

"Thanks guys. Don't wait up for me." Rocco's attempt at humor was always well received; however, they could only manage a half-hearted smile. There was a sadness in their eyes that told a different story. A person's eyes are said to be the pathway to the soul; however, for these particular souls, they were filled with anger and sorrow.

Libby slowly wheeled Rocco out toward the courtyard to await his family's arrival. Passing Dr. Raines and Nurse Maggie, Rocco raised his right arm in joy. He could only raise one arm because the other was wrapped tightly to his body. "Doc, my family's coming again today. Isn't it great?"

The doctor peeled his attention away from a hospital chart he had been studying, one of the several troubling cases of a patient not improving quickly enough. He put his hand on Rocco's shoulder to comfort him and smiled. "Yes, it is, Rocco. Have a nice visit but don't get too excited. I'll check your bandages later today."

The young soldier remained animated and waved his good hand in response to the doctor's request. "No worries about that, Doc. Hey, Nurse Maggie, you're looking especially gorgeous today, doll. When are we going on a date? You can't say no forever."

Maggie Reilly, a kind and loving woman in her late forties, laughed at today's version of his daily flirtation. "OK Romeo, I think you need to focus on someone your own age." A nod and a wink in Libby's direction emphasized her point. The older nurse had the appearance and emotional resonance of a caring maternal figure, who had a natural ability of connecting with her children, that is to say, the hospital's patients and staff. A person couldn't help but feel good and safe when near her.

Rocco's eyes sparkled as they stopped for a moment to chat. "No way. These young girls don't know nothing about having fun. No offense Libby. Just wait until these bandages come off. We'll go dancing." Rocco scooted his hips in his wheelchair as much as the pain would allow to emphasize his point.

Maggie waved her index finger in jest at her youthful paramour. "You naughty boy. What are we going to do with you? It's a good thing you're cute. Libby, please put our Romeo next to the roses. It's especially sunny there now and the buds are blooming full today."

The young nurse continued the trek to the courtyard. "Yes, I will. I have the place already picked out."

Rocco bellowed with delight. "Oh boy. It looks like I got two girls!" Turning his head to gaze at Libby as he was being wheeled away, our young hero gave the object of his affection a subtle wink and whispered. "Don't worry, you're still my best girl. I'll try to let Maggie down gently."

The motherly nurse laughed at Rocco's humorous indiscretion. "You're such a rascal." Her laughter was abbreviated by thoughts of her own boys fighting in the Pacific. She took a deep breath and sighed. "Poor soul. I hope he is going to be OK. He reminds me of my boys." One son was island hopping his way to Tokyo with the rest of the First Marine Division. The other was a sailor on the Enterprise, the Big E, the toughest ship in the Navy. Boys quickly became men on the decks and beaches of the South Pacific. The bonds these men formed would last a lifetime, but only another mother could imagine what it felt like to send her child off to war. That invisible umbilical cord remained attached no matter where they went, affixing mother to child through eternity.

Dr. Raines nodded his head in agreement with Maggie's sentiments but was discouraged by his patient's slower than desired mental recovery. "If he doesn't improve, we may need to send him to Pilgrim in New York, and none of us wants that." They both looked at each other, helplessly looking for comfort, not only for Rocco but for their own peace of mind. Suddenly, however, with a hint of anger rising within them, Maggie shared her thoughts, "Those bastards got what they deserved."

Dr. Raines stared resolutely at Rocco being wheeled away and agreed. "Damn right. I hope they burn in Hell."

Libby set up Rocco in a prime location to await his family. The sun's radiance created a halo that surrounded him, showing others in the yard that day how exceptional he was. Walking back to the main ward, the young nurse reflected on Rocco's tragic story. She turned to look back at this brave soldier and remained motionless, staring at a young man who had gone through hell and survived. Tears rolled down her cheeks as she reflected on what happened to him. It was something that could never be forgotten.

At that moment, Joe, a new volunteer at the hospital, noticed Libby from across the courtyard and waved to her. His greeting went unnoticed. Puzzled at the lack of a response, Joe ambled over to her and gently touched her shoulder. "Hey, are you OK?"

Lost in her own thoughts, Libby was startled upon hearing Joe's greeting. The young nurse clasped her hands tightly against her chest and shouted. "Ahhhh!" She slowly regained her composure with a recuperative exhale and several taps to her chest. "Oh, hi, Joe. Just lost in my thoughts. You scared the heck out of me. No fishing today?"

"No, I thought I'd spend a few hours with the boys today. Some could use a bit of extra attention." Joe nodded in the direction of Rocco. "But I see one already has yours."

Libby blushed and smiled. "Oh stop."

Joe then asked a question that the young nurse wasn't expecting. "Do you know that young man's story? You may know what happened at his last battle, but do you know his whole story?"

She was puzzled at the question. "No, but how do you know?"

Joe shrugged his shoulders. "Ah, my angel, let's just say I know a lot about these young warriors. Each one of these men has a remarkable story but Rocco Farfalla has one that Hollywood would kill for. It's the sort of story that would leave a person cheering one minute and crying the next. It may shake your faith in humanity and the Almighty. Would you like to hear it?"

Libby quivered in her response while attempting to steel herself to hear Joe's account of Rocco's life. "Yes, please, but I don't understand how you know…"

At this point, Joe noticed someone familiar staring at him from the opposite end of the courtyard, making him extremely uncomfortable. Joe interrupted her question mid-sentence. "Let's do this another day. I just remembered I need to be somewhere."

"OK, I need to get back to the ward anyway. Maybe we can meet tomorrow?"

"Sure, tomorrow or the next day. I'll find you. Until then, be well and keep a close eye on our young friend. I know I didn't have to tell you that last part." Joe snickered with his last statement.

Libby tilted her head and looked sideways at her friend. "You seem to know a lot of things, don't you? It's a little odd."

Joe laughed. "Don't worry, I'm a friend to both of you." His mood changed quickly as the familiar individual moved closer to him. He became more and more uncomfortable with each passing second. He quickly excused himself. "But I need to go right now."

Libby turned to walk away, still saddened by the prospect of hearing Rocco's story. Libby suddenly felt ill at ease with each step she took; a premonition of danger came to her. She felt she was being watched carefully and with bad intention, but by whom? Her radar defense was on full alert. Her body shivered with a coldness more appropriate for a raw January morning, not June. She stopped and scanned the courtyard to see if she could find anyone suspicious. Her attention ultimately became focused on Joe speaking to someone. She could see the outline of a nurse's uniform. Libby took a step toward them, angling her head to catch a glimpse of the nurse, but she couldn't make out who the person was. She was pointing her finger at Joe in a manner of a parent or teacher scolding a child. Joe shrugged his shoulders as a child would do to proclaim his innocence. Noticing that Libby was moving toward them, Joe motioned to the nurse that they needed to depart. The two quickly slipped away into the building before Libby could take another step towards them. Their hastiness to exit the courtyard piqued her curiosity of finding out the nurse's identity and the topic of their animated discussion.

Libby remained momentarily frozen in place pondering her misgivings about this unknown colleague. Questions shot through her mind in rapid fire. *Who was she? What did she want? Why was she with Joe? Was she the reason for her anxiety and uneasiness?*

Libby centered her mind by thinking about Rocco. At that moment, thoughts of him made her feel more at ease for some reason. It was as if someone had just planted the thought in her mind. She wished Joe was able to tell Rocco's story. She knew it would be a remarkable chronicle of a man with whom she had fallen in love. Parts of it were known around the ward, but the whole horror story would have to wait for Joe's recital.

The only other person who knew Rocco's story was Rocco, but he was lost in a world of delusion and guilt. Libby glanced at Rocco waiting patiently in his wheelchair for his family to come for a visit. Bowing her head, she could only think about the extreme sadness buried deep in his soul. She whispered to herself, "How did he get to this point?" Libby did know two things; Rocco loved his family, and he would do anything for them.

Several days later, Joe left a mysterious note for her at the nurses' desk.

> *Libby, meet me in the chapel at noon today. I want to tell you*
> *Rocco's story. This may sound strange but don't tell anyone.*
> *– Joe*

Naturally, Libby found the note odd. Why was he being so secretive? Was it because of what Rocco did or was it because of that mysterious nurse he was speaking to in the courtyard the other day? Who was this nurse? She had seen her around the ward recently, often near Rocco, but every time she tried to approach her, the nurse would conveniently slip away. Clutching the note tightly, Libby continued to reflect on the note's meaning. Her thoughts raced repeatedly over the same questions. Why? What? Who? Over and over, she asked herself these questions, but ultimately knew there wouldn't be any good answers until noon.

As requested, Libby kept silent about the meeting and made her way to the chapel at the appointed hour. Opening the heavy wooden doors slowly and reverently, the young nurse found Joe sitting in a pew and staring peculiarly at the crucifix. His manner wasn't contemplative or supplicative as one would expect in a chapel. Rather, he looked more perplexed and bewildered, seemingly uncertain of what stood in front of him. At one point, Joe shook his head and exhaled dismissively.

Libby walked up beside him quietly and stretched out her hand to tap her friend on the shoulder, but Joe knew she was coming. "Good morning, angel. Or is it good afternoon?"

"How did you know it was me? Did you hear me? I was very quiet."

Snickering flippantly, Joe slid down the pew to make room for his friend to sit. "Oh, I have eyes in the back of my head."

Libby was slightly annoyed at Joe's irreverent attitude. "I guess so. Well, I'm here. What do you want to talk about? And why so secretive?"

"I'm sorry for being mysterious but the walls have eyes and ears. No one can spy on us in here."

"What does that mean? What does this have to do with Rocco? All this cloak and dagger stuff belongs in a movie. Please, just tell me what you have to say."

Joe regretted his comments. "Forget about the walls, angel. I'm sorry for saying anything. Sometimes, I have a big mouth." Joe leaned back in the pew. "But I do want to talk to you about Rocco and to tell his story. He reminds me so much of my youth, growing up in Portugal. I am having a little difficulty gathering my thoughts."

Libby leaned toward Joe and touched his hand gently. "I see that his story has affected you and it's not going to be easy for you to tell; but please, will you try for me?"

"Angel, for you I will."

Family

What can someone say about a daily existence of grey and rust, twin offspring of a decaying world? Scrape and peel, scrape and peel. That was Rocco's place in the world, all the while hoping for something better, something pure. They said America was the land of opportunity. For his family, he never abandoned that dream. It's the reason a teenage boy left behind his old life in Italy and came to Boston with the goal of earning enough money that could extricate his family from a life of abject poverty and misery.

Puglia is a beautiful region in Southern Italy, but it's a land trapped in the jaws of an unforgiving history. Conquered many times over the centuries by foreign powers because of its strategic location in the Mediterranean, Puglia's people persevered through so many hardships and tribulations that it produced a people bonded together strongly as family. *Alla famiglia* was a familiar expression amongst her people to celebrate the strength of their bonds.

Conquerors came from all countries to own a land located at the center of the Mediterranean and to take advantage of its rich soil. Hannibal came from Carthage to wrest control from the Romans. From the defeat of Hannibal, the Roman reconquest, the ultimate fall of the Roman Empire centuries later, and the havoc wreaked by barbarian armies, the land would become a flash point between the two main superpowers of the Dark Ages: the Byzantines — the inheritors of the Roman Empire in the East — and Saracen Moors. Religion and greed would drive the actions of competing armies for centuries as they would continue to do into the modern age.

Eventually, other European nations came as well to re-establish Western European dominance. War and misery became collective elements in the history of Puglia; however, her people persevered and grew stronger.

Hard work and poverty were the common ingredients of life's daily soup with tragedy sometimes mixed in. Many looked for an escape from this reality to a new existence, one that would offer some semblance of prosperity and peace. For Rocco, this escape meant working the Trans-Atlantic ships sailing from Naples and taking immigrants to America. It was decent money for a 14-year-old. Actually, anything more than zero was decent money. Rocco was big for his age and could easily pass for someone much older. Then again, a lot of people from Southern Italy looked older. It was a natural outcome of a life of hard work and poverty that could weather the bodies but not the hearts of the Pugliese.

While the money he sent back home was a welcome contribution to the family's finances, it wasn't always enough to help support a mother, father and two younger sisters. Papa, an experienced cobbler, worked as much as he could, however, the pains he felt in his hands from the wounds he suffered in the Great War limited the amount of work he could do. There were days when his hands resembled claws rather than something human. There were candlelit nights when a loving wife would rub oil on his hands at the end of a long and grueling day, trying to soothe the agonizing pain he was feeling. For the entire time, this strong and beautiful woman would sing a love song to her husband who would fight the pain with grimaces but never complain. Mostly, he would stare at his wife and express his love for her. "Valentina, why are you with such a helpless man? I married the most beautiful girl in Tranquillo, and she got the runt of the litter. I am not worthy of you."

Valentina always had a comedic and loving response to this question. "Matteo, what could I do? I was defenseless to your charms. You always made an extra effort to work in front of my parents' house and find a way to take off your shirt. *Mascalzone — you rascal. Ti Amo.*" Her gentle laughter would fill the room.

Matteo would sit mesmerized, staring into her eyes as she continued to sing a love song to him, never stopping her healing touch. *"Anch'io, ti amo, amore mio — I love you too, my love."*

On special Sundays after the harvest, father and son would form an unbreakable bond, making their locally famous homemade wine. Matteo would laugh that drinking their wine was the best way to put hair on Rocco's chest someday. Well, it didn't work. His son's face and chest remained as smooth as a baby's bottom, a reflection of the innocence of this young man's soul.

His father never wanted a journeyman's life for his son. Something stable and productive was always his dream. Working on the ship was not something that made Rocco's dad happy. "Rocco, you need to find a nice girl some day and have a big family. It will be the best time of your life."

The young lad was always quick to respond, "Girls, they're crazy. They always bother me." What else would a 10-year-old say? As Rocco loaded more grapes into the wine press, Matteo couldn't hold back his laughter at hearing his son's response. Taking a moment to stop working the manual wine press, Matteo slapped his young son's back,

"Well, I guess we should have named you Romeo." He knew the apple didn't fall far from the tree.

Rocco continued, "Oh, please stop, Papa. Girls make me sick. They are only good for giving me a headache."

Apparently, the fairer sex's attraction to Rocco was evident at an early age, just like his dad. Packs of young girls would follow him home after school, giggling and trying to get his attention. "Girls, go away. Why do you have to haunt me?" Rocco's friends would laugh at his plight and make kissing noises with their pursed lips to taunt the girls and their friend. Rocco wasn't amused. He would just shake his head and continue his walk home, ignoring the taunts around him.

There was, however, one girl that stood out amongst all the rest. Her name was Antonia, and she was exceptionally beautiful. She had the kind of beauty for whom men went to war so ferociously in centuries past. One could easily imagine her as a modern-day Helen of Troy, although in a more impoverished situation. Her dark eyes, glistening under her raven-haired locks, melted the hardest of hearts. Even Rocco was enchanted by her, but not enough to sway him from his stated opinion of the female gender.

On one of their walks home from school, Antonia ran ahead of a pack of girls and sidled up next to Rocco. Their friends roared at the two presumed paramours with glee. One of the girls yelled, "You better be careful, Rocco. It looks like you'll be seeing the priest next."

Red-faced, an embarrassed Antonia spoke softly to Rocco. "I'm sorry for my friends. They think they're funny." Snapping her head around to face the pack, she shouted firmly, "But they know they're not."

"That's alright. My friends are no better. No one should make fun of you." Rocco's unease with the conversation was evident. He tried in vain to not look in Antonia's direction, keeping his head bowed and eyes focused intently on the cobble-stoned road, but it was to no avail. He eventually turned his eyes upward to his beautiful companion and smiled sheepishly. For the remainder of the walk home, the two young friends ignored the cackles and taunts from the pack following them, and for a moment, Rocco actually enjoyed the company of a girl. There's a first time for everything, including the initial spark of young love.

Rocco and Antonia would become best friends over the next few years, growing closer as the seasons passed. In him, Antonia saw the boy of her dreams who would someday become her husband. Rocco, on the other hand, saw a friend, but only a friend, who knew him best. Ultimately, this friendship could never translate into love. His mission was clear, and nothing could get in his way. He had to take care of his family. Rocco couldn't stand seeing the pain his father bore from his old wounds each day. He had to do something, even if his parents didn't fully support his plan.

On the day he left for America, our young hero was barely sixteen years old. Rocco's parents and Antonia joined him in the town square to wait for the bus that would take him to the port in Naples. They were making one last effort to convince him to stay. The village, as a whole, was not immune to the sadness of the day. They were joined by other families who had their own fathers and brothers emigrating to a new land. Most had tears in their eyes as they said their goodbyes. Rocco's father tried to convince him that he didn't have to go and that he didn't have to shoulder this burden alone. His mother cried in an unsuccessful attempt to get Rocco to change his mind, "Please don't leave. You're still my baby. Look at Antonia. She's heartbroken. Think of her at least." Their grief would never be alleviated.

Looking intently at his mom, Rocco tried to ease her pain. "Don't worry. Once I've earned enough money, I'll be back for you, Papa and the girls. I'm going to be a big success. You'll see. A big success."

Turning to a weeping Antonia, Rocco could only muster an apology and wish that her dreams would come true, but it would be without him. "You deserve a person who will love you and only you. I wish it could have been me, but you deserve the best."

A grief-stricken and devastated Antonia was inconsolable. The young beauty responded as she wiped the tears from her eyes, "But I don't understand. This is so cruel. How can you do this?"

Rocco had no words to temper the pain of the moment. Nothing could be said. The path forward was set in stone and irrevocably put into motion.

When the bus drove into the square, everyone hurriedly and tearfully said goodbye. Once on the bus, Rocco bowed his head and closed his eyes. He couldn't bear seeing their weeping faces any longer. His heart ached.

Now, how did our young hero get to a life of scraping paint off warships in the Charlestown Naval Yard? After several passages back and forth across the Atlantic, Rocco had decided it was his turn to stay in the land of plenty. He was able to find lodging with an uncle who had immigrated to the US a decade earlier. Uncle Ciro was Matteo's brother whom Rocco had met on a couple of occasions during his visits back to the village. In those days, Italian fathers would go to America to earn money and establish a home before bringing over their families. It was an indelible part of the Italian immigration plan. Over the years, these men would take the long sea voyage back to visit their families and provide enough money to sustain them between visits. It was a long and tiring endeavor, but it was worth it in the end. These men thought of family first and foremost. An interesting outcome of his uncle's visits was the birth of another child nine months later.

Based on Uncle Ciro's recommendation, Rocco was able to get a laborer's job in the Charlestown Navy Yard. A typical day for him was toiling for nearly ten hours — lifting, scraping, sweeping, and painting. It was backbreaking work. Rocco performed any task without complaint because he had a mission to achieve. His family was in his thoughts daily, and nothing would get in his way. He was the hardest worker in the yard and his bosses took notice of a determined young man that welcomed even the more difficult jobs.

During the last few years, the yard's foreman took a liking to Rocco and got him a plumbing apprenticeship that others had fought hard to obtain. After about seven years of sweat and tears, he had saved as much money as physically possible, while still being able to have some fun as a handsome young man who dated the prettiest women in the neighborhood without getting serious with any of them. Settling down was not an option. His primary focus was getting his family to the US, in complete harmony with the other Italian expatriates.

Rocco, or Rocky as his American friends called him, was about to become a citizen of this new home too. It was a home that he grew to love, but trouble was on the horizon. War was raging around the world, but it wasn't here, not yet anyway. It was late 1941, and there was still hope in his heart for the safety of everyone's family that remained in Italy. This hope, however, was fading with each passing day. Information, however insignificant, was reaching the immigrant community, but it didn't provide sufficient comfort as to the health and well-being of their families. The stress was taking a toll on the people of the North End, Boston's Little Italy, where Rocco lived.

Mezzogiorno

On a particularly mild autumn day shortly before the bombing of Pearl Harbor ushered in America's entrance to the war, Rocco was working on an old battleship's boiler and reminiscing about his last visit home with a fellow Italian expatriate.   Recalling these types of memories would sustain all the immigrants working through the long arduous days at the yard.   Mental images of their families played through everyone's mind.   Two years earlier, in the summer of 1939, Uncle Ciro and Rocco ventured back to Tranquillo to begin the final process of getting their families to America.   Five years had passed since he had left for America, but it seemed much longer to Rocco.   His mother and father had aged fifteen years in five.   Their daily struggles trying to make ends meet had grown so increasingly difficult that Matteo had taken odd jobs in Naples when he couldn't work his chosen trade.   He still had sufficiently strong arms and legs to carry construction equipment and debris.   The work was backbreaking, but he never complained, because he had a family for whom he needed to provide.   He would be away for weeks between the harvest seasons to earn additional money to supplement the profits gained from their small farm.

On the sea voyage back to Italy for this last visit before the world imploded into six years of mayhem and death, the hope for peace was dimming each day. Newspapers from all locations around the world had been debating the threats and consequences for each side. What nations needed more land or security? Who was responsible for Germany's defeat in 1918? Who was responsible for the bad peace treaty that ultimately saw people turn to fanaticism and radicalization? Scapegoats were found with the most extreme conclusion and discriminatory action. It would later come to be known as the Holocaust, where millions would perish because of their religion. The US newspapers tried to understand and report on the dangerous political and social atmosphere; however, the pending war was seen as a European problem and had nothing to do with America. The US experience during the Great War, while 3,000 miles away from home, had a dramatic effect on the psyche of the nation. Isolationism was the leading mandate for most Americans and was embraced by both parties. Europe was seen as the old homeland, something they wanted to leave behind. America was their future. The US had no business intervening in wars thousands of miles away. That naivete would be shattered on December 7, 1941.

Arriving at the village, Rocco savored the sights and sounds of his old home, but now he felt more like an outsider. After years in America, life in Tranquillo seemed alien to him. Life in America became his point of reference now rather than the village of his birth.

Rocco's mom, Valentina, kept the house and worked the farm along with their two beautiful teenage daughters, Noemi and Annabella. Like most mothers of the *Mezzogiorno* — Italy's descriptive characterization for its hot southern region, where poor families tirelessly worked their small farms under the heat of a blistering sun — Valentina had a lot of responsibilities placed on her shoulders, the true source of power in an Italian home. She was a warrior for her family and never backed down from anyone. While she wore many hats, she was never distracted from the critical task of keeping the village boys away from her daughters, or vice versa.

People said that Noemi and Annabella were the prettiest girls in all of Italy. Their raven hair flowed over tender, olive-colored skin that had yet to show signs of the distressed life that had been so prominent in the appearance of the other villagers. They were mirror images of their mother as an adolescent, and the boys were crazy for them. Rocco's sisters played the coy role perfectly as they teased and flirted with their local admirers. Daily, a crowd of boys would show up at the Farfalla home looking to help with chores, forsaking their own responsibilities at home to impress the objects of their affection. In this way, the girls were able to keep their youthful appearance and to avoid aging prematurely; the boys did their work for them. These young paramours had no chance of success with the sisters. What's the old saying, the boys were punching above their weight class?

Ultimately, Valentina would chase them away. *"Ragazzi, per favore, andate a casa!* Boys, please go home!"* Her pleas would become particularly more urgent when Matteo was expected home soon. But they would always return. The risk was worth it in their eyes. Italian boys in love could cause their share of headaches. One boy, Giovanni, stood out from the rest.

Giovanni was a muscular boy with chiseled features and black wavy hair. His one blemish was a scar across his right cheek caused by a donkey's kick several years earlier. Giovanni's father had been untying one of their donkeys from a cart upon returning home from the market. The young paramour frightened the animal when he walked too closely behind it. A quick and powerful kick grazed his face but was sufficient enough to leave a scar that stretched from ear to nose. He was lucky to be alive, and he learned that day never to walk too closely behind a nervous donkey.

While scarred, Giovanni still had a sparkle in his eyes and a boyish charm that attracted the village girls. Unfortunately for him and similar to Antonia's experience with Rocco, the attraction for Noemi was that of best friends, but that didn't prevent him from trying to win her heart. Whether it was on days of walking home from Mass or running through the fields to avoid daily chores, Giovanni tried his best to capture Noemi's heart.

Rocco took notice of the young man's interest in Noemi during his visit in the summer of 1939. Giovanni's interest concerned him sufficiently enough to pull his sister aside one evening before dinner and instruct her not to marry anyone. "You cannot marry Giovanni or anyone else here. Otherwise, you wouldn't be able to come to America with us."

Noemi didn't like being ordered. She pointed her finger at Rocco and delivered a firm and direct response that showed her contempt of her brother's command. "Listen Rocco, you're not my boss. I can do what I want. I'm seventeen years old now, a grown woman who can think for herself."

As amusing as it was to hear Noemi claim her status of adulthood at the ripe old age of seventeen, Rocco had difficulty accepting that his sisters were growing older. He preferred to think of them as young, prepubescent girls playing with their dolls. Despondent, he tried to reason with his unyielding sister, but he knew he had lost the fight.

Seeing a concerned reaction in her brother's face, Noemi realized that Rocco wasn't trying to control her. Rather, she appreciated that he was speaking from a place of love. She continued in a more relaxed voice and with hands clasped gently in front of her. "Well big brother, you don't have to worry about Giovanni. He's just a friend."

Rocco raised his hands in surrender and smiled awkwardly. "OK, OK. A fighter to the end, aren't you?"

An uncomfortable silence enveloped the two siblings until it was broken by their mother's shout. "Everyone, come in! Dinner's ready. Girls, grab a bottle of wine from the cabinet for Papa."

Rocco's attitude suddenly changed at hearing Mama's voice. Valentina was a fantastic cook, and he couldn't wait to eat. "Mama has cooked a wonderful meal and the smells from the kitchen are driving me crazy."

Wrapping her arm around his waist, Noemi hugged her big brother and laughed. "Yes, let's eat before you decide to tell me what to do again."

Rocco sighed in agreement. Both siblings beamed as soon as they saw the feast Mama prepared. While not an expensive meal by any stretch of the imagination, it was one the Farfalla family prized above all, *pizzagaina*. While the meat and cheese stuffed pie was a dish traditionally served at Easter, *pizzagaina* was a family favorite and a special treat for Rocco. Mama always said meals should be prepared with one critical ingredient, love. All of her dishes were made that way, and this one was made for extra-special reasons. The whole family was together, and happiness reigned supreme over the family.

Laughter filled the home that evening. All the problems of the outside world were left at the house's doorstep. All that mattered was a family bonded together physically and spiritually in joy and peace.

Later that evening and after enjoying Mama's delicious home-cooked dinner, Matteo asked Rocco to join him outside. He wanted to talk to his son about the seriousness of the current situation in Europe. With his gaze firmly fixated on the moon shining brightly that night,

Matteo heaved a sigh of regret. "My son, I wish you hadn't come back. You're not safe here. They'll come and take all of our boys for the army. My heart won't be able to stand seeing you go off to war." Peering down at his damaged hands, his voice quaked. "I fear its brutality will change you from my sweet boy to…to…a hardened and battered soul. No, no, please God, no."

Rocco tried in vain to reassure his father. "Papa, don't worry. There's always the threat of war. Do you really think the world is crazy enough to have another war? It's only been twenty years since the last war. People couldn't have forgotten everything that happened. This new crisis will pass too."

"No, my son, it won't. The last war was never finished. Old grudges and extreme pride are a recipe that will be the death of us all. An old soldier can recognize the bitter aroma of blood and war filling the air. War is coming soon, very soon."

Rocco slouched against the house's exterior wall and gently kicked a small stone that lay next to his foot. He contemplated his father's warning before attempting to lighten the conversation. "Papa, let's enjoy this evening and worry about war tomorrow."

While the drums of war were far away from Tranquillo that night, Rocco couldn't sleep. He had never seen his father so upset and worried. Papa was such a strong man that any display of negative emotion was a rare occurrence. Rocco decided to take a walk around the village in an attempt to clear his mind of his father's warnings. He wandered the cobblestoned streets of the village aimlessly for nearly an hour and noted the serenity of his home. He thought, how could war be a reality for such a tranquil place? Was Papa right? No, he's just worrying too much about nothing. These thoughts echoed through his mind as he finished his journey.

Rocco entered his home quietly so as not to disturb anyone's sleep, but he soon took note of the sound of crying coming from his parent's bedroom. He stood motionless in the kitchen, his heart breaking with every sob. It was his father crying for God to keep his boy safe. "Dear God, please protect my sweet and innocent son. War will ruin him. Please, please, please." The sobs were heartbreaking for a son to hear.

He could hear his mother passionately trying to console her distraught husband. "Matteo, please trust in God. He'll take care of our son. I know it. I feel it in my bones." Her voice gradually tailed off into a more somber tone. "Rocco is an innocent young man. Heaven knows war has no place in his heart."

Rocco couldn't bear it. He had to go outside to give his parents the privacy they deserved. He lay on the bench in front of the house looking up at the sky and thinking about his father. He knew he had to leave Tranquillo soon and return to Boston to alleviate Papa's fears. Falling asleep an hour before the sun rose did not offer any solace to the young man. Rocco's thoughts about Papa's warnings turned to nightmares and a restless slumber. He recalled stories that the veterans of the Great War had told him. Images of death, limbs torn from shattered bodies and soldiers screaming in pain haunted him. It was horrifying.

As the sun's rays burst over the horizon, Mama opened the front door to allow fresh air to circulate through the house, the ancient equivalent to modern air conditioning. "Rocco, what are doing out here? This is no place to sleep. Your back must be killing you."

Rocco rose to an upright position to allow Mama to sit next to him. "I'm OK. I was just enjoying the morning air."

Mama sat down next to her son and tried to be cheerful. She didn't want to reveal to him that she knew the reason he had spent the night on the bench. She gently caressed his overgrown and messy hair, which at this point looked more like a bird's nest. "Well, it is a beautiful morning, but we need to do something with this hair."

"Oh, Mama. I like my hair." Rocco tried in vain to fix his unruly mane, but he soon surrendered. It seemed his hair had a mind of its own and refused to cooperate with its owner. "Alright, I'll get a haircut for you, and only you."

Mama laughed. "For me? I can't imagine the girls in Boston like this shaggy mess on your beautiful head."

Rocco's face turned beet red at his mother's teasing, which resulted in Mama's laugh growing louder and more festive. She pinched his cheeks gently to emphasize the joy of the moment. "I knew it. You have a girlfriend back there, don't you?"

Rocco joined in on the fun. "Girlfriend?"

"Ahh, there's more than one! I didn't know Casanova was my son." Mama's laughter was contagious, afflicting Rocco with a case of uncontrollable giggles. It was a beautiful morning that Rocco would never forget. Staring out at the horizon, mother and son enjoyed a dreamlike and carefree moment, where there were no worries of another terrible war that could be worse than the previous one.

Little did Rocco know that this would be the last day he would see his mother alive, because later that morning his father had arranged for him to travel to Naples to catch the next boat back to the US. After a hurried breakfast, Papa frantically ran out of the house like a person whose hair was on fire. He wouldn't say why or where he was going, but the family would know once he returned. Papa wanted to make sure he could get his son a ticket for the afternoon bus to Naples.

Papa walked slowly up the hill on his return home. He could see his family waiting for him. A look of sorrow filled their eyes. Valentina hugged the girls tightly with each of her arms, while Rocco stood to the side. They suspected where Papa had gone.

The family patriarch approached, subdued and with a purpose. "Well, I guess you have an idea of where I went this morning. Rocco, I bought you a ticket for the afternoon bus to Naples. There's a boat leaving for New York tomorrow. You need to be on it. There were people in the piazza talking about getting their sons out of Tranquillo as quickly as possible. War is coming and you have to go."

Rocco wasn't happy abandoning his family. "I won't go and leave all of you. I want to help."

Tearfully, Mama was quick to respond. "Your father is right. You're in danger here, not us. We'll be OK my sweet boy. We'll be OK." She hugged her son tightly and was soon joined by the rest of the family.

Rocco cried as he felt the unconditional love that came from their tight embrace. He tried to reassure them that things would get better. "I love you all. Let's hope that the threat of war will pass soon. The next time I'll see you, we'll all be in Boston. I promise." That afternoon, Rocco left Tranquillo for the last time before war came to his home and his family with ferocity. Tragedy would remain inseparably bonded to Puglia and its people as it had for centuries.

Back in Boston

Rocco made the long sea journey back to his adopted home, one that he had grown to love. A voyage by ship in those days provided an individual sufficient time to contemplate the past, present and future. For Rocco, it would be several weeks of torture. Would the past become present in the form of another world war? What did the future hold for his family and the people of Tranquillo?

Terrible thoughts ran through the young man's mind. He recounted the veterans' stories of the Great War. The old soldiers had talked about their personal experiences with no variation in tone or emotion. Their souls and bodies were hollowed by the ravages of a war never seen before. They spoke of living for months in filthy trenches infested with rats and lice, watching a buddy being dismembered by an artillery shell or experiencing the madness of a frontal assault on a pack of machine gun nests. Quiet periods were equally scary times for these men. False interludes of peace were breeding grounds of fear and dread for inactive minds that anticipated the horrors of the next battle. Oddly, as if they had practiced their storytelling together, each tale ended with "I hope nobody has to go through that again. Nobody." Several of these men would stare blankly after telling their personal experiences. Interestingly, some didn't want to talk at all; they chose to remain silent.

What could Rocco do with so much idle time on his hands other than worry and fret about things out of his control? Nothing. A trip lasting several agonizing weeks felt like months. Unlike others on the voyage, most of his days were spent at the ship's stern looking at the horizon in the direction of his family and old home. He had difficulty picturing the future without seeing what he left behind. The past gripped him tightly. Anxiety and fear overcame his every waking and sleeping moment. He often tried to envision a peaceful resolution to the current crisis. It didn't work.

Over the course of the coming weeks, Rocco developed his own personal philosophy of the world. How could the older generation forget the atrocities of a war that ended only twenty years earlier? He surmised that it was easy for people to justify their actions and to forget the lessons of the past when it suited their cause. Living in the past wasn't difficult; it had become second nature for many. One of its key ingredients was to find someone to blame, a scapegoat for all the problems they faced. It was easier to blame someone for life's ills than to look inward for an answer. If everyone had this philosophy, there would never be immigrants searching for a brighter future. The natural world would be stuck in neutral, devouring itself. These thoughts replayed themselves in his mind, even as he tried to convince himself that his family would be safe.

Finally, the ship arrived in New York City where Rocco then caught the train to Boston's South Station. It was a short walk back to the North End and to the other Italian expatriates. Along the way, Rocco shouted greetings to old friends. First, he saw Vito, the fisherman. "Hey Vito, how's today's catch? Anything good?"

Vito yelled back and waved his fish oil-stained hat. "Rocco, welcome back. How's the family? Great to see you back. The newspapers are saying war is close for the old country."

"Don't believe everything you read. Everything's going to be fine. It's great to be back home." Rocco smiled as soon as he spoke the word *home* so effortlessly. It had dawned on him that America was his home now and he was happy.

Vito smiled and raised his arms cheerfully. "From your lips to God's ears. I hope that's true. We don't need another war."

The American public wanted to stay out of the war. Most felt it was none of their business. This feeling permeated every level of society across the nation. One event would change that conviction and the country forever.

He continued his trek back to his apartment and stopped to say hello to several other friends. Seeing these old friends, *the guys* as he called them, was a welcomed distraction from the thoughts that plagued him during his journey home. He promised to meet up with some of them later for a beer and to talk about the news from the old country.

The neighborhood girls who were enamored with the young man were also on his path home, although he tried hard to avoid them. It had been a long train ride from New York, and he just wanted to go home to sleep. After all, Rocco was the most handsome and desired young man in the neighborhood and one whom many local mothers dreamed their girls would marry. The prettiest girls who attracted Rocco's attention were Lucia and Giulia. Both were raven-haired beauties, the kind of which reminded him of the girls from the old country. Lucia was the more intense and demanding of the two. Going out on a date with her wasn't just going to a movie or on a slow walk along the waterfront. It was dinner, dancing, and more dancing.

Walking past Lucia's house, he picked up his pace while trying to not look like a cartoon character. It was a classic flop. Lucia was standing with a group of women in front of her building and was wearing a pretty red floral dress that matched her fiery and seductive personality. She made sure Rocco saw her. "Rocco, you're back! I hope you weren't thinking of running past my house to avoid seeing me." She walked halfway into the street and placed her hands on her hips in a pose so powerful it would have made Superman jealous.

Startled, Rocco knew he was caught red-handed, but he tried to recover the best he could. He walked over to Lucia quickly to mitigate further torment. "Lucia, sorry, I didn't see you there. It's been a long trip and I'm half-asleep."

Lucia shook her head in disbelief. "Ya, ya, nice try. Do you really think I can't tell when you're lying to me? But I forgive you. Are you coming by later tonight? I've missed you. Not sure I should though, with the way you treat me." Lucia pushed her lips into a pout that made her more alluring to local prospective suitors.

Rocco was outgunned. "Of course, I will come by tonight, but I may not be good company. I'm really tired." He placed extra emphasis on his exhaustion and got the answer he wanted.

"OK. Go rest and be ready for a date tomorrow, because we'll be dancing." After making her point, she walked slowly toward her beau and leaned in seductively. Pressing her lips against his ear, Lucia offered further enticements. "And who knows what else we'll do?"

Rocco smiled sheepishly. "Ohhh…ok…g-g-great. I'll see you tomorrow." Rocco turned and walked away, content in the knowledge that he didn't need to see his firecracker of a girlfriend that night but also looking forward to a potentially good time tomorrow.

The relationship with Giulia, on the other hand, was more relaxed. There was no pressure for an expensive night out on the town. She enjoyed being in Rocco's company most of all. But none of the girls he dated ignited a spark in the young paramour's heart like the one he would get at Camp Edwards several years later. That one would be forever special.

Rocco avoided another potential confrontation, since Giulia's apartment was a couple blocks away and was not on his path from the train station. While he didn't expect as fiery a reception from Giulia, he didn't want to risk it, because she and Lucia both had marriage on their minds. Like many young men, Rocco wanted to avoid marriage like the plague. Only a father holding a shotgun would convince him otherwise.

Rocco knew juggling these two girls was going to get tricky very soon. They were getting older and would ultimately be looking for a commitment soon. This young man, however, couldn't think of anything else other than the safety of his family. Everything else would have to wait.

Rocco went to bed thinking of his dates that weekend, first with Lucia on Friday and then possibly with Giulia on Saturday. Neither he nor anyone else could ever have imagined how the world was about to change overnight. It was a day that would transform the world forever. He awoke late in the morning on Friday, September 1st, having had his first restful night's sleep in weeks. Opening a kitchen window to get some fresh air, Rocco was surprised to hear a great deal of commotion coming from the street below. Leaning his upper torso out of the window, he scanned the several groups of people engaged in spirited conversations to understand what had happened. The cacophony created by the growing crowd of people shouting at each other was too difficult to penetrate. Rocco went back into the kitchen and turned on the radio, hoping that it would offer him some relevant information. He got what he was looking for but not what he wanted to hear. Germany had invaded Poland in the early morning hours, and Great Britain and

France were threatening war in defense of their ally.

Rocco slumped into the chair next to the radio, not believing what he was hearing. He sat motionless, unable to express his shock at the dramatic turn of events. For this young man, it was the first of three events over the next two years that would impact his life and set him on the path of returning to his ancestral home; however, it would be as a liberator and executioner.

Italy Joins the War

On a tranquil summer day in June 1940, nearly a year after the start of the war, and with Italy not yet an active participant, Noemi and Giovanni, two would-be paramours, lay on a hillside staring at a clear blue sky. "Noemi," he whispered softly to the object of his affection, "one day, I will build a beautiful house on this hillside for you. It will be the envy of the entire village."

Noemi smiled, but her attention focused on two birds flying above, performing an aerial mating ritual. The similarity to their situation was not lost on her. "Gio, you've tried so hard to win me. Maybe someday, you will find the right girl, but for today you and the male bird flying above us won't succeed. You're like a brother to me and I don't ever want to spoil that."

Giovanni sighed but refused to concede defeat. "But tomorrow's another day."

"Yes, it is, and so is the day after tomorrow."

They turned to each other, while still lying on their backs, and burst into laughter. The bond was too strong to be broken by unrequited love.

The spontaneity of the moment was a beautiful example of the attachment the two shared.

Slapping his stomach, Noemi joined in the fun. "You can always make me laugh, but you've been eating too much pasta lately. I know Rosa likes her boyfriends with meat on their bones. There's hope for you yet." The laughter rose a few more decibels.

As the merriment subsided, the mood turned serious. Chewing a long blade of grass, Giovanni posed a sobering question, "What do you think will happen? I don't understand what's going on. Will Italy go to war too? Some of my friends are already in the army."

Noemi, her eyes focused once again on the sky, responded with confidence. "Never. What does it have to do with us? The fascists need not worry about Italians, but only Africans." Her response was based on the lessons all Italian school children were taught.

Giovanni carefully pondered his beautiful companion's comment along with all that he had learned in the country's fascist youth camps over the years. Like any good fascist regime, Italy's government focused heavily on the hearts and minds of the young to cement their power. "I guess Mussolini is going to resurrect the glory of ancient Rome. Look at what he's done in less than 20 years to modernize Italy's armed forces to be a triumphant colonial superpower. The ships of Italy's navy have been built to ensure our nation's power was projected throughout the Mediterranean. The British can't stop Italy from reaching its destiny. His dreams of a reborn empire started in Ethiopia and Northern Africa. Do you remember my Uncle Carlo? He died during the war in Africa five years ago, and they called him a hero. I guess his death was good for the Motherland. Do you think so too?"

Noemi, however, knew better. Perhaps, it was the letters Rocco sent home describing his new life and the perspective of the American newspapers on the approaching doom for all of Europe. An intelligent young woman, Noemi had an opinion or comment on every topic. Her mood changed to exasperation. "I wish these ambitious men would worry about *us* first instead of *glory*. There is too much pride in their hearts. A mirror must be the favorite piece of furniture for these peacocks."

Giovanni was troubled by Noemi's statements and nervously turned his head to his friend. These types of revolutionary ideas being expressed so openly were seen as a threat to the regime. Anyone speaking these words would have been considered a traitor to the motherland and dealt with harshly. "Amazing! I wish I had your confidence and courage, but you can't say these things out loud."

Suddenly, their attention was directed to a disturbance in the distant sky. "Giovanni, what is that sound? Where is it coming from?" The startled adolescents rose to their feet quickly and searched the sky intently, confused at what they were hearing.

"Noemi, look! There are planes flying toward us. Are those our planes?"

Noemi pointed to the sky. "Yes, they're fighters and bombers of the *Regia Aeronautica*. They are flying to the west."

Giovanni raised his hands to his head, his face showing signs of intense alarm. "Noemi, where are they going? What does this mean?" Pausing momentarily to watch all the planes pass over, the two agreed to run home quickly and find out what was happening.

In the town *piazza*, Mayor Pavone stood in front of the municipal building wearing a fascist sash and preening like a peacock. With his chest and jaw thrust outward in a manner that would have made Mussolini proud, the mayor addressed the crowd with a thundering voice and energetic movements of his arms. He announced with joy that Italy had declared war on France and had joined her Axis partner Germany in attacking a common enemy. "The nation was going to participate in the glory of conquest and in the defeat of a corrupt neighbor and its criminal democratic government! We will free the people of France!"

Shocked and confused, the crowd moaned its collective disapproval. Some families had already lost loved ones in the invasion of Ethiopia in 1935. These poor villagers never understood the reason for the nation embarking on a quest to resuscitate the Roman Empire. Families who had sons already conscripted into the army whispered amongst themselves and wrung their hands in nervous anticipation. "Is France our enemy now? Does this mean we have to fight the British too?" Most of the people in the crowd were parents who worried about their boys. "Why is this happening?"

Soon, the grumblings turned to cheers once well-placed fascists in the crowd yelled their approval and exhorted the others to do the same. "The gangsters in France and Britain asked for this! They tried to control and suppress us!" The rest of the assembled mass would not dare to contradict them. It wouldn't have been healthy for them. The villagers roared their uncomfortable approval as a reflex of self-preservation. The fascist police were standing around the square, watching everyone closely. No one would dare step out of line.

The icing on the cake was the local marching band striking up the *Giovinezza*, the fascist party anthem. The crowd sang along. The mayor's goal of rousing the crowd in support of the nation's destiny was achieved; however, they couldn't imagine what fate would bring for the people of Tranquillo before the war ended. The decision-makers believed that war was the only answer and defeat was impossible. Fascist hubris was also on full display in Rome that day.

Separately, Mussolini, the nation's caustic and prideful *il Duce*, spoke to a throng of cheering Romans who had no idea what the future held. As his fascist representatives had done in Tranquillo and all over

the nation that day, he passionately rallied his legion of Black Shirts —
Italy's paramilitary wing — to seize the day and defeat the Western
democracies who had been trying to suppress the Italian people. When
he spoke about the nation's sons being sent to foreign lands, *il Duce*
captivated the crowd with his description of the armed force's
capability to easily defeat the enemy; however, history would tell a
different story. *Il Duce's* confidence and projection of power in June of
1940 was mirrored by all of his lackeys throughout the cities and villages
of Italia. No one could have known that when the war came to Italy's
shore three years later, her people would experience the horrors of war
firsthand. It would be an intimate experience shared with millions of
other victims of this tragic war.

Once the band stopped playing its fascist tune and Mayor Pavone
shouted to the crowd one last exhortation for victory, the villagers
dispersed slowly to their respective homes. Families muttered
pensively to themselves as they made their way out of the town square.
No matter what the mayor said, they knew difficult days were ahead.
Soon, their sons would become cannon fodder on the deserts of North
Africa, the rugged mountains of the Balkans, and the icy killing fields
of Russia.

Noemi found her parents and sister working their way through
separate groups of villagers who were walking home in a daze.
Giovanni's parents were with one of the groups. The teenagers
hurriedly ran up to them. Noemi couldn't contain her emotions.
"Mama, Papa! What does this mean? Will my friends need to go? Will
they make you fight again? What about Giovanni?" The fear in her
voice was sufficiently audible for others to hear. Tears were now
streaming down her face. Her father attempted to calm her down to
avoid the undue attention of the fascist police. Matteo, the loving father
that he was, hugged his daughter and stroked the back of her head.

"*Principessa*, don't worry. The war is far away from here and they don't want an old man like me. They don't need our young boys like Giovanni yet either."

Noemi still held on tightly to her beloved papa. "What do you mean 'yet'?" Even though she hadn't turned eighteen, she couldn't be appeased so easily.

Her father responded quickly, "Giovanni is too young. He's still a boy for Heaven's sake. The war will be over before he's drafted and trained. Trust me." He gently caressed his baby's hair and repeated his strong belief on the matter. "Trust me. He will not go to war."

Giovanni's father agreed that the village shouldn't worry. "The war is far from here. Who wants to conquer Tranquillo? It's not Paris." Gentle laughter broke the tension of the moment completely.

Matteo, however, knew better. One battle won would only feed the hunger for greater glory that this regime desired so intensely. He imagined a ravenous wolf, jaws open and blood dripping from its fangs, moving from one captured prey to another for an unabated feast. He tried to hide his emotions from his daughters and wife the best he could. For now, Noemi was satisfied with his response. "I believe you, Papa." The fascist police, who had begun to approach the loud teenager were satisfied too. They nodded in approval to Matteo's handling of the matter and returned to scanning the crowd for malcontents.

The loving father turned to both families with arms raised. "Let's go home and have some dinner."

While Giovanni and the other young men would not be conscripted that day for the war with France, 1941 would be different. There would be battles in North Africa, Greece and Russia. By the time the war ended four years later, there would be an abundance of hardship for the participants. Boys from many countries would not come home, including several local youths who met their frozen fate at the Battle of

Stalingrad, along with many other Italians. Giovanni's destiny, however, lay in North Africa.

Names of battlefields that were not known by most of the world's population before the war would soon become hallowed ground. Places like Guadalcanal, Dunkirk, Normandy, and Stalingrad would remain part of humanity's psyche and lexicon for generations to come.

Waiting Game

For the next year, the people of Boston's North End agonized over their families and friends back in the old country. While Italy had not gone to war in 1939, they knew Mussolini would ultimately want to share in its spoils. The fear of war weighed heavily on their hearts and minds. Sunday Masses were full of parishioners praying that their kin would not be harmed, and that the war would bypass both their ancestral and adopted homes. The prayers got stronger and more dire when Italy decided to join the war in the summer of 1940. This marked the first of two tragic events over the next 18 months that would lead Rocco and other young men of the North End down a terrible path. The second event would culminate with the bombing of Pearl Harbor and America's entry into the Second World War.

While this Boston enclave of Italians knew of the bigotry facing their place as immigrants in a new land, Mussolini's entrance into the war brought increased scrutiny of their lives. Since the beginning of the large waves of Italian immigrants that had entered the US forty years earlier, these people had never had the welcome mat rolled out for them. They were dark-skinned mongrels, WOPs, dagos, liars, thieves and plenty of other derogatory terms placing them in a subhuman status. Most were from the *Mezzogiorno* — the heel of Italy's boot — where they were looked on with equal disdain by their own Northern countrymen. But these people persevered. They were too strong to fail. The ideals and promises of the American Dream lived in their hearts and no bigot or pompous fascist was going to stand in their way. Their old lives as doormats were over. The ancestral bonds joining the North Enders as one family were unbreakable. These people always stood upright and tall; now, they stood taller. Centuries of misfortune had prepared them well.

On several occasions, Rocco and his friends would have a run-in with a group of drunken bigots on their way home after a night out in Scollay Square, an old area of Boston situated next to the North End that was known for, shall we say, its colorful nightlife. Burlesque houses and taverns dotted the landscape for the enjoyment of its adult visitors.

On one particular occasion, a drunken moron, barely able to stand, leaned up against one of his buddies and slurred his insults in Rocco's direction. "Hey, greaseball, what the hell you doing around here? Teddy, Mikey, I bet you these garlic eaters are looking to mug someone. Can't trust any of them, especially their women. They'll rob and screw you at the same time." The group of drunkards laughed contemptuously, agreeing with their friend's disgusting sentiments.

That last comment, however, stopped Rocco dead in his tracks. He had heard the other crap before, but this crossed the line for him. His friends told Rocco to forget it, but he couldn't do that.

Rocco walked up to the loudmouth drunk slowly and sized up the situation. There were five of them to the two with him. In a calm and firm voice, he approached the offending party, who all the while continued to flaunt an air of smugness and cockiness. "So, you're a tough guy, huh? You know a lot about people too I suppose. What if I give you the first punch?" Rocco barely moved his head and stared at each with malicious intent. "Are you or any of your boys interested?"

The one named Teddy, who was the most formidable looking of the five, moved forward slightly and he was immediately met with a right cross that broke his jaw. The color on his drunken friend's face turned pale as he stood and watched his compatriot collapse to the cobblestoned pavement. Rocco didn't wait for a response. He now directed his attention to the loudmouth bigot, but before he could deliver his punishment, the inebriated man fell to the ground and wet himself, pleading to be spared.

"Please don't. I was only kidding."

The other three men stood silently and in shock. They did not try to intervene.

Rocco laughed at the now pitiful sight lying before him. "Boys, pick up your buddies and go home. There's been enough fun for tonight. Now beat it!"

Rocco felt a small crowd forming around him. He clenched his hands and prepared for another fight, but what happened next surprised the young men. An elderly man, a stranger and definitely not Italian, stepped forward and offered his hand to Rocco. "Well done. Stupidity in the world is limitless. Don't let these idiots ruin your night. Unfortunately, you'll probably run into others equally stupid in the future, but remember, not everyone is. The world has hope."

Shaking the man's hand, a new friend was made. "Thank you, sir. I appreciate that."

The three North Enders walked another ten feet before Rocco stopped and looked nervously around the square. He asked his friends if they noticed a peculiar odor in the air.

His friends shrugged their shoulders and stated that they smelled nothing.

"Really, you can't smell that odor. It smells like some sort of rotten incense, if that's possible. And it feels like someone is watching us." By then, the crowd had turned away from the men and attended to their own affairs. Rocco had another rush of adrenaline course through his body, stimulating his heartbeat and raising the hairs on the back of his neck. Rocco's radar was up, but he couldn't see anyone staring at them.

His friends repeated their response and wondered if he was alright. Perhaps, the fight and the constant stress of worrying about his family unnerved him.

"Never mind, let's get out of here." That was the first time, but not the last, that Rocco would have similar uneasy feelings.

The group continued their short walk home, silently contemplating their confrontation with bigotry. The answer was simple; nothing more needed to be said. That evening, Rocco showed his friends that bigots had a pack mentality and that you could ignore them, but at some point, a man needed to stand his ground. These types of incidents became less frequent as time passed, perhaps because bigots began to lose ground to the good people out there, just like the elderly man said. Perhaps, people got used to one another and realized the stupidity of a bigoted mindset. This had to be true, Rocco thought, because of the friends and relationships he developed after many years working on ships and living in America. While the North End had offered him a safe and familial atmosphere similar to Tranquillo, Rocco's exposure to new things and people, and their experience with him, proved to be life-changing. Affirming the progress being made, Rocco smiled as the group passed the numerous Italian restaurants and pizza shops brimming with non-Italians. At that moment, our young Italian American saw hope for the future.

Over the succeeding months, Rocco endured the monotony of daily life at the Navy Yard as well as the constant and unchanging drumbeat of Lucia and Giulia to marry. The year 1941, however, would be a turning point for Rocco and all Americans. He would be sworn in as a citizen and the US would enter a war that was in its third horrible year. The US and its place in the world were about to change, and the change was going to be dramatic.

Birth of a Warrior

December 7th, 1941, began like most other Sundays. It was a seasonably cold and blustery day in Boston. Many people had gone to church, and later on, they filled the cafes for lively discussions and gossip. Rocco, who always elected to sleep late on a day off, didn't go to Sunday Mass. Working at the Navy Yard was tough physical labor. Any free time that wasn't spent having fun was used for sleeping. Regardless, he did his praying in private. He didn't feel the need to do it in church as others did. It wasn't because he didn't believe in a higher power or going to Mass. Rather, he always thought he had better things to do with his free time, which wasn't uncommon for young men of his age.

Rocco was sitting with his friends in one of the busier espresso bars, drinking an afternoon coffee and trying to stay warm. They never imagined that their lives would be forever changed in an instant. A news alert cut into the musical broadcast to report that the Japanese had bombed Pearl Harbor. All of the café's customers stared at the radio in disbelief. Total silence permeated the bar except for the bleak and cold tone of the voice coming from the radio. Everyone remained frozen in place, motionless and listening to the full report. After the conclusion of the news broadcast, the café remained eerily silent. People didn't know what to say. It was like the power of speech was ripped from their bodies after a solid punch to the gut.

After a few moments that must have felt like hours to each person, one of Rocco's friends grumbled. "What the hell! I can't believe those bastards did it. They really did it. I just can't believe it." Others around the table and café joined in and asked whether they should join the Army or Navy now. A shout from the back of the crowd was heard loud and clear from an imposing North End man. "Forget them, I'm rejoining the Marines. Semper Fi, boys."

Rocco walked home somberly to contemplate his next steps. His mind raced through a sleepless night as he considered his options. He spent the next few days working at the yard in a zombified state. Having been sworn in as a US citizen a month earlier, he was worried about his new home as well as his old home. He knew he had to do something, but he was torn. Could a person rush to the aid of his new home and knock his family down in the pecking order? Was this allegiance mutually exclusive? Was he being a traitor to his own family? He had received little information from them since his last visit two years earlier. He needed guidance from someone or somewhere. The universe would soon provide that answer.

Several days after Pearl Harbor, the fascist leaders of Germany and Italy, in their infinite stupidity, declared war on the US. Japan had been the sole focus of US ire immediately following the attack, declaring war only on that nation. This extraordinary event, a declaration of war by Germany and Italy, provided a clear path for the US to join the war in Europe and for Rocco to achieve two goals simultaneously.

As soon as he heard the report of the war declaration, the prospective warrior ran to his boss and told him what he was going to do. Rocco grabbed his supervisor, an elderly Irish-American man, by the shoulders to express his resolve. "Danny, I'm signing up. There's no way I'm sitting this out."

The old man held on to Rocco tightly. He had come to see him through fatherly eyes. There was something about Rocco that reminded him of his own son, who had died of cancer a decade earlier. "I figured this day would come. There's a ton of crazy people in the world hellbent on controlling everything. These people are pure evil." Danny pulled Rocco into a long hug and his voice trembled at the thought of losing him. "You've got a pure soul that I don't want to see changed by war. But you gotta do what you gotta do. Keep your head down and remember us in Boston. Go on, son. God protect you and your family."

With his elderly friend holding tightly still, Rocco shed a tear for him. He knew how genuine his feelings were. To lighten the mood, the future soldier inserted a little levity and bravado into his response. "Don't worry. I'll write you. I'm going to take out Hitler and Mussolini, personally." That last part brought a snicker out of Danny. As the two men broke apart from their embrace and Rocco turned to leave, he found it peculiar that Danny and his dad had the same feeling about him going to war. What did they know? Should he really be worried about his future and surviving the war? Rocco put those thoughts out of his mind. He had business that needed his attention; specifically, saving his family and fighting for his new country.

Rocco sprinted to the local recruitment office. He wanted to join the Army because he knew it would be the best way to get back to Italy and to ensure his family's safety. Joining the Marines wasn't an option. It would be a direct path to the Pacific and completely away from one of his goals. As important as the Pacific War was, Rocco knew he had to stay true to both his new and old homes. There was no doubt in his mind that Europe was his destination.

He passed his physical with flying colors and within a few days, he joined a busload of young men — it's a more accurate description to call them boys — who were transported to Camp Edwards for basic training. His first trip to the camp would be markedly different from his next one. Here, these boys would meet recruits from other New England states. If it weren't for the war, they probably would have never met.

Rocco spent the next three grueling months getting his body, mind, and soul into combat shape. Many of the boys often complained that the drill instructors worked them so hard that they had no strength to fight Hitler. After each long day, the boys walked in a half-zombie state back to their bunks, too tired to moan about their sore bodies. It was said that the DIs had a special knack for pushing their recruits to the edge of their physical and mental capacity, but they had a job to do too. Turning these boys into a finely tuned fighting machine weighed on the minds of the DIs with each command. "Move faster! Keep your head down! Do you want to get your melon shot off? Get over the wall now, now, now! Adolf's guys have been fighting this war for two years. Do you think they're waiting for you with ice cream and balloons? Move! Move! Move!" The world was on the brink of Armageddon and these boys needed to grow up quickly. The First World War, for all its tragedy and death, would be more like a fancy-dress party in comparison, an opening act to the absolute horror show to come. Perhaps the First World War never ended; it was paused for twenty years to allow more young men to be born and placed on the butcher's bill.

The daily grind quickly turned to a monotonous rhythm of torture and torment that no one ever envisioned. Repetitive drills on the obstacle course and long marches with full backpacks, followed by intense hand to hand combat training, exposed the recruits to the realities of what they would soon be facing.

During these weeks, Rocco developed a friendship and camaraderie with a wide assortment of young New Englanders. Vermont Green Mountain Boys joined Maine Lobstermen and tough Rhode Islanders, as well as boys from across the country, to form the backbone of an army that would take the fight against fascism across many battlefields. All of these recruits started their journey naïve and doe-eyed, even the so-called street-smart tough guys from the Eastern cities. Soon, their experiences in a hellish war would open their eyes wide and forever change their lives. These men, however, would become a family bonded in blood, sweat and tears when they marched off to war.

While thousands of miles away from the fighting, soldiers' families would not be immune from the effects of the war. They too would experience the pain and suffering of husbands, brothers and sons. Death comes in many forms. It can be physical, spiritual or emotional. It would take perseverance, tenacity and that original naivete to bring soldiers back home intact and united with the Trinity, the three-sided essence of life. In this union, Heaven, Earth and its binding spirit are joined together in harmony. Upsetting this balance drives people to the darkest regions of despair.

At Camp Edwards, there was one local Massachusetts boy with whom Rocco developed the strongest bond. Jimmy Harrison was from South Boston and had a reputation for being tough as nails and having a heart of gold. He had a fondness for beer and swing music even though he couldn't dance. Jimmy was Rocco's best friend, and they were inseparable. Rocco spoke so much about how beautiful his sisters were that Jimmy would love to tease him. "Hey, beautiful huh? Wait until they see me. Maybe I'll come home with a bride." Jimmy knew talking about his buddy's sisters would make him feel more at ease, even in jest.

Rocco always returned a deadpan response to Jimmy's teasing. "Won't work. They like to dance."

The two met on the bus ride down from Boston to boot camp. It was a meeting that exhibited the character of the man who would become Rocco's best friend.

On the bus, there was an especially ignorant and rowdy group of guys looking to establish themselves as the alpha dogs of the recruits. As always, there is only one person who can be the real alpha, the rest being lackeys powered with fake courage that comes with their inclusion in the group.

Eddy, the alpha bully, made a point of picking on the smallest guy on the bus. He cut an imposing figure, standing close to six feet tall. He made his way to a seat behind Tony, a nineteen-year-old boy from East Boston who weighed no more than 140 pounds soaking wet. Eddy rustled Tony's hair and laughed heartily. "Hey, looks like we have an escapee from Munchkinland? Are you here to represent the Lollipop Guild? Or are you looking for Toto?"

Tony attempted to stand up and fight back. "Hey, what the hell?"

Eddy's friends made sure that didn't happen. Two guys in the seat directly in front of Tony pushed him back into his seat. Eddy placed his hands on Tony's shoulders and mocked his prey with his massaging hands. "Easy kid. You don't want to get hurt on your first day. Don't be a stupid WOP."

Rocco and Jimmy were sitting together on the opposite side of the bus, a couple of rows behind the situation. The two had barely spoken for the entire bus ride up to that point, except for the general grunt of hello when Jimmy sat down. Upon hearing Eddy say WOP, Rocco moved to get up. "Excuse me, do you mind moving for a second?"

Jimmy responded calmly and directly. "No, please allow me."

Rising up slowly from his seat, one of Eddy's lackeys noticed him getting up and nodded at Jimmy's direction to warn their presumed alpha dog. "Hey, looks like we got brave one here."

Eddy turned his attention to the potential oncoming threat, although his actions showed he had no fear. He had more guys on his side, or so he thought. "Well, what the hell do you want?"

Jimmy grumbled. "I want you to sit your ass down, or I'll put you down." He never minced words; the direct approach always worked.

The other two guys moved to the aisle as Eddy looked to confront Jimmy. "Are you serious, you Potato Head?" This miscreant evidently was an encyclopedia for hate speech and derogatory terms — one of the best ways to dehumanize an individual.

Jimmy furrowed his eyebrows in frustration. "Well, I warned you." With a single punch, the bully of the bus was knocked out cold and fell back into his seat.

The two lackeys lost their courage quickly and jumped back down in their seats. The whole bus watched as Jimmy slowly moved closer to them. Sliding down into their seat and wishing they could turn invisible; they glanced sideways at the kid from Southie approaching their row.

Jimmy bent down with his forearm resting on the back of the bench where the two misguided fellows were now sitting and became somewhat philosophical. "Now, I know you really don't think this is a way to act, right? There are two ways your lives can turn out, on your feet or on your ass. Following an idiot like the sleeping prince over there will put you on your ass more times than you'd want. Nobody will be your buddy when this guy runs. That's what bullies do, either from responsibility or from a bigger threat like me. Guys like you will always be left holding the bag. We'll have plenty of fighting to do soon against Adolf's boys. That's what we need to worry about. Not this stupidity.

So do we have an understanding?"

The two men replied nervously and in unison. "We... we... understand."

Jimmy turned to leave. "Good, now we can get back to business."

He returned to his seat next to Rocco. Nothing was said until Rocco broke the ice a few moments later. "I never knew philosophers had a strong right cross. I thought you guys were gentle."

The two new friends burst into laughter. This friendship would carry them through difficult days in boot camp and then through Ranger training in Scotland. This was only the first phase of training that would turn boys into men and into a machine of war. The nation's top recruits, which included Jimmy and Rocco, were selected to join the Rangers, an elite service in the US Army. Men were chosen for the Rangers based on their impeccable character, mental stability and physical performance. Our two young Bostonians outshone all others in their recruitment class. Their selection was an easy one for the camp commanders to make. For Rocco, it was another step on his path to reaching his family. The assignment was a perfect recipe for achieving this goal, because the Rangers took on the toughest tasks assigned to the infantry and often worked behind enemy lines. The universe and Rocco were seemingly aligned and in balance, but he didn't know yet how cruel the universe could be.

Scotland

By the summer of 1942, the two Bostonians arrived in Scotland to start their Ranger training under the tutelage of seasoned British commandos. The Brits had been in the war since the beginning and had valuable experience to teach the *Yanks*. This term was used freely, affectionately, and sometimes with derision by the locals to call Americans. It was generally accepted kindly by the boys. It was, however, met with the disapproval of soldiers from the Southern states and Boston for different reasons. The Civil War, or the War Between the States if you are from the South, had ended seventy-seven years earlier and remained an indelible part of the US historical lexicon. For Bostonians, it was driven by their celebrated rivalry with New York City and the cities' baseball teams.

Jimmy and Rocco were joined in Scotland by guys coming from other states spanning the entire country. Each had his own unique personality and background. There were husbands, fathers, bachelors, and sons. There were machinists, accountants, teachers, police officers, farmers and more. Some were bald while others had wavy hair. Some were skinny while others were muscular. There were Southerners,

Northerners, Mexicans, Irishmen, Italians, Poles, Jews, Catholics, and Protestants. All were individuals from different walks of life and backgrounds that had one thing in common. Purely and simply, they were Americans getting ready for their part of the looming battle.

These men had grown accustomed to the small, isolated world of their hometowns and neighborhoods. Only Rocco had seen more of the world because of his prior work on a trans-Atlantic transport ship. But even for him, the small world encapsulated in the narrow streets of the North End was about to grow exponentially larger, yet more intimate and dangerous.

Strong friendships formed quickly amongst the men as familial bonds soon developed. Death was knocking at the front door and fighting for your brother would make enduring the horrors of war easier but never more palatable. To maintain his mental stability, Rocco had heard it said that a soldier went into battle with the belief he was already dead and that protecting his brother was one of the things that might help keep a person sane in an insane situation.

Rocco became friends with many of the men, but he was particularly close with the members of his squad. These men developed such a close connection that they decided to name their group the Wolfpack, a brotherhood of men on the prowl dedicated to drinking whiskey and capturing the attention of the fairer sex. For as dangerous as their name sounded, they were just harmless, young men stretching their wings in a new land.

The founding members of the Wolfpack included Cody "Cowboy" Davis, a rodeo champion from Wyoming who loved horses more than people. Unfortunately for him, Cowboy was born fifty years too late; he wouldn't be riding a horse into battle.

Billy "Shortstop" Kaplan hailed from Brooklyn and loved baseball. Watching the Dodgers play at Ebbets Field and eating a handful of hot dogs loaded with mustard was all he talked about.

Tom "Tommy Gun" Ryan from Chicago could crack jokes faster than a machine gun unloading its magazine. While everyone was defenseless against his wit and barbs, none felt uncomfortable or offended. He had an odd way of making others feel at ease.

Ted "Reaper" Wills from Tennessee had never left the family farm until boot camp but was the best soldier in the division. He was the squad's bedrock when trouble was on the horizon and promoted to company sergeant by late 1943. He was one heck of a soldier.

Manny "Hollywood" Ramirez came from Los Angeles and worked in a major movie studio. He was the suave member of the pack who had a way of charming women.

Last but not least, there was Ethan "Gunslinger" Wilshire, who was part Comanche and a full-blooded Texas Ranger in civilian life. This warrior could shoot the leaf off a branch from a hundred yards away in the blink of an eye. His lone soft spot was for his girlfriend, Margie, his Yellow Rose as he called her.

The Wolfpack formed a lethal fighting group. Not all would make it out of the war alive, but their memory would remain embedded in the souls of the survivors for eternity.

Through months of training in the Scottish Highlands, the British commandos brought out the best qualities of the American soldiers and fashioned one of the finest fighting forces the world had ever seen. They could see that once let loose into the war, the Rangers would run through brick walls and all manner of obstacles to complete the mission, win the battle and get home.

By the beginning of November, the division was waiting for its orders. The Wolfpack was enjoying a night out at the local village pub. There were rumors that North Africa would be their landing spot. The time for preparation was over. The war was about to get real.

The pub was uniquely named the Bloody Abbot. It apparently got its name from the head of a local monastery who joined the Scottish rebellion centuries ago and was skilled in two conflicting arts — redemption and warfare. Rocco and his mates developed a taste for Scottish ale visiting the pub on the weekends and soaking in the ancient atmosphere along with their overflowing pints. The food, like haggis, for the most part would remain a mystery for the Rangers. They weren't fans of sheep organs, although they were told it was a tasty dish. Only a few daring Rangers would try it, and then, only as part of a bet.

The last night before they received their marching orders, Rocco and Jimmy were sitting at the back of the pub contemplating the destination of their first mission. The division was told to be ready to leave at a moment's notice. While they didn't know where they would be going, the Rangers knew they would be heading into the jaws of the beast.

Taking a drink, Jimmy took note of Rocco's serious expression and silent introspective mood. "Hey, buddy, where are you right now? Want to join the party?" He pointed to the guys carousing with a group of elderly men whose sons were off fighting the enemy in North Africa and Burma. For these fathers, having a drink with a young man made them feel closer to their own sons. They were soldiers during the First World War and knew what was waiting for the young Americans on the battlefield.

Rocco shook himself out of his funk and managed an uncomfortable smile. "I'm alright, Jimmy."

Jimmy placed his hand on his friend's shoulder to offer some reassurance and spoke to him in a strong and comforting tone. "Don't worry. Your family has got to be safe. They are nowhere close to the fighting. We'll get to them soon enough."

Rocco seemed to accept his buddy's confidence. Placing a hand on

Jimmy's shoulder, his attitude changed quickly. "I know. You're right. They are far from the battlefield. Hey, we are going to teach those bastards a lesson, aren't we? They won't know what hit them when they meet the boys from Boston."

Rocco's bravado was not lost on Jimmy. "You got it now. We have miles to go, but we'll get there. Just don't do anything stupid like getting your butt shot off." Jimmy punctuated his last comment with one of his belly laughs that everyone always found infectious.

"You can bet on that. I'll just make sure to duck behind your big ass when the shooting starts. They won't be able to see me. I'm not sure how you did it with all the training we do, but I think you gained a few pounds drinking these pints." Rocco rubbed his friend's belly in jest.

Jimmy had gained a little weight, but he was nowhere near being classified as overweight. "It's a good thing I'm a churchgoer, or else I would tell you to shove this glass somewhere tight."

The two buddies burst into laughter. Rocco removed his hand from his buddy's shoulder and pointed to their mates. "Let's go join the party. After you, my lordship." For the time they were in Great Britain, the two Bostonians enjoyed teasing each other by putting on airs of nobility, the last two individuals anyone would think of as being highborn. The irony is that these men were princes in their own way, one that the Trinity held dear.

"Right, squire. We need to have some fun tonight." Little did they know it would be the last fun the guys would have for a long time.

Making their way over to the bar where the other soldiers were drinking and reveling with their newfound Scottish friends, Rocco suddenly had an odd feeling that hit him like a lightning bolt. An uneasy sensation stopped him dead in his tracks. He could sense someone staring at him. Searching the bar, his eyes became fixated on a darkened corner where no one was sitting or standing. Puzzled at not seeing anything or anyone, Rocco furled his brow and stared intently into the pitch-black corner. "Hello, is someone there?" The young soldier got no answer in response. "Hello, is someone there?" Again, there was no response, but he could smell something unusual in the air around him. It smelled like something was on fire, but he could see no smoke or flame. "I know someone's there."

Rocco took a couple of steps toward the corner before his friend stopped him. Jimmy had noticed his buddy had stopped several paces behind him. "Hey, what are you doing? The party's over here." Catching him in one of his giant bear hugs from behind, Jimmy startled Rocco out of his puzzled state.

"Alright, alright, I'm coming."

"What were you looking at? Are you seeing ghosts or something?" Jimmy stared into the corner as well and wondered what his friend saw.

"Nothing. I thought I saw something. My mind was just drifting again I guess." Jumping on Jimmy's back, Rocco's attitude flipped back to having fun. "I need a shot of whiskey and you're buying."

"Dream on, lightweight. Dream on. You can't handle whiskey. How about a ginger ale?"

"Well, as long as it's got booze in it. I'll drink it right now."

Pushing up against the bar, Jimmy ordered shots of whiskey and beers for his buddies at the bar, including several of the locals out of respect for their sacrifice during the war. He was always a generous person, who never pinched a penny, but not the best at giving a toast. "Slainte, here's to swimming with bow-legged women. Boys, let's get the job done and get home safe." Well, the toast was half good.

Rocco added his sentiments as well. "*Cent'anni, amici.* May you all live a hundred years."

The men slammed their drinks to the bar and continued the revelry. Tommy Gun provided his opinion of Jimmy's toast. "Geez, Iceman, you burnt the hell out of that toast. At least Butterfly recovered for you, big fella."   Rocco was nicknamed Butterfly because of the tattoo on his chest of a red, white and blue butterfly emerging from a cocoon. *The boys had no clue that Farfalla translated to butterfly in English. They just thought he liked butterflies and was patriotic.*

Gunslinger roared. "Tommy Gun, you've been asking for a maulin' all week from Iceman. You poked the bear one too many times." Gunslinger was referring to how Tommy Gun loved needling his Bostonian buddy for just about anything. Jimmy was a good-natured soul and always took the ribbing in stride.

While it was difficult to get on his bad side, he did have one and it did pop out once or twice when pushed hard, but not this time. Jimmy, who was called Iceman because of his pre-war occupation of hauling large blocks of ice for old refrigerators, lifted his mouthy buddy over his head in jest. "Really, how do you like my toast now?"

Tommy Gun shouted loudly. "Really good! Really good!"

Jimmy threw him to the floor like a rag doll. "I thought you'd change your mind."

Laughter erupted in the bar and the rest of the evening was incident-free, although Rocco couldn't shake his uneasiness completely. Intermittently, he would glance back at the corner to see if anything was there. He wasn't successful.   In due course, his attention turned to thoughts of the oncoming battle in North Africa, the presumed destination for his platoon and division, and not a darkened corner in a Scottish pub. He knew he had to think of himself as being dead, but he couldn't do that. He had to get to Tranquillo, alive and ready to fight.

Demon of Dreams

The Rangers fought their way through North Africa and Sicily, and onto the Italian mainland. They suffered their share of casualties with some never making it back home. Fortune smiled on Rocco's platoon as none of the Wolfpack suffered major injury before landing in Italy. They knew it was only a matter of time before their luck ran out and a shitstorm would hit them. It was purely a matter of odds. There was no way they would all get back home to their families alive or undamaged; however, a flicker of hope remained in each soldier's heart.

Photos of wives, sweethearts, moms, dads, and family members were held tightly in their chest pockets, and memories of the good old days occupied their thoughts when not engaged in the fury of battle. Downtime, the common description of the period between battles, became serene moments for the men to recenter their focus and mental health; otherwise, they would fall to pieces under the immense strain that war can inflict on a person. Now that the Rangers were in Campania, and just to the west of Tranquillo, Rocco's thoughts were on his family's whereabouts and situation. *Were they safe? Were they still in Tranquillo? How have the last few years treated them?*

Well, the quick and simple answer to the last question was *not good, not good at all*. The Farfallas and the people of the Mezzogiorno were not spared by the ravages of this war. The last three years had been difficult; however, the recent months proved to be monstrous. The populace of Tranquillo di Puglia maintained the ancient hardiness that was ingrained in their souls through centuries of enduring trials and tribulations. They endured for the most part, but one event would prove too evil even for the strongest person to survive, either physically or mentally, sound and sane.

Up until the summer of 1943, Sicily and mainland Italy were spared the physical ravages of war. Previously, the war had more of a psychological impact on the populace and region. The war had been in far-off places like the frozen plains of Russia and the burning deserts of North Africa where their sons were suffering or dying. Now, the battles were being waged in their backyards. Their false sense of peace and isolation was about to end and with disastrous consequences. The snow globe that was Tranquillo would be forever shattered by the fury and cruelty of mankind. Their lives had been difficult and demanding yet they prevailed. The immediate future, however, would be even less kind to them, and while many good people would be broken physically by the horror to come, their spirits could never be. The Pugliese, like other Italians of the Mezzogiorno, were survivors.

By 1943, the war had been raging for over three years. Several local boys who were drafted into the army had died in the fighting in North Africa and Russia, including Noemi's best friend Giovanni. It was said he had died gloriously fighting the British, but the truth was much different. Giovanni was one of four soldiers killed by an airplane strafing his truck that had run out of gas. The young men had also run out of ammunition and were defenseless to the attack. Local fascists at home didn't want embarrassing facts about their military enterprise to be known for fear of impacting the morale of the Italian people. If it became known that the government couldn't supply the army adequately or even protect their sons, there would have been a mass uprising. All communication from the front had to be closely monitored and censored by Rome to ensure all references to defeatism and negativity were removed. So, stories of heroism were created to maintain control of the country and to keep Italians uneducated about a war being lost. Propaganda extended the misery of these innocent souls. Giovanni's story became one where he and his squad held their positions from advancing British tanks, ultimately forcing the enemy to retreat. Sometimes people will believe the silliest and most farfetched story, because if they were to question this alleged *truth*, it would represent a loss of hope and a surrender to fear. Their boys would be dead and lost. At least, they had a tiny glimmer of hope, albeit a manufactured one.

For the Farfalla family and the citizens of Tranquillo, their full participation in the war had been a waiting game. Every week mothers and fathers would go down to the town square to listen to the casualty reports. The town mayor would read aloud these reports to the gathered mass of worried townsfolk. "Albanese, Marizio. Killed in action. Amici, Daniele. Killed in action. Barone, Francesco. Wounded in action." The mayor would read through the list alphabetically until he reached the end. On the day when Giovanni's name was reported, it came as a punch to the stomach to Noemi and the boy's family. "Patria, Giovanni. Killed in action." A large shriek came from the boy's mother. "No! No! *Il mio bambino! Mio figlio!*" Cries swept across Giovanni's extended family and friends.

Noemi stood motionless and in shock, unable to understand or accept the news. "Papa, is this a cruel joke? He can't be dead. He asked me to marry him before he went away, but I couldn't marry my best friend. I said no. Why did I say no?" Her voice trembled and increased in volume with each spoken sentence. Her mental and physical state approached hysteria, as she collapsed into her father's chest and paternal embrace. "Papa, I said no! I said no! Why did I say no?! He died and I said no. Why, Papa, why?" In her distress, she had seemingly linked his death and the refusal to marry him. Grief had transformed into guilt for the young woman.

Matteo held onto his daughter tightly and spoke softly into her ear to calm her down. "Noemi, this is not your fault. Giovanni knew you loved him. On the day he left, he told me that you refused his proposal, but he wasn't giving up. He looked at me with that silly crooked smile of his and I knew he wasn't going to give up. Know that you were in his heart, special to the end."

"Did he really say that, but...?"

"Yes, he did. No more buts. This is not your fault. We can't control life. Sometimes, bad things happen to good people and it's not their fault. We must endure life's challenges like we always have, with dignity and as a family."

"Thank you, Papa. I need to go see his mother. Annabella, would you come with me to talk to Stella?"

Valentina grabbed Noemi's and Annabella's hands to provide the support a daughter could only get from a mother. "We'll go together as a family. Right, Papa?"

"Right, Mama."

Walking toward her friend's grieving mother, Noemi thought about the days she would go visit her to see how she was doing. Both of her sons were in the armed forces. Giovanni was in the army while his brother Carlo was in the navy. She would help Stella around the house and ensure they had enough food. With both sons away from home, they needed help once in a while. Not to mention, they loved seeing Noemi.

By the time the Farfallas made their way through the shocked crowd, Stella had calmed down somewhat, but it would have been better described as settling into a state of detached numbness. In a monotone voice, she spoke softly to her son's would-be wife. "Noemi, Noemi. Our Giovanni is dead. Now we only have Carlo. Valentina, can you believe this?"

Noemi and her mom hugged Stella tightly and the three wept in one another's arms. Stella turned to look at Noemi and reconfirmed her strong feelings for the young woman. "Noemi, you are a special light in the darkness. Giovanni saw it. Don't ever lose it. Do you hear me? Don't ever lose it."

"Thank you, but I think it was Giovanni that made me special."

Stella smiled tenderly for her young friend. "He will always be special and so will you."

Other townsfolk joined the group to offer their condolences to the grieving parents. After a few minutes, the crowd dispersed to their respective homes to contemplate the news of the day, firstly, the shock of hearing the names on the casualty report, and secondly, the relief for their sons' names not called. It was an odd feeling to be happy and sad at the same moment. A sense of guilt was felt by the fortunate families. After all, the whole village was one family. This contradiction would remain for the entirety of the war.

Every week, the emotions of Tranquillo betrayed its name. Families gathered in the town square to listen to the casualty reports. Some came to hear about their sons while others came in support of friends. The fear and distress were always the same, but the town's emotional state would begin deteriorating the day after the next reading of the weekly announcement. It became a repetitive machine-like existence for these families where the horror was in both knowing and not knowing the truth of their sons' situation. In their hearts, they knew they couldn't trust the government officials, but what choice did they have? They would manufacture all types of atrocities. Their minds called up images of sons lying dead in a North African desert hellhole, or their limbs being ripped from their bodies on the frozen Russian tundra.

These images and ones of their children being eaten by the crows became nightly terrors brought to parents, courtesy of the Demon of Dreams. To fight against the demon, who had a propensity of sitting on a victim's chest while inducing its nightmares, they prayed to the Virgin, the Patron Saint of Tranquillo, to protect them and their boys until they could return home. They prayed hard, very hard to keep their sanity intact. For the demon, this war provided a veritable human feast, a smorgasbord of misery for its sustenance, devouring each morsel of the dreamer's nightly agony and sorrow. The innocence of their souls provided a tasty *dolce* to aid in the consumption of the main course. World War I was merely an *aperitivo* — an appetizer — in comparison.

Family members would say that victims of the demon appeared to be caught in a nightmare, writhing in bed trying to scream. They would see loved ones with their mouths opened wide, but eyes shut tightly. The appearance of panic and outright fear was displayed for all to see. A muffled, almost inaudible scream was the only sound coming from the sleeping quarry, who could only be awakened by being doused with water — a nocturnal baptism. It was at this point that the demon would lean closely toward the dreamer's face, nearly eye to eye and mouth to mouth. As one can imagine, this had the intense effect of inducing greater panic in the victim to the delight of the parasitic entity from Hell.

Stella suffered these night terrors most of all. The demon took special delight in torturing her for some reason. Perhaps, it knew of the bond Stella shared with Noemi, and ultimately Rocco, not that anyone would have known at the time that he was considered special by the evil powers waging spiritual warfare on humanity for millennia. During one of these night terrors right before they got news of Giovanni's death, Stella's husband, Antonio, had difficulty shaking his wife out of her nightmare. "Stella, Stella, wake up! Wake up!" His pleas didn't get the immediate response he wanted. Grabbing and shaking her didn't work either. Nothing worked, until he ran to the kitchen for a pail of water. He remembered that water would do the trick just as it had a couple of weeks earlier.

When Antonio poured the bucket of water onto her and finally was able to pull his wife out of her hellish torment, he claimed to have heard a loud hiss followed by one word being spoken in the darkened corner of the room. "Delicious."

Alarmed, Antonio looked at the pitch-black corner of the room and made the sign of the cross. "God protect us. Who's there? Who's there?" He shuffled his feet and inched closer to investigate the location of the voice. Cautiously extending his arms to feel for the source of the voice, he continued to inch forward until he was startled by Stella's call to him.

"Antonio, what are you doing?"

Antonio slowly turned his attention away from his immediate objective to his wife. He tried to keep one eye on the corner of the room as he directed his focus back to her, but he soon surrendered his search. "Nothing. I thought I heard something. Never mind, how are you? You had another scary nightmare." A dutiful and loving husband, Antonio sat next to her on the bed. He gently stroked her hand to comfort his wife of over twenty-five years.

Stella, like all sleeping victims, had awakened in a state of confusion and panic, only remembering snippets of her nightmare. "I'm alright. Just a lot of crazy things playing in my brain, I guess. My goodness, it feels like my head was beaten like a drum." She tapped her head several times to emphasize the point.

Antonio laid in bed and embraced his wife tightly. "Well, maybe we can sleep late today. The daily chores can wait."

Stella smiled, secure in the arms of her beloved. "Maybe, I should have bad dreams every night."

Antonio laughed. "Maybe. Maybe." Soon, they fell back into a deep sleep laughing like young lovers.

Through all of this torment, Stella and the people of Tranquillo did what they always did, persevered in the face of any hardship thrown their way. They fought against the evil plaguing them as their ancestors had for centuries, with determination and resilience. After each nightly terror, the hardy townsfolk carried on with a single-minded purpose, the safety and security of their families. There's a reason why an Italian raises a glass in a celebratory toast and shouts those familiar words passed down through the generations. *Alla famiglia* embodied the priority of family above all.

For the Farfallas, the demon had no power. It was only when Italy declared war on the US that they became somewhat concerned. Before the US entered, they were content in the knowledge that Rocco would not be in harm's way. But even with Italy having declared war, they knew he was safer 4,000 miles across the sea than in Tranquillo. They had no idea that he was determined to make his way back home as a soldier in an invading army.

In early September of 1943, villagers gathered in the town square to hear the weekly war news and casualty reports from the local officials. The mayor shouted for all to hear; however, his fascist regalia was noticeably absent. "People of Tranquillo, Italy has surrendered unconditionally to the Allied Governments with the promise of fair treatment. People of Tranquillo, the nation has been saved from the darkness of hate and death. God save the king." In an instant, one-time fascists suddenly became monarchists in their praise of King Emmanuel. It's amazing how a person's political affiliation can change so quickly.

The gathered crowd was shocked to hear the news. Finally, they realized all the lies that Mussolini's government had been feeding them for years. Suddenly, a junior official ran out of the town hall. "Mayor, mayor, the Allies have landed at Salerno. Fighting is now happening on the Italian mainland."

Then, another person ran out to the mayor. Instant relief turned to anguish with an additional report that Italian soldiers were engaged in battle with German armed forces, the fearsome Wehrmacht, who were attempting to disarm their former Axis partners. The villagers didn't know that Hitler had ordered his soldiers to take control of Italy to prevent the US and its allies from gaining a strong foothold in Europe through the Italian peninsula. Fighting would be village to village if necessary. There would be no retreat.

Italy's rocky and mountainous terrain provided an excellent defensive advantage for the former Axis partner. The fighting was going to be fierce and horrific. Victory was not going to be an easy or swift proposition. It would be hell on earth with soldiers fighting for yards of earth and rock. The Demon of Dreams was smiling that day, because the future was going to bring a feast of nectar and ambrosia filled with sufficient fear and sorrow to sustain it for a century.

On the day following the announcement, Matteo left the village to complete work at the ancient abbey on Monte Cassino. Matteo and several other men of the village had returned home for a short break after three months of hard work there. It was a job that would take nearly a year to complete and required the work of skilled craftsmen. The abbey's masonry required repair and due to its age, the work would have to be done slowly and carefully. It was decent money, and Matteo couldn't pass up the opportunity to financially support his family, regardless of the recent war news. He thought his family would be safe and he wouldn't be far too far away if anything should happen.

Matteo and the other men were saying their goodbyes to their families before making the trek back to the abbey. One of the men had an old truck that was being used for the trip, although there was sufficient doubt it would survive the whole journey. The Farfallas hugged each other strongly as they always did.

"Noemi, Annabella, please take care of your mama. I won't be too far away. I'll come right back if anything should happen."

The girls shed tears for their father, the man who was the embodiment of unconditional love. Noemi spoke first. "Papa, do you really have to leave? I feel something bad is going to happen. I feel it in my bones. We want you to stay."

Annabella cried her agreement and held her father tightly. "Yes. Please stay. We don't need any money. We need you. I won't let you go."

Matteo cradled each of his daughter's faces as a tear rolled down his cheek. "Aww, my babies, I've been through Hell already and Heaven doesn't want me yet. Be strong."

Turning to the love of his life, his *inamorata*, Matteo had little or no words to express how he felt. He could only embrace her. Valentina spoke for him. "My love, the days will feel like months until you return. But don't worry, all will be well. Return to us safely."

"I will. I will."

The men jumped into the truck and started the journey back to the abbey.

The girls waved to their father. "Bye, Papa, bye! Please finish quickly! We love you!"

Little did the girls know that this would be the last time they would see their father alive. Valentina cast a classic stoic image as she tried to hide her fears from her family. Looking at her daughters, Valentina smiled uncomfortably to conceal her fear of losing her beloved husband. Noemi, however, couldn't be fooled. Holding her mother's hand tightly, she sought to reassure her worried parent. "Mama, I don't think we need to worry. Papa will be back home in no time. I have faith."

Hell on Earth

A week later, a mechanized detachment of Wehrmacht soldiers entered Tranquillo to set up a defensive perimeter. They arrived in large trucks pulling howitzers and machine guns. The lead vehicle stopped in front of the town hall to establish control of the situation. The commanding officer, a captain by rank, stepped out of the car to survey the town square and to visualize a defensive perimeter. Once he completed his survey of the town, the captain turned to the mayor who had come out of his office to meet him. "I assume you are the town mayor."

"Y-y-yes I am."

The captain hissed a statement of fact to all those present. "Well mayor, people of Tranquillo, we now control this town. Don't get in our way and no one will be hurt. Don't step an inch out of line. We are your friends, and we want to keep it that way." He then screamed orders to his men. "Defensive placements around the square, here, here and here! I want a sniper in the church tower and machine gun nests at the two entrances into town! Get it done! The enemy isn't far away."

The recently reformed fascist mayor sought to assure the captain that the village was peaceful and that its residents wouldn't cause any trouble.

"I know you won't, or else." The captain grinned and tapped his holstered Lugar to emphasize the obvious threat his men posed. "I will be commandeering the town hall for my quarters. Please arrange lodgings for my men with the local villagers. I want a listing of all residents and an inventory of the central grain warehouse. My men need to eat too, and I know you wouldn't want to see old friends who are protecting you from invaders go hungry now, right?"

"Yes, of course. Don't worry captain. We'll make sure your men feel comfortable and welcomed." The mayor scurried into town hall with his assistant to obtain the requested information.

"Lieutenant Lang, please escort our friends inside and lend a helping hand. Please be delicate. Remember these are our friends and allies." The captain's pronunciation of the word 'friends' sounded more like a threat and not a promise of peace. He topped off his greeting by flashing a grotesque smile to punctuate the danger of the moment.

The lieutenant followed the two men into the building to make sure there was nothing underhanded going on, since they were of the opinion that Italians, especially Southern Italians, can't be trusted. How odd it is for the same stereotype to follow people around the world. Whether they're in the New World or the Old, Southern Italians were viewed similarly — devious and untrustworthy.

The mayor instructed another assistant to run to the bell tower and ring the town bell. The ringing of the bell in a certain way acted as a sort of emergency notification to all residents to gather in the town square.

A crowd made up mostly of older men and women made their way to the square with their sons. Their daughters were left behind, because they didn't want the girls to be seen for obvious reasons. It was a matter of protecting them from unwanted advances and potential danger. Defensive walls were raised around each family's hearth and home.

"People of Tranquillo, I am Captain Hoffman. We are here to protect you from the invaders. Depending on the route the invaders take up the peninsula, we may be here for a month or for only a few days. Until then, stay out of our way, but continue to work and complete your daily chores. Additionally, the mayor has arranged accommodations for my men in your homes. I expect they will be treated courteously. That is all."

The townsfolk grumbled amongst themselves at the prospect of housing soldiers. Stella walked up to Valentina and whispered to her discreetly so as not to seem suspicious. "You need to hide Noemi and Annabella. Send them into the back fields where no one will look."

Valentina spoke softly to her friend and without moving her head. "I know. This is terrifying. We need to walk slowly back to the house and hide the girls quickly."

Stella took Valentina by the arm and walked out of the square in a deliberate and steady manner, without making eye contact with the soldiers. "*Piano, piano* — slowly, slowly. Nice and easy."

Homes were selected based on their strategic location to the two main roads into town. Soldiers arrived at each house and informed the owners of the army's expectation of complete cooperation.

The two mothers made it back to the house and carefully opened the door. Once inside, Valentina called for her daughters, but not too loudly. "Noemi. Annabella. I need you to pack up a few things quickly and to go hide in the back fields for a few days. German soldiers have taken over the town, and we need you girls to hide. Each house will have a soldier sleeping there."

Noemi stood silently because she knew why her mother wanted them to hide. Annabella, who was still a little immature for her age, didn't comprehend the potential danger. "Mama, I don't understand why we need to…"

With tears streaming down her cheeks, Valentina cried and stared intently at her daughter. "Annabella please listen to me. You are so young and beautiful. You, you, you…". Her voice quivered unrelentingly, and her hands shook in panic.

Noemi grabbed her sister's hand and caressed her cheek with the other. "Don't be naïve Bella. We need to go."

Fear consumed Annabella as she stared at the front door. She was about to let out a scream until Noemi stopped her.

"Bella, no!" Placing her hand over her trembling sister's mouth, she tried to simultaneously silence and comfort Bella. Being a compassionate and astute sibling, she knew her role at that moment needed to be more maternal than sisterly. Noemi explained that both were going to be safe, and Mama would not be hurt either. "Shhh. Easy Bella, easy. We are all going to be safe. There's nothing to worry about. This is sort of like the game we used to play, you know when Mama and Papa would try to find us, but we didn't come out until they surrendered." Noemi slowly removed her hand from her sister's mouth.

"Then why are we leaving? I don't understand." Anguish was still clearly evident in her face and tone.

"Oh, it's so we're out of the soldiers' way. We don't want to be a distraction. Let's face it. You are the prettiest girl in town. Well, next to me anyway." Noemi pulled away slowly and continued to hold her sibling's hand.

The two sisters giggled, and Annabella slowly regained her composure. "OK, I believe you, I guess. But how will we know when it's safe to come back?"

Mama answered swiftly. "Stella or I will come for you. No one else. Do you hear me? No one else. Now go quickly."

The girls made a hasty exit out the back door and into a hiding spot where it was easy to view their home while remaining undetected. The location was known only to them. It was used by the two girls to hide from their mother when they wanted to avoid chores. It was an area of overgrown shrubbery and packed with large trees. It was easy to hide and go undetected.

Soon after the girls left, the Wehrmacht lieutenant, accompanied by the mayor's assistant, banged on the front door with a determined authority. Valentina and Stella were startled at the intensity of the knock. Valentina shuddered a short response. "Y-Y-Yes, who is it?"

The mayor's assistant responded. "It's Marco. I'm here with a soldier who will be staying with you for a few days. Please let us in."

Stella opened the door. "Good day, Marco. I was just leaving."

"*Ciao, senora.* We'll be by later today with your house guest."

"Fine, let's hope he's quiet. I need my sleep."

The men walked into the house and greeted Valentina. Grinning like some sort of evil cartoon character, the lieutenant introduced himself and the young soldier. "*Senora*, I am Lieutenant Lang, and this is Private Schmidt. Please arrange quarters for him."

The juxtaposition of the evil grinning officer and the innocent, baby-faced private was astounding. The officer's presence created a parfait of creepiness and testosterone that was so thick a butcher's knife couldn't cut through it easily. A jackhammer would have been more appropriate. Valentina knew he was trouble.

The private, on the other hand, seemed harmless, but why wasn't this boy in school back home instead of a war zone about to be pushed to his mental and physical limits? Matteo was once this young before he went off to war and lost part of his essence, the life spark that separates humanity from beasts. The ability to dream and to expand one's mind exponentially was unique to mankind. Beasts don't dream; they lie in wait to pounce on and devour their prey. Sometimes, these beasts were the prey, being eaten by a predator that was one step up in the food chain. What a pity, she thought, that another boy was destined for the war's meat grinder.

"Yes, of course." She pointed to a spare room off the kitchen for the young man to get settled. "I assume I will have no trouble too."

The lieutenant laughed mockingly at the perceived absurdity of the comment and exited the house, slapping the gloves he was holding in his right hand against his thigh. "Never, *senora*, we are your protectors. Are we not?" The threat meter just hit ten.

Over the next few weeks, the soldiers would leave and return to the village several times. Their movements were based on Allied troop activities along the long and rocky front in Campania, the region which Tranquillo straddled on its western side. As soon as the soldiers left, the local girls would return home from their hiding places, every time without fail. It became a dance that the soldiers were well aware of, but ultimately, they didn't care. There were real problems in front of them, namely several enemy divisions. While a partisan uprising had sprung up in Italy, there was no indication that one was in operation in or around this village. So, they didn't pay any attention to missing girls.

An odd thing that did happen during this time was the development of a maternal bond between Valentina and Private Schmidt, or Hans as he preferred to be called. Just 18 years old, Hans was the embodiment of the perfect young gentleman, calm yet politely inquisitive. With blonde hair and blue eyes, he looked like he fell off a Hitler Youth poster, but this belied his true nature. He was a sweet and innocent teenager in whom any parent would take pride.

Breakfasts were the best part of her day, where she could sit and chat with the young man who became a surrogate for her son. Hans appreciated the relationship being a substitute for the mother he left behind. He needed a reminder of a motherly and loving connection to maintain his sanity, something that would stay with him during the fight to come.

On one such morning, Valentina asked to know more about her young house guest. "Hans, please tell me about your home. Your mama and papa. Who are they? Are they like you?"

"They are normal people. Really average. Father is a mason, and my mother is the real head of the family. My parents love to dance and have fun. They hate to take life too seriously. I have two younger brothers and two older sisters. My brothers are real hell-raisers, but my sisters are the complete opposite, quiet and beautiful. I miss them all."

"What a big family! Your mama must have her hands full."

Hans laughed. "Yes, she does. She really does."

The banter would continue for the entire meal, a serene distraction from the realities of the outside world. It came as a shock when Hans raised a point that Valentina wasn't expecting. "You know, your daughters will always be safe. I wouldn't let anything happen to them but it's better they stay in the hiding spot in the field by the trees." Hans winked as he gathered his equipment; his unit was moving to another defensive location in another village closer to the front.

Valentina was startled at hearing the young soldier's comment. "Thank you. Rocco, I mean Hans, be safe."

Hans understood why she mistakenly called him Rocco. He gave her a big hug and exited the home into an uncertain future. It was his time to join the fight. A week later, his division was racing back to Tranquillo and retreating from an oncoming onslaught of a powerful Allied attack. The villagers didn't know what was happening. The sound of intense gunfire and bombs exploding were heard and seemed to be getting closer to them.

German soldiers hurried into town to set up another defensive position. One of these soldiers, whom Valentina recalled as one of Hans' friends, ran to the house. "*Senora*, I don't have much time." Interrupting his greeting, a bomb exploded just outside of town causing many in the vicinity to duck their heads.

"Yes, what is it? What's happening?"

The soldier answered hastily. "We are retreating to another town. Hans… Hans is dead. He asked me to tell you that he appreciated everything you did for him. I need to go. You all need to get out of here."

Valentina stood in shock as the soldier sprinted away. Hans had left an indelible mark on her soul. The battle continued to rage nearby, inching closer to the once peaceful hamlet. She took no notice of neighbors running past her with personal belongings in the opposite direction of the explosions and in a futile attempt to get out of harm's way. They were leaving before getting caught in the crossfire. Upon hearing the explosions, Noemi and Annabella emerged from their hiding spot and rushed back into the house. The commotion of the running villagers added to their disorientation caused by the proximity of the explosions and gunfire. They screamed and tugged at their mama to get her to move and act.

Noemi screamed, "Mama, we have to leave! Mama! Mama!"

After what seemed like an eternity, the girls were able to shake their mother out of her catatonic state.

"Yes, girls, we need to go. We'll go, we'll go to the abbey and find Papa. We'll be safe at the abbey. It's a holy site. Bella, go pack some clothes for us."

Matteo was unable to return home since the time he had left as the fighting made travel too perilous. The Wehrmacht did not want any Italian men moving around the countryside for fear of a partisan group forming. Monte Cassino was the safest place to be.

Bella ran into the house and started packing a bag with the bare essentials, while her mother ran to the kitchen to grab a small amount of money hidden behind a loose stone in the wall. Mother and daughters met in the kitchen and quickly made their way to the front door. Valentina carefully looked outside to make sure there was no sign of danger. "Girls, quickly, we need to run to the other side of the village. Keep close to me and don't look back. Let's go."

The family raced down the road along with other villagers fleeing the chaos of war. The rat-a-tat-tat of gunfire could be heard coming from the southern part of Tranquillo and the battle was growing increasingly louder and more intense. This was where the so-called invading forces were engaged in a life-or-death struggle with the Wehrmacht.

The commotion and turmoil experienced by the crowd running for their lives was made significantly more terrifying by the increasing intensity of the battle and nearby explosions. Parents held screaming children tightly, while others picked up friends who had fallen onto the hard cobblestone streets. The crowd formed into a pack of stampeding bulls rampaging through the ancient narrow passage out of town. Nothing could stop them once they got moving, although some villagers were left behind, including Stella and her husband.

If only the villagers had known that the invading army was Rocco and his Rangers coming to liberate the village… He had returned to save his family and his hometown, but no one could have imagined it was him, a native son of Puglia. War had come to Tranquillo, and it was scary. Each step away from home was a step toward an uncertain future and a possible death. Escalating screams and numerous twisted ankles suffered on the cobblestone road highlighted the mob's panic and anguish. Disorder and mayhem were surely their companions.

So Close

In the days and weeks leading up to the Battle of Tranquillo, Rocco had been sensing an invisible hand guiding his Ranger company back to his hometown. It was too coincidental and convenient for his return to be so dramatic. Only a contrived Hollywood B-movie would have scripted such a scenario. Every turn on the battlefield away from Tranquillo would be reversed in short order. The men in his company attributed these constant changes to the confusion of fighting in a significantly mountainous land where danger lurked around every bend.

On the morning of the attack, Rocco's Ranger company was encamped about five miles to the southwest of the Tranquillo. They were awaiting orders to move north with the objective of capturing Rome. Rangers were to be the vanguard of the attack on the left flank. Their goal was to seize a critical promontory overlooking Naples Bay and to generate enough mayhem to divert the Wehrmacht soldiers away from other sectors along the front. The overall objective of this strategy was to create an opportunity to achieve a significant Allied breakthrough and open the road to Rome. It had been a tough fight so far, and the troops needed some good news.

Rocco's squad was resting near a tent where the sector's US Army commander was reviewing the battle plan with his staff. They were all huddled around a table studying a map indicating where the attack would take place.

Jimmy spotted Rocco staring oddly at the group of officers inside the tent. His friend's puzzled expression worried him. "Rocco, what are you looking at? Is it another one of your bad feelings? You know I don't like it when you get them. It's way too spooky."

Shortstop took notice of the situation too. "Looks like his radar is going off."

Cowboy was lost in his own world, thoroughly engrossed in reading the most recent edition of Stars & Stripes. There was a story of a recent battle in the Pacific that interested him; his brother was in the Marines and had been part of the Navy's island-hopping campaign.

Gunslinger was standing next to Shortstop, cleaning his rifle. He knew when Rocco got those strange feelings that there was going to be a fight. "Oh boy. The last time he looked like that, we were on the road to Messina, and that was one humdinger of a day. You know that was the day I first began to think we had some sort of heavenly protection. Not one of us has hit the butcher's bill yet, and that's all the way through North Africa, Sicily, and here. Just a little blood spilled. Can't be explained any other way. Rocco, what's the story? Are we protected by the angels or something?"

Rocco slowly redirected his attention from the men in the tent to his friends. His response was as chilling as it was pausingly brief. "Or some…thing." Getting up to walk away, the young warrior from Puglia felt a little faint, but Jimmy was able to catch him before he hit the ground.

"Are you okay?"

"Thanks Jimmy. I'm fine. Just needed to stretch my legs a little. They must have fallen asleep. I guess I was sitting too long. Jimmy, take a walk with me."

The two Boston brothers-in-arms walked slowly away. Rocco's inner turmoil was clearly visible to his friend. "Hey buddy, what did you see?"

"I don't know what I saw. Can't explain it. There was an officer in the tent whispering into the general's ear. I had never seen him before, but he had a strange look on his face and a sort of weird smirk. The general seemed like he wasn't aware of the guy's presence or was in some sort of trance, but he had to know he was there. The officer was whispering to him for God's sake. Every so often, the general would nod his head, apparently agreeing to what was being said."

"Could you hear what he was saying?"

"A little. Most of what he said was gibberish, but I did hear him tell the general to send us to Puglia to finish off the enemy troops there. But when he finished speaking and backed away from the general, something odd happened. I swear he looked right at me and saw that I was watching him. He stared at me intently with this puzzled and pained expression on his face. You know what happened next? He winked."

"Winked?"

"Yes, winked! He then put his finger to his lips and said, 'Shhh,' before slowly backing away and out of sight. Can you freaking believe that? I don't know where he went because there's no opening in the tent there."

Jimmy had learned not to be surprised by what Rocco saw or said. They had been through a lot in their journey from North Africa, Sicily and Southern Italy, but this story caught him by surprise. "Holy crap! That's crazy!"

Rocco fixed his eyes to the distant horizon and weighed what he had just seen. "Jimmy, it feels like some power has been guiding me toward something, and I can't say if it's the hand of Heaven or Hell. It's like I'm a passenger on a bus, and it won't let me off until I reach my final destination. And you guys are along for the ride unfortunately."

"Don't overthink it. Why would Hell want to take you somewhere and keep all of us safe too? Hell has no power over you."

Rocco wasn't convinced. "Maybe, just maybe. Well, we'll see what fate has in store for me, for us. I think our next stop is Puglia."

The two friends walked back to their buddies to await the forthcoming orders. It was no surprise to Rocco when the unit commander told them of the change in plans. "Puglia is our objective. We're gonna clear out the remaining forces around a town called Tranquillo. The general wants his best men to make sure there are no foul-ups. Let's get going in ten."

Rocco wasn't surprised but still a little shocked at hearing that his hometown was their destination. The squad immediately stood up and stared at their buddy. Tommy Gun was the only one who could muster enough strength to speak. "Butterfly, what the hell is going on? This is really weird. Did you know?"

"No, I didn't know. But everything's gonna be alright and airtight, like it's always been. We got a job to do." He spoke to the guys, his buddies, while staring at the ground and avoiding eye contact. This was his way of trying to convince everyone, including himself, that there was nothing to worry about. It didn't work. There was something to worry about. They could see fear written on Rocco's face, no matter what he said. They never saw him worry about anything before this moment.

Cowboy approached Rocco to reassure his friend. "Like we always say, it's gonna be alright and airtight, like a cold beer. It's just another mission. That's all."

One by one, all spoke up. "Yup, alright and airtight."

What these warriors didn't know was that this wouldn't be the last time Rocco would see the officer from the tent. He would be seen once again, but he'd be in a different uniform and with a renewed purpose. Rocco's torment and his descent into madness was just beginning. Born of horror and deeds so dreadful that it would shake a person's faith in humanity, this madness would produce a reaction in an otherwise innocent and kind-hearted young man that was beyond comprehension. Newton's law states that *"every action in nature has an equal and opposite reaction."* In Rocco's case, his reaction would be far from equal. It would be unimaginable and life-altering.

Soon, the division was on the move with Rocco's company taking the lead. As the men piled into a truck, they noticed a distinct heaviness and odor in the air that weighed on them. Gunslinger stared at Cowboy, while both men rubbed their chests. "Do you smell that? What is it?"

"I don't know what it is, but it's putrid. My lungs feel like they can't take in enough air."

Shortstop agreed. "This is crazy. It's like I can feel the air."

Rocco and Jimmy could only stare at each other. They knew in their hearts that Hell was coming.

Tommy Gun jumped into the conversation quickly in his own jovial way. "Sorry guys, that was me. Beans for breakfast are a killer." His joke had an immediate calming effect and lightened the tension in the truck. Soon, they were off on their trek to the battlefield.

Jimmy looked over to Tommy Gun and covered his face to pretend he was blocking his friend's noxious fumes. "Well, at least you don't have to change your underwear before the battle. Why would you want to ruin another pair if you could avoid it?"

The truck erupted in laughter. Tommy Gun laughed the hardest.

The Rangers were ready for battle.

The journey to Tranquillo was eerily silent, not a word was spoken by anyone despite the bumpy ride on rough, mountain roads. The trucks carrying the Rangers stopped several miles outside of the village. The men would have to make the rest of their way on foot and in secrecy. They didn't want to give the enemy troops advance warning of their attack.

Once the battle got underway, the assault was so swift and ferocious that the Rangers were able to gain the upper hand quickly and overpower the defenders in short order. An unintended effect of the attack's success was the total fright that it sent through the village. Not understanding what was happening or having the opportunity to speak with the Rangers, the villagers grabbed their children and belongings and ran in the opposite direction for self-preservation. Their liberation veered violently into a pathway of continued captivity in servitude to overwhelming fear and panic. They fled to what they thought was safety, but their journey brought them further into the jaws of the beast. Just another day in Puglia.

The Rangers entered Tranquillo cautiously to ensure there were no remnants of the Wehrmacht units left behind. Jimmy had to hold Rocco back to prevent him from running foolhardy into his hometown and into danger. Once the all-clear signal was given and he was released from his friend's grip, Rocco was off like a jackrabbit toward his family's house.

He ran into the house, nearly breaking down the door. "Mama! Papa! Where are you? It's me, Rocco! I've come back for you! Noemi! Bella! Can you hear me?" He rushed to the garden and continued to call out their names. He even checked the old hiding spot the girls knew so well. "Girls, are you here?" He frantically ran from one side of the garden to the other. Nothing. No one could be found.

Running back through the house, Rocco found several of his old neighbors, including Giovanni's mother, Stella, outside. They were all shocked to see the return of a familiar face. A crowd of old friends who hadn't made it out of the village during the battle formed around Rocco. Stella came forward to embrace the young warrior. She wanted to make sure it wasn't an illusion, or some sort of evil spirit come to prolong their agony. She had been injured by some flying debris and was now being assisted by her husband. "Rocco Farfalla, is that you? Is that really you?"

"Yes, it is, *Zi' Stella*." As a matter of respect, young villagers would often refer to elders as aunt or uncle. "Where is my family? Are they safe?"

"Oh, my child, if only they had known you were coming. If only they had known, this would have been a happier reunion."

"What do you mean? Where are they?" Panic consumed him now.

"They ran out of town along with the retreating soldiers. We all tried to get away. No one knew what was happening. There was so much confusion with all the bomb explosions and guns shooting."

Rocco immediately ran to the opposite end of the village to see if they were there. Stella and the others tried to reason with him, but he couldn't be stopped. "Rocco, they aren't there. They're gone. Please wait."

Running at full speed and still holding his rifle, he yelled back at the villagers. "I have to see for myself."

Arriving at the end of the village, Rocco saw the retreating infantry and the fleeing villagers. The soldiers were abandoning the temporary defensive positions they had set up for an anticipated continuation of the offensive on Tranquillo. They soon realized that no further attack was forthcoming. It became apparent that the villagers fleeing with them had become a human shield. The Rangers stopped their offensive to prevent further civilian casualties. The risk wasn't worth the reward of capturing a few remaining units of enemy troops. Grabbing a pair of binoculars from Gunslinger, who had run with him to view the retreating troops, Rocco looked intensely at the scene and saw some villagers climbing into military trucks. He thought he noticed his mother and sisters getting in one of the trucks. "No, wait! Don't go with those bastards! Gunslinger, I was so close. Why is God doing this to me? Those sons-a-bitches are using them as protection."

"We'll get them, buddy. It's just not safe to do right now."

Rocco tuned Gunslinger out as he continued scanning the landscape and watching his family ride away. "I was so close, so close." Still looking through the binoculars, he caught sight of the creepy officer he saw in the general's tent earlier in the day. This time, however, he was wearing the uniform of a Wehrmacht officer and was whispering in the ear of a lieutenant. Unknown to Rocco at the time, it was Lieutenant Lang who had scared Valentina earlier. The captain of the unit had been killed in the attack. The scene was the same as before, the lieutenant nodding his head mechanically in response to what was being said. When the creepy officer finished whispering in his ear and backed away, Lieutenant Lang yelled several orders, and the trucks were quickly on the move with their civilian passengers.

Rocco muttered to himself. "Holy crap. It's him again. Who is he?" Momentarily, the sinister officer looked right at Rocco as if he knew the young man was watching him. He smirked and winked at him once again; however, this time he tipped his hat and waved goodbye to his eavesdropping foe. Commander Creep, as he came to be known, turned and walked into a patch of trees and disappeared.

"Oh my God, Gunslinger, did you see that guy? He walked into the woods and disappeared?"

"No, what guy?" The Texan responded in his best West Texas

drawl. "Butterfly, are you okay buddy? You look shakier than a newborn colt."

"Yeah, I'm fine. Guess I'm just seeing things."

Rocco ran back to his boyhood home to talk to the other villagers and to see if he could gather any information on his family's destination. He surmised Stella would be most knowledgeable, so he went directly to her first. By this time, she was being treated by a medic and was sitting on the bench in front of her house. "Hey, how's she doing?"

"She's okay. She had a bullet fragment stuck in her arm, but I was able to remove it. Didn't even make a single sound while I was taking it out. She's one tough lady." The medic smiled at Stella to acknowledge her courage.

Rocco responded emphatically. "You have no idea, kid. I'll take it from here." The medic ran to another civilian needing help. Since there were only minor casualties to the Rangers, the division medics had ample opportunity to assist the villagers. Each felt fortunate that no one died that day. It seemed that Providence was smiling on Tranquillo, or so they thought.

Rocco couldn't hold back his anxiety. He rapid-fired a set of questions, hoping to get some level of comfort from a still stunned Stella. "*Zia*, please tell me what you know. Where are the Germans taking my family? I didn't see my father with them. Where is he? Do you know? Do you know?"

"Easy *Bello*, I can't understand a word you said. Did you ask me where your family is going?"

"Sorry, yes."

"Well, your mama talked about going to Monte Cassino. That's where your papa has been working to repair the abbey's masonry."

"Monte Cassino? That's over a hundred miles away. How did she think they were going to get there? Magic carpet?"

"Don't be fresh. Your mama did what she thought was right. Both Noemi and Bella are with her at least, and I didn't see them get hurt."

Rocco rubbed his forehead vigorously and paced frantically back and forth in front of his old neighbor. "But they are stuck now behind enemy lines and it's going to be a slugfest all the way up to Rome. All the fighting we've seen so far is a pretty good sign of what's in front of us. How can I get to them?"

"Ahh *Bello*, we have to have faith in the Holy Mother and the saints. They won't let us down." This was odd considering the Holy Mother and saints didn't save Giovanni from a terrible fate, but the Pugliese will always be Pugliese. "Look, you almost got to them today. You'll get to them another day. If we don't have faith, then what do we have to lean on during the bad times?"

"You make it sound so easy."

"It is, when you believe. Now, I've got to lie down. It's been a tiring day."

Stella's husband escorted her inside to rest, while Rocco thanked her for the positive outlook. Something was guiding him to his family. Perhaps, it was Providence or the Madonna who were his guide. Maybe Commander Creep was an unknown saint sent from Heaven to help him. He was so close in reaching his family, but next time, he would need to try a little harder.

The error of that day pointed to Rocco and old friends misreading the path he was on. At Tranquillo, Rocco had entered a crucible whose entire focus was to toy with every fiber of his being and to prepare for his slow descent into madness, death, and rebirth. By the time he found out the truth, the consequences of his folly of not recognizing the evil standing in front of him would be tragic. He was right about the slugfest to come. The Allies' journey up to Monte Cassino would take several more months. It would be a hundred miles of blood and death, where men would die for yards of rock and dirt. Italy's terrain was a defending army's dream. It was packed with ragged hills and mountains for which the Allies paid dearly. Over these months, the Farfalla clan would learn more about horror than most families would experience in generations.

Crucible of Madness

Valentina and the girls, as well as the other villagers accompanying the retreating soldiers, were removed from the trucks after travelling about twenty miles from Tranquillo. The soldiers told them there was no reason to hold onto them any longer. They had served their purpose as human shields.

"*Raus!* Everyone, get out!" Lieutenant Lang barked his orders. "*Raus! Raus!*" There's something about the German language that made commands seem scarier than others. "I don't care where you go but stay out of our way, or else. Now go!" Placing these civilians in harm's way was seen as a good strategy for the defensive battles to come. During the winter and spring months of 1944, it would be a main factor in impeding the Allied efforts across a treacherous and expansive front line, which came to be called the Gustav Line, and it was exactly where Commander Creep wanted them. A slow-burning fuse had been lit to capture Rocco's soul, and he was already beginning to feel its effects.

Once removed from the truck and pushed to the side of the road, the small group of villagers, numbering around thirty, discussed where they should go. One by one, they expressed their opinions.

"Let's go East. It's safer there. All the fighting is near Naples to… to the West."

"How about we go back home? I thought I saw Americans."

"How do you know they were Americans? It could've been anybody you saw. Your mind is playing tricks on you."

Opinions volleyed back and forth until a shout was heard from the back of the crowd. "Let's go to Monte Cassino. It's an abbey. No one will get hurt there." Nobody, but Noemi, turned to see who spoke; their focus remained fixated elsewhere. Noemi, not recognizing the voice, unsuccessfully scanned the crowd.

"Yes, the abbey! That's right. We'll go there." The bark of an elderly man was immediately and reflexively followed by those of his family.

Valentina agreed. "That's exactly where we should go. My husband is there. We'll be safe there. The Heavenly Father will protect us."

Shouts of "let's go" and "no" permeated the hillside. Refugees in their own country, the now stranded villagers argued intensely and set off an indecipherable cacophony of symphonic proportions. Disharmony and discord ruled the day, until a momentary lull allowed the mysterious voice to be heard again. "Why don't families go in the direction they think best?"

Noemi raised her voice. "Who said that?" Angling her head and peering around her neighbors in the crowd, she tried in vain to locate the origin of the unfamiliar voice. "Who said that? Can you step forward?" A great feeling of unease developed in Noemi at the sound of the voice. Something didn't sit right with her. She found the voice to have a certain menacing tone that didn't seem to register with the others. The atmosphere on the hillside became suffocatingly thick with danger.

The crowd murmured and was still undecided about what to do next. At first, everyone appeared confused and then frustrated by the latest recommendation. The tone of the debate continued to rise as they tried to decide the best course of action for all to take. Still wanting to remain together, old friends did not want to split up the group. The mysterious voice shouted again. "Let each family decide!"

With the crowd at an impasse, the decision suddenly became unanimous in an instant. "Yes, let each family decide for themselves." Shouts of "yes" now passed from person to person with some still arguing to keep the group together.

Noemi and Bella clung tightly to their mother. Believing there was safety in numbers, the girls were frightened by the splintering of the crowd. About ten villagers agreed with the decision to go North and to the abbey. The rest scattered in different directions with most deciding to return to Tranquillo. It was their home, and they felt they should have remained there, for better or worse.

For the third time this day, Commander Creep stealthily accomplished his mission. He kept Valentina and the girls on the path to Monte Cassino, but why? What was his game? Was he a puppet master controlling people like marionettes on a string? Commander Creep would be seen again in Camp Edwards, where his name and insidious identity would finally be revealed to our young hero.

Over the succeeding weeks and months following their escape from their home village, the small group of refugees inched their way toward Monte Cassino. The path to the abbey through Campania to Lazio wasn't an easy one as they stayed one step ahead of the intense battles being fought. It was a daily replay of terror for all involved. It had been a tortuous journey for the group, travelling from hillside to hillside, cave to cave and abandoned home to abandoned home. They foraged for the little scraps of food they could find. They ate the little bits and pieces of food that soldiers left behind, and often even the inedible fodder normally allotted to farm animals. This was the sad nature of their journey from Tranquillo to the abbey.

Approaching the base of the mountain where the abbey was situated, the madness of war surrounded them, but fortune seemingly favored the Farfalla family. While emotionally distraught and pushed to the limits of sanity, they had remained uninjured physically. Several of the other travelers, however, could not claim such fortune. A few days earlier, the group was making its way along a path that was within a few miles of the abbey. Unfortunately, they wandered close to a Wehrmacht infantry regiment and were run off the road by several speeding trucks.

The German soldiers were preparing defensive emplacements for an expected attack on the abbey, which provided a strategic position overlooking the valley below and the path to Rome. Naples and most of the Campania region had already been captured, and the Allies were pushing their way up the peninsula against a ferocious defense. Fighting was taking a heavy toll on the armies on each side, and the Normandy landing was still months away. A breakthrough on the Italian front was needed by the Allies to help bring the war to a speedier end and produce a lasting peace for a world exhausted by two global wars in less than thirty years.

The group was in complete disorder. Mayhem was the ruler of the day. The soldiers were yelling at them to get out of the way, or they would be shot, civilians be damned. Suddenly in the skies above them, a squadron of fighter planes and bombers appeared. The air force was coming to soften up local defenses and to bomb the abbey. The Allied leadership feared that the abbey was a key strong point for the Wehrmacht, and they couldn't risk leaving an enemy force behind their advancing armies on the way to Rome. It had to be addressed, or so it was believed.

During the air raid, several planes pulled out of their tight formation escorting the bombers. Their objective was to attack and eliminate the defensive fortifications ahead of advancing Allied forces. The fighters strafed these positions with machine gun and rocket fire, causing many of the soldiers to scatter when their ammunition reserve was hit and exploded. It was a stunning display, killing many soldiers and several of the civilians who were not able to get to a safe distance. A sad day was going to be made horrifically sadder for Valentina and her daughters in the coming days. They would soon discover that Matteo, beloved husband and father, had also been killed, although it wasn't because of the bombing. This war's deadly tentacles reached everyone, and no one was safe.

Whether bombing the ancient abbey was strategically sound or whether the Wehrmacht had sufficient strength encamped there to justify it had been hotly debated at the Allied headquarters. War is the opposite of sanity for even the most well-intentioned person, and hindsight is a superpower shared by many. What can't be debated was that the bombing left a gaping hole in the Farfalla family.

Valentina and the girls survived the attack; however, they found themselves separated from the rest of the group. Unable to locate the others safely, they sought refuge underneath an overturned donkey cart several hundred yards away to wait for the fighting to stop before continuing their journey. They spent the night there not knowing how much danger lay in front of them or where their friends were. In the coming days, they would experience the highest and lowest points of emotion. *Danger* would not be wearing a uniform that Italians were taught to fear. Rather, it would come from a place never expected. Commander Creep had done his job well. Hell's prey was being delivered to the trap and the hunters were close behind. The path was laid to be slow and indirect, a veritable labyrinth designed to break down the travelers' spirits and emotional state.

Day by day, terror lay in front of them with the beast following their every move. Throughout their walking journey, Noemi had a feeling of impending doom that no one else shared. Though unseen, the beast's power could be felt. She would ask the others in her party for their opinion, but everyone thought she was just imagining things. The common responses were, "Here we go again, Noemi's seeing ghosts."

On the day before the attack, Noemi was particularly disturbed as the remaining members of the group pressed their journey onward to the abbey. Her distress grew as she continued to swivel her head from side to side and back to front, scanning her surroundings to find the object of her suspicion and anxiety. Unable to find anything out of the ordinary, well anything out of the ordinary for a war zone, her mind raced with terrible thoughts of being attacked by wild beasts. Death, terror, and screams echoed in her dreamlike and panicked state, until in an instant, she stopped dead in her tracks. A hideous odor had suddenly overtaken her. "Mama, do you smell something odd? I think there is something bad following us. Do you see anyone?"

Her mother reached the point of exasperation and turned back to face her daughter. She couldn't lose her strength. Otherwise, her children would lose hope quickly. "I see no one, *bambina*. Please stop worrying. Everything's going to be fine, alright?"

"You say that every day, but we have been walking so long. It feels like we've walked around all of Italy. Something's not right."

"Mother of God help me! Noemi, please stop worrying. It's been a long trip, but we are close to the abbey now and we are out of danger."

"But...."

"No more 'buts.' Enough is enough. *Basta!* You're going worry yourself into an early grave. We're almost there. Your papa will be so happy to see us."

Noemi begrudgingly acquiesced, but her fears remained embedded deep within her. The tragic irony of her mother's last comments would soon be realized. The beast was near, and it would be walking on two legs. Its form would be a gang of men, more inhuman than human, committing a level of atrocities that would make the most hardened heart weep.

On the morning after the attack, Valentina and the girls started their journey to the abbey again. When they arrived at their destination and ended a long journey from Tranquillo, their lives would be forever changed, because it was there the world would come crashing done on the Farfallas. Coming down the side of the mountain where the abbey was situated was a stream of people attempting to escape the next aerial attack. The prior attack had already caused damage, and no one was going to take a chance that Providence would protect them. There were monks and laborers abandoning the ancient hilltop refuge.

Valentina recognized a friend of Matteo running swiftly with a group of other laborers. Her husband was nowhere in sight. She waved her arms and shouted. "Mario, is that you? Mario!"

"*Dio mio!* Valentina, Valentina! What are you doing here? It's not safe. We have to leave."

"Mario, where is Matteo? Where is he?" Her pleadings were met with an old friend's blank stare. "Why won't you say something? What happened? Why can't you speak? What are you hiding?" The decibel level of her voice rose with each question, bringing her to the point of delirium. Her children now pulled close to her and clung to her tightly, sobbing uncontrollably. "Is he...is he...?" The distraught wife and mother couldn't finish her last question.

Mario reached out his arms toward the sobbing trio but struggled to speak. "Valentina, girls, I...I...I don't how to say it. He's dead. Matteo's dead."

The sobs turned to shrieks for Noemi and her mother. Bella, however, backed away silently, shaking her head and in a state of shock. The sight of the three traumatized family members was heartbreaking for a shattered Mario. "I'm so sorry, so sorry."

Valentina gathered sufficient strength to ask the specifics of her beloved's death. "When did it happen? How did he die?"

"He died about three months ago."

Noemi cried as a stunned Valentina remained still. "Three months ago? We have been on the road for so long and he was killed three months ago? That can't be true. It's unbelievable."

"Your papa was carrying some construction materials up to the abbey that day. My old friend was helping me pull some of the heavier materials up the side of the mountain. One of the items was a short section of a drainage pipe. He was mistaken for a partisan by a young soldier who thought the pipe was a weapon. He died instantly. For some reason, a few of the materials we stacked inside the abbey walls tipped over. I rushed in to see what happened. It was odd because we were so careful. Your papa told me to take care of restacking the materials and that he would finish bringing up the last of the items. And then boom, he was gone. I'm so sorry. It should have been me. It's my fault."

Valentina assured Mario that it wasn't his fault. "No, no. If you had died, then your children would be fatherless now too. Fate can be cruel." The now widowed Valentina stared blankly into the distance — emotionless and numb.

Mario hugged Valentina tightly. "We have to go. I heard another attack is coming and that there is a crazy group of soldiers operating behind the lines. We're going to get caught in the middle of a battle. Each side wants the abbey. Girls, please hurry. There isn't a lot of time."

Valentina pulled Bella by the hand while Noemi followed close behind. "OK, let's go."

And off they went, hoping to reach safety. Unfortunately, violence and heartbreak were going to visit the family again very soon, but this time the action and impact were going to be more medieval.

Inhumanity

Many countries were fighting for the Allied side on the Italian front. The Nazi regime had invaded so many countries that finding friends to help defeat a common enemy was fairly easy. Besides armed forces from the US and Great Britain, there were soldiers from New Zealand, Poland, Brazil, and Free France. Part of the French contingent were soldiers from their colonial empire, including Gourmiers, tough North African mountain warriors.

These men were renowned for their fighting skills and the ability to withstand the harshest conditions without complaint. Gourmiers functioned as a proficient fighting machine, seemingly born for the rocky Italian battlefield. This force had no peers, and no one wanted to tangle with them if they didn't have to. Often working behind enemy lines, their objective was to secure strategic mountain and hilltop locations, positions that often required the most resilient and toughest warriors. Unsupervised, these men had freedom of movement and to operate on their own terms. Their only problem was their reputation for extreme behavior when dealing with civilians or noncombatants. This behavior was apparently not fully regarded by their commanders in consideration of the main objective of the war; specifically, to defeat the fascist forces plaguing Europe. Recalling the old adage, if they didn't see it, then it didn't happen. Later, changes would be made when witnesses came forward, and bad behavior could no longer be overlooked in totality. It is entirely comprehensible that war can be blinding, willfully or not.

Unknown to the refugees from the abbey, Gourmiers were operating several miles away and laying a path of devastation and terror to open the road to Rome. The stalemate along the Gustav Line had become a meat grinder for all of the combatants. A breakout was needed.

At a different point along the line, Rocco's Rangers were quickly making their way to the abbey. Rocco had two objectives that day. First, the enemy's defenses needed to be significantly degraded, and second, he needed to get to his family. He had a premonition that they were so close now. Failure was not an option for him this time.

Meanwhile, Mario, Valentina, and the girls moved to the East of the abbey, the direction that they believed would be safest. Having walked for a couple of days with minimal rest, they looked for a comfortable place to shelter for the night. A drizzle of rain made their search more urgent. Just as the sun was setting, the group came upon an old farmhouse that appeared to have recently been abandoned by its owners. Noemi saw the door had been left open. "Hey, the door's wide open. Let's see if there's anyone inside."

Mario stopped Noemi from entering the house. "Wait. Let me go in first." He cautiously peeked inside the house through the open doorway. "Hello? Is anyone home? Hello?"

Hearing no response, Mario slowly walked through the house. "Hello, my friends and I are from Tranquillo. We are not dangerous. Is anyone injured?" Still, no answer was forthcoming, but he did notice that the house appeared to have been ransacked and stripped of all its food. This should have been a warning sign for the weary traveler, but he was exhausted.

He called to Valentina and the girls to come inside. "It's safe to come in. Looks like the owners left in a hurry." Always the gentleman and respectable individual, he picked up several chairs, which had been tipped over, and returned them to their rightful place at the kitchen table. "Please come in. Let's try to relax for a little bit."

Noemi's internal radar was fully engaged, and her defenses were on high alert. "What happened here? It doesn't look like the family would have done this to their home. Someone else did this. Maybe, it was the Germans. This place is a complete mess. We should leave. Mama, we should leave now!" Noemi placed extra emphasis on her last statement and pointed to the broken dishes on the floor.

Mama was too tired to listen clearly to the wise pleadings of her daughter. "Noemi, please I'm tired. I need to rest a little bit."

Mario brought a chair to Valentina and offered his perspective to allay any fears the family may have had. "Please sit, sit. I think we're safe. Anyone who did this is long gone. Since there's no food left, nobody will be coming back."

Bella fervently agreed. "Yes, why would anyone want to come back here? Noemi, stop worrying. I know it's funny coming from me, but you worry too much."

The two sisters hugged each other and laughed.

Noemi walked over to her mother and held her tightly. She realized everyone was exhausted and needed to get a good night's sleep. "Sorry for being such a worrier. Mama, let's get some rest. Hopefully there's a bed big enough for the three of us."

They went to sleep still grieving over the tragic loss of a husband and father, but the family was also at ease with a feeling of security.

Unfortunately, the house would soon be transformed into an inhuman mouse trap for the group. Four innocent lives would be plunged into hell on earth, a terror no one should ever experience. The beast was winning.

The Farfallas snuggled into the bed in the largest bedroom in the house. Mario threw some blankets on the floor to sleep near the family just in case someone did return. The four unsuspecting souls lay quietly and rested their weary bones, contemplating the long day's travel. The moon shone brightly through the window and added to the sense of an idyllic and peaceful room.

A question that Valentina hadn't asked yet concerned Matteo's burial. She summoned up the strength to ask her friend about her husband's final resting spot. "Mario, please tell me where Matteo was buried. Is it beautiful there?"

"Yes, it is quite beautiful. He was buried in the abbey courtyard in a shady spot underneath a large cherry tree. Everyone loved Matteo. No matter how much his hands hurt, he had a smile on his face and a kind word for every person he met. Even the abbot loved him, and he was one strict man. God's lucky to have Matteo now."

"Thank you. It's good to know he wasn't alone at the end. He had you." Valentina held her girls tightly in a maternal embrace and thanked God for keeping them alive. She really didn't believe God was designating who should live or die. Rather, it was a spiritual security blanket to hold onto in times of emotional distress. Seeing Bella had fallen asleep, she turned to a still-awake Noemi and whispered softly, "Can't sleep?"

"No, I was just wondering where Rocco is right now. I need to see my stupid brother. I hope he is safe and happy wherever he is."

"Me too, me too."

Suddenly the door burst open, and Hell rushed in.

Bang. Boom. Bash. It was like a stampede of cattle rampaging through a glass factory, producing a fury of sadistic pandemonium with every step.

Six soldiers of unknown origin and wearing foreign clothing charged into the room and attacked Mario first. Startled by the sight and sounds of these men pushing quickly into the room, Mario had no time to react and defend himself. He succumbed quickly after repeated bayonet stabs into his stomach. Again and again, these mad men plunged their blades of steel deep into their prostrate victim. The echo of evil laughter filled the room.

One spoke contemptuously of their victim. "Another pig for the pit."

Another responded and laughed harder. "At this rate, the pit will be full by morning."

All Mario could say while he expired was a hushed one-word question. *"Perche?* Why?" Why indeed, the old family friend from Tranquillo didn't know how fortunate he was to have suffered a quick death.

The soldiers immediately turned their attention from the initial target of their mayhem and rushed to the women huddled in bed. Two soldiers slipped on the bloodied floor in their attempt to seize the main objects of their despicable desire. It would have been comedic if the succeeding events weren't so tragic. Terror seized the bodies of the three defenseless victims and paralyzed them with fear. The girls cried as they were violently pulled from their mother's embrace. "Mama! Mama!"

"Oh, my God! Leave my daughters alone! What are you doing? Please stop! Please stop!" Valentina reached out for her babies but was held back by two of the soldiers. Her motherly pleas for her children were answered only by sounds of malevolent glee.

These soldiers, the dreaded and fierce Gourmiers, were the ones who had been battling successfully behind enemy lines to secure the area around Monte Cassino. They had lost some of their companions capturing, losing and then recapturing key hillside targets. After a tough and challenging week of work, it was playtime; however, the way these men defined play it was more like *slay-time*, and the Farfallas were about to feel its life-shattering effects.

"No! Please stop! What are you doing? Where are you taking them?" Valentina desperately pleaded for her crying daughters. Tears streamed down all of their faces now. Four of the soldiers dragged the girls outside and headed to the barn to do their awful and monstrous deed. For these men, this was seemingly an inseparable ingredient of war. Satisfying their carnal needs was as necessary as it was to kill an enemy in battle, both of which were seen as indispensable functions in warfare.

Bella was thrown into the barn kicking and screaming and was immediately followed by Noemi. The two sisters hugged each other and cried profusely to the amusement of the soldiers, who poked and prodded the siblings with their rifles. Noemi shouted. "Please stop! Why are you doing this to us?" Once again, like the response to her mother's pleas, only laughter was returned.

One of the soldiers pulled Bella onto his lap and pulled her hair back to get a better look at her beauty. *"Bella!"* The animal knew the word for beautiful in Italian, shocking his young, intended victim. He gently rubbed her cheeks, further escalating his aroused state. A grotesque and evil smile formed on his face.

Their abhorrent sense of playfulness continued for several minutes, until one of the other soldiers loosened his belt and headed toward Bella. The situation suddenly became grimmer and more desperate. Noemi realized what was going to happen next and appealed to her captors to set her sister free. Being several years older than Bella, she now knew what these animals wanted, and always the protective sister, she wanted to defend Bella with her honor and her life, if necessary. "Please, I'll do whatever you want but let her go. She's just a baby. No, please, please."

Noemi's panic grew by the second. She tried to focus on the faces of these men, but all she could see was their giant eyes, which glowed like incandescent lamps. Struggling to break free, she lost her grip on sanity. The faces of her captors appeared formless and exaggerated, almost inhuman. Every second that passed became more surreal for the young victims. The sounds of laughter and of clothes being torn permeated the room, manufacturing a shroud of despair that asphyxiated the young suffering siblings. Cries turned to silent paralyzed gasps for air.

Torn from their bodies were the blue and red sweaters that Rocco had brought to them from Boston during his last visit in '39. Although at the time they were large, the sweaters fit them perfectly now.

Bella shrieked hysterically. "My sweater! You're taking everything from us. Stop! Don't do this!"

It didn't matter who was first to be assaulted. All that mattered to these fiends was the gratification and pleasure that came from the assault, but it seemed Bella was going to be first. Bella was bent over a bale of hay and held down by two soldiers. The first beast was about to plunge himself into his victim when a bomb exploded nearby, surprising everyone in the barn. Dust and shards of hay filled the room. Confusion and lust now reigned in synchronized harmony.

The other soldiers who had remained in the house with Valentina burst into the barn. While their friends in the barn were harassing the girls in their own terrible and playful way, the other two were treating the victim of their assault more ferociously. The bastards knocked out

Valentina's teeth with the butt end of a rifle for reasons that would have been obvious even to the most innocent of souls. The strike to her mouth knocked out Valentina as well as most of her teeth.

"Look at this little pig. I guess you hit her too hard. Wake up now little pig. Wake up now." The soldier gently slapped her face to awaken her from unconsciousness. "Ahhh, that's a good little pig. Wake up, wake up."

Valentina slowly regained consciousness and reached for her mouth to assess the damage. Feeling a lack of teeth in a mouth full of blood, she moaned and looked at her captors in horror. One soldier pulled her battered body from the floor and onto her knees in front of his friend.

How can an individual, an alleged member of the human race, think of performing atrocities on another? Is it because of some unfulfilled desire to exert dominance on perceived beings of lesser value, the ultimate bully? Or is it because of an old or recent wrong that needs to be avenged, indelibly, a generational fight to pay for the sins of the father? Perhaps, it's just a dormant and intrinsic feature of mankind that's triggered by the beating drums of history and the perspective of one's ancestors, ultimately forming in a vendetta by the growing mob with no regard for life. Facts no longer exist. Rather, the past is disrupted by opinion. A spiritual, or supernatural, lethargy can easily envelop a person, forming callouses around his heart and beckoning him to react reflexively on impulse. Indifference to see, hear and understand others encases humanity. The beast satiates itself on mankind's cruel apathy, the sloth is an easy prey. Could the explanation be that simple? No, it can't be. Bad behavior is learned, and the battle can last a lifetime.

The soldier couldn't contain his excitement as he struggled to remove his belt and open his pants. After muttering a few indecipherable words to the laughter of his companion in crime, he was ready. It was time to complete their abhorrent assault on an innocent soul; however, a German 88 shell would interrupt their festivities. The soldiers dove to the ground and took cover behind the bed, pushing Valentina to the far side of the room and knocking her unconscious again.

One of the soldiers, the apparent leader of the squad, inched his way to the window while keeping his head down. "I see some activity down in the area we cleaned out yesterday. Leave her for now. Let's regroup with the rest of the men. Now!"

Rushing into the barn, the leader shouted an order to the others. "We need to go. It looks like we missed some Germans. Where are the two girls you brought in here?"

"There, hiding behind the hay." Two soldiers grabbed them as they attempted to escape. "No, no, little pigs. You're coming with us."

Noemi and Bella cried out. "Please stop. Where's Mama?"

The leader spoke firmly and pulled Noemi close to him. "Mama is dead. Now shut up or you'll both join her."

The girls froze in place and in shock at hearing of the death of their saintly mother. The other soldiers could be heard jeering and mocking the girls with catcalls referencing the Italian colonies of Libya and Ethiopia —apparently to justify their treatment of these young women. Because of the language barrier, the girls could not truly understand what they were talking about. Noemi and Bella were violently and unknowingly paying for their nation's colonial conquests in North Africa.

The soldiers forcibly pushed Noemi and Bella to the door. The girls went out first, just in case there were any Germans in sight. Thrown to the ground, they were not hit by gunfire. This convinced the soldiers that it was safe to proceed. Taking hold of the girls, they made their way toward the gunfire, keeping low to the ground to avoid gunfire. Apparently, these fiends could think with both heads simultaneously.

Valentina awoke, unsure of what happened and questioned how long she had been out. It could have been minutes, hours, or even days for that matter. She raised her hands to her head in an attempt to shake the cobwebs from her brain. She quickly noticed that the bastards' handiwork rendered her mouth a bloody mess, but she was not dead. Shocked at seeing the amount of blood in her hands, panic gripped the mother's soul. Mama immediately thought of her children and struggled to call out to them. Tragically, she mumbled several toothless cries in vain. "Noemi! Bella! Where are you? Girls, do you hear me." Her heart sank when no response was returned.

The sun was peeking out over the eastern horizon, so she surmised that she must have been unconscious for several hours. Running to the courtyard and heading toward the barn, she continued to scream for her children. "Noemi! Bella! Answer me, please! Mother of God, where are they?" The distraught mother scanned the yard for any sight or clue for what may have happened to her daughters.

Still hurting from the abusive treatment and her head throbbing in pain, Valentina hobbled into the barn and continued to call out for her babies. "Girls, are you here?! Girls?!"

Then, her greatest fear came true. Walking toward the far end of the barn, she saw her daughters' torn and bloodied sweaters on the floor. There was no doubt. The store tag from Boston was still sewn into the collar. "No! It can't be true. It can't be true." Falling to her knees, the mother's wretched wails filled the barn. She was abandoned by the world and Heaven, and now she was left alone to grieve. Her daughters and beloved husband were dead, and she didn't even get a chance to say goodbye. "Rocco, where are you? I have nothing — nothing left."

Valentina gradually became quiet, her body turning into an empty cadaver. She noticed something hanging on a post next to one of the stalls, and it became her sole focus of attention. Mama knew what she had to do, needed to do. There were no options, other than to end her misery. Life was pointless. She raised her arms to Heaven and cried. "If only Rocco had been here to help me, if only! My son! My son, where are you?!"

But her son was close, which made the events of the day even more heart-breaking, if that were possible. Rocco's squad had made it to the foothills surrounding the abbey a day after his mother and sisters. Fighting was still occurring in various hot spots. The Rangers were tasked with taking out German 88s that were in the village next to the abbey. They had also heard that the Gourmiers were in the vicinity attacking Wehrmacht mountain posts from the rear. Entering a nearby village where the abbot and his staff had sought refuge to avoid getting caught in the middle of a battle for the abbey, the Rangers drove into the undefended town. It was early evening, and the town had been through hell already. They had no energy to fight or to ask if the Rangers were good or bad. It was plain to see that they were battered and exhausted.

The Ranger commander ordered his men to proceed carefully and to aid anyone needing it. "Looks like these people need some food and first aid. I want everyone to share his rations. Rocco, head over to the church and ask what happened here." Sending him was the obvious thing to do since Rocco could speak Italian.

Rocco ran to the church and rushed in. There, he found the abbot kneeling in front of the altar with his head buried in his hands appealing to a God that hadn't been listening to his prayers lately. Rocco immediately noticed that he was in anguish and reached out to touch his shoulder. *Mi scusi. Sei tu il prete di questo villagio? Stai bene?* Excuse me. Are you the priest of this village? Are you alright?"

His spirits raised, the abbot turned to the young soldier and smiled. "You speak Italian?"

"Yes, Father, I'm originally from Puglia, a small village called Tranquillo."

Abbot rose and hugged his new friend. "You don't know how happy you've made me right now."

Rocco let the priest hug him longer to extend his moment of joy, but he needed to gather some intelligence for his Ranger detachment. He pulled away slowly from the priest. "Father, what happened here?"

"Hell came through here last night. We prayed for deliverance, but it seems God was distracted with other people's problems." The devout man stared desolately at the crucifix above the altar. "Why? Why? Why?" His monotone, mechanical voice added to the misery of the moment.

"What do you mean?" Rocco implored the abbot for more information. "Who came through here?"

"Soldiers speaking a strange language that I had never heard before came through here and exploded like Vesuvius. They were a band of marauders from Hell who came through here yesterday and released an eruption of destruction and mayhem, like the ancient Vikings of a thousand years ago. They took particular delight in beating the men and taking the women out into the fields. We couldn't stop them. Nothing could stop them. Not even the Germans."

His worst fears were coming into focus. Rocco understood what happened and who had brought Hell to this village. "Father, tell me. My name is Rocco Farfalla. Was my family here? Did you see them?"

The stunned abbot stared at the young Ranger. "Rocco Farfalla? Your name is Rocco Farfalla? This is astounding. Providence has brought you to us. I knew your papa."

Rocco seized on the word that scared him immensely. "Knew? What…What… do you mean?"

The abbot placed a reassuring and comforting hand on his shoulder. "Yes, your papa was killed. He was shot carrying materials into the abbey. He was mistaken for a partisan. He died quickly, my son. He felt no pain."

Rocco broke down at hearing the news and fell to his knees. "Oh, oh, oh." These barely audible sounds were the only words he could form. Taking a minute to recover, he implored the priest for information about his mother and sisters. "Did you see my mother? I was told she was coming here with my sisters. Did they make it here?"

The abbot froze upon hearing his question. With all that happened earlier, he had forgotten about Valentina and the girls.

"What, what is it? Please tell me!" Rocco's anxiety rose along with the decibel level of his voice.

"Child, they were at the abbey yesterday. They're headed east to avoid the fighting. I think an old friend of yours is with them. Mario, Mario Fiorello."

Rocco's mood improved. "Yes. I know him. Mario's an old family friend."

"They'd be travelling along the main road. They should be near Collina Verde by now." The abbot held back some information, not knowing whether Rocco's family was in further danger or how he would react. The marauding soldiers had headed in a northeasterly direction, so he didn't think he needed to alarm the young man. He thought they stood a good chance of being safe, but he underestimated the unpredictability and constant fluidity of modern battle. He never considered that these men would have altered their path to Rome, another premature nail in the coffin of innocence and peace.

"I have to get to them, but how? An enemy division moved in

between us and Collina Verde today. We are going to have to fight through them. Father, thank you." Rocco shook the abbot's hand before running back to his division commander.

He found the Ranger leader conversing with other officers in the town square. Before he could give his report, the division commander ordered everyone to get ready to move out. They had to attack a Wehrmacht division that had just moved into the area.

The Rangers were scrambling back to their units and jumping in the various trucks and jeeps on which they rode into town. They had no tanks with them. These men would have to do the job with no armor support, although angels would be flying P47 Thunderbolts in the skies above.

Jimmy saw Rocco running toward him. "Hey, what happened?"

"We're moving out. We have to take out that enemy division to the east. Jimmy, I know where my family is."

"You do?"

"They were here yesterday. So close, so close. They're in a town called Collina Verde that's not far from here, but we have to get through that damn division first." Rocco's excitement made him appear almost giddy.

"Easy does it. Keep your head buddy. We'll get to them but first things first."

"Ya, I know, I know. But there's something everyone should know. You know those mountain soldiers from… from… what's the place? Well, they're the ones that caused all the damage here before we came in. It seems some of the women were abused. What's the word?" The innocent young soldier didn't even know the right word to describe the situation.

"Oh wow! Raped? Are you serious?"

"Dead serious."

Jimmy shook his head in disbelief. "That's insane. Well, the boys are here and ready to kick ass if we have to. Let's get this party started."

Jimmy and Rocco climbed into the truck and joined their buddies. They were all still alive and unhurt. The boys were in a particularly jovial mood. Cowboy and Gunslinger were debating which actors made the best western movie.

Cowboy asked for Hollywood's opinion. "OK, Hollywood, you worked in movies. Who's better, Roy Rogers or Gene Autry?"

"Don't ask me. I don't think I ever saw any of their films. Come to think of it, I prefer gangster movies."

Gunslinger chimed in quickly for the native Texan. "It's easy. Gene Autry is the best, period and end of discussion. How do you think I was able to convince Margie to go on dates with me? We'd go to Gene Autry movies because she said he was the best. And I don't disagree with my Yellow Rose." Gunslinger smiled heartily.

Cowboy heartily disagreed. "No way. Roy can lasso a calf with one hand and shoot six bullseyes with the other."

Tommy Gun, who had been arguing separately with Shortstop about who was going to win the World Series in '44, was puzzled at hearing Cowboy's declaration. "Bullseyes? Is that even a word? I think you've both been hit with too many cow chips in the head."

The truck erupted in laughter. As always, men enjoyed turning into boys when good-natured ribbing was the dish of the day. Their mood turned serious once they saw Rocco. He had a cold and determined look on his face. They knew what that look meant; the team was in for a hard fight.

Hollywood, sitting opposite Rocco, noticed that his friend looked worried. Jimmy winked at the man from the City of Angels as a signal to help out his buddy. He leaned in toward Rocco and smiled devilishly. "Hey Butterfly, cheer up. We're here to save your ass like we always do. Who doesn't like a good Hollywood ending?"

Knowing the boys had his back, Rocco felt at ease. "I know. I know."

The next twenty-four hours would be unforgettable for the Rangers. Some would never go home, while others would never be the same. Rocco had a date with destiny in Collina Verde, and she was not going to be kind. But first, he had to get through a powerful obstacle that wasn't going to be overcome easily.

il Forno

For the next twelve hours, the Rangers saw their most intense fighting of the war. The Allied forces were facing seasoned German Army veterans. Some thought they were facing the dreaded Hermann Goring Division, one of the fiercest fighting forces in any army. To the Rangers, it didn't matter, because they had a job to do. The trucks delivering the men to the battlefield all came to a halt once they got to their predetermined destination. Reaper, arguably the best soldier and sergeant in the Army, barked orders to his men. "OK. OK. Everyone let's go. Let's go. We're taking positions on the right flank. We have to move."

All the men jumped to their feet, leaped off the truck and followed Reaper to their spot along the line. The Rangers had the privilege of leading the charge again, the so-called tip of the spear for this offensive. Their job was to disrupt the enemy's flank and to create sufficient confusion that would allow for reinforcements to be reallocated there. Hopefully, this would then lead to a weakening along other parts of the line.

Their pre-battle ritual started like it had before every fight, with Jimmy staring up to the sky and requesting help from Heaven. "St. Michael the Archangel, defend us in battle." While of different faiths, the boys had become accustomed to starting every battle this way. It provided a sense of comfort to the point of superstitious belief that they would be protected from harm. After all, Ike did call this a crusade against the evil of fascism.

The offensive started with a massive artillery barrage and was followed by a ground attack. For the aggressor, the sights and sounds of an artillery bombardment could be equally frightening and spectacular. For the receiver, they were horrifying, but to some these became a mundane and routine part of war. Eventually, if a soldier was subject to enough shelling and lived, he would come to find it ordinary, like army rations. As sad as it was, Hell on Earth became a typical day for these warriors.

The day started well for the Rangers. The division was able to advance along their line with limited casualties. Several hours into their advance, Rocco's squad ran into a tough obstacle, a staggered and tiered emplacement of machine gun nests. The squad came to an open field that was eerily quiet. Reaper gave a firm command. "Boys, be on guard. I don't like this."

Cognizant of the danger of mines and booby-traps, they walked slowly and cautiously through the field, while searching the area for any enemy movements. Each soldier understood that the serenity surrounding them was fictitious, and that danger lurked nearby. In an instant, the false peace was destroyed. The pop-pop-pop of machine gun fire echoed across the pasture, sending men diving to the ground and taking cover in the high grass that encompassed the field. Reaper yelled, "Hit the dirt!"

Tommy Gun was hit first, a shot to the head. He was killed instantly. Another Ranger was ripped to pieces when he tried to get to his injured comrade. Hollywood took a shot to the shoulder and was writhing in pain, but he was still alive at least.

Cowboy cried out. "Medic! Medic! Here, keep your head down! Hollywood got hit."

A medic crawled up to him faster than a jackrabbit and attended to his wound. A dose of morphine helped to calm the wounded warrior. "Easy, fella. Stay with me."

Cowboy was distraught. "Doc, is he gonna be alright?"

"Yes, he's gonna be alright. He'll have some nice scars to show the ladies back home. But I need to move him now." Doc and a fellow medic moved Hollywood from the battlefield to safety.

Cowboy yelled out his anger. "Those bastards got Tommy Gun and Hollywood!" He attempted to raise his head and charge the enemy emplacements for revenge; however, the heavy machine gun fire prevented his movement. The Rangers were sitting ducks.

Rocco knew something had to be done. He heard the sounds of someone whispering next to him. "Rocco, get up and fight. Your friends need saving. Don't worry. I'll be with you."

Rocco turned his head to see who was speaking to him, but he only saw his Ranger brothers ducking for cover. "What? Who's that?"

The voice hissed an ominous threat. "Rocco, look at your buddies. They're all going to die today if you don't get up and move. Jimmy's going to be next."

At that moment, Rocco acted on pure instinct, without concern for his own welfare. He had wondered whether he had supernatural support and protection for what he needed to do. Perhaps, there really was a God who was lending a divine hand and guiding him to his goal, namely, the rescue of his mother and sisters. What else could explain the lack of injuries to him or his buddies up to this point? The truth he didn't recognize was that this perceived support, while supernatural, was far from divine. Would he find out in time that he was under the control of the original puppet master, the Light-Bringer, the Morning Star?

Rocco steeled his nerves and yelled to Jimmy. "Enough of this crap!" He jumped to his feet and ran toward the first of three nests. Running zigzag, side to side, to prevent the machine-gunners from getting a bearing on him, he sprinted across the open field holding his rifle with both hands. It was an inspiring sight for his buddies. They couldn't believe he wasn't getting hit, not even a scratch.

Reaper was in shock. "Butterfly, get down! Oh my God. Get down!" His pleas went unanswered.

Rocco lobbed a grenade into the first nest and killed the three men there in a snap. Turning toward the next emplacement about thirty yards away, the young Italian-American Ranger took a deep breath and restarted his sprint. Zigzagging right and then left, Rocco's heart pounded heavily against his chest wall. The enemy soldiers looked on in disbelief. He could hear shouts in German directed at him. *"Tote ihn! Tote ihn!* Kill him! Kill him!" Although he couldn't understand what they were saying, he knew it wasn't a welcome greeting. The daring soldier pressed onward fearlessly.

The Rangers, seeing this, jumped into action and followed their buddy. Jimmy rose first. "Let's go. Let's go. We can't let him have all the fun." Gunslinger let out one of his patented rebel yells, signaling to the boys to jump up and sprint across the field. There was no stopping them; their brotherly connection was bonded in steel.

Rocco made it to the second machine gun nest. He shot the first soldier right between the eyes but had to deal with the other two men in hand-to-hand combat when his rifle jammed. Turning his rifle around, he used it like a baseball bat with swings that would have made Ted Williams proud. The second nest was out of commission.

Rocco had to improvise for his jammed gun. He looked around the nest quickly and picked up the machine gun that was still loaded with an ammunition belt. Now, he made a dash to the last nest.

His jaw tightly clenched, he never uttered a word throughout the entire attack on the three nests. His silence made the assault even more inspiring to his buddies and yet equally terrifying to the defenders. After killing the last man, Rocco collapsed into the entrenchment, not understanding how in the hell he did it. He looked to the sky and offered his gratitude while his heart pounded from the exhilaration of his unbelievable action. "Thank you. Thank you."

The rest of the squad caught up to Rocco quickly and joined him. One-by-one, each man collapsed in the foxhole and sat next to his superhero buddy. Each squad member had similar observations. "Holy crap! That's the craziest thing I ever saw. What got into you?"

Jimmy approached his friend and knelt in front of him. "How did you do it? You've got an angel on your shoulder. That's for sure."

Rocco barely had any strength to speak and leaned his forehead against his burly brother's chest. "I don't know. It felt like my heart said screw it and took over my brain. Something told me that nothing was going to hurt me. Thoughts of my family and the boys just kept on driving me to run faster and faster. Getting hit wasn't even a thought in my brain. Hearing bullets whiz past me sounded like I was surrounded by a swarm of bees that wouldn't, couldn't sting me. I became judge, jury and executioner." Jimmy and the rest of the Ranger squad remained silent and motionless while Rocco finished his story.

Jimmy stared down at his friend's head, waiting for him to say something else, but no more was said. Rocco had spoken all he could. He had no more energy to expend.

Jimmy patted his shoulders as added assurance and comfort to a friend who was in distress. He could feel his Boston brother trembling underneath his calming touch. "You've got us too, brother. You've got us too." Rocco sobbed quietly, knowing how lucky he was to have him as a friend. This would be a feeling he would have again before his journey ended.

Just around the corner, a wicked curveball was waiting to be thrown at Jimmy and the squad. Tommy Gun was dead, and Hollywood had nearly joined him on the butcher's bill.

The Rangers barely had a minute to recover when suddenly a runner approached the squad with a new objective to support a unit that had gotten trapped behind enemy lines. "Hey, where's your sergeant?"

Gunslinger pointed to Reaper, who was standing next to Cowboy several feet away. "Ease up, son. He's over there."

The runner handed Reaper a note from division command. "Sergeant Wills, you've got orders to link up with the Allied mountain forces about five miles down the road at Rally Point Able in Collina Verde. Their support unit got hit hard and won't be able to help them. Intelligence tells us there's an old farmhouse near the main road heading into town. You need to link up with them there."

"What, we're on the move again?"

"Yes, sir. It looks that way. Division asks that you get there fast."

Reaper responded to the private sarcastically. "Don't call me 'sir'. The stripes are on my arms, not my shoulders, son." He always enjoyed tweaking guys not in the squad. Sticking the letter inside his jacket, he saluted the young soldier. "OK, we'll get it done, *again*." He placed an extra emphasis on 'again' since it had become habit for Division to lean heavily on his squad.

Reaper grunted the orders. "Alright guys, listen up. We've got another job. No rest for the weary."

Shortstop wasn't thrilled. "Are you kiddin' Sarge? After what just happened, we gotta get into another fight?"

Annoyed, the beleaguered sergeant answered swiftly and pointed in the direction the team needed to go. "Stop your bellyaching. This isn't a Saturday afternoon walk in the park. We need to push north along this access road but to stay on this side of the lake. A bunch of mountain soldiers are in a pickle in Collina Verde." Rocco's head popped up at hearing the name of the town as he remembered what the abbot told him. His eyes were opened wide now, and his heart raced faster and faster with each successive beat. He knew he was close now, but in the back of his mind he thought of the recent assaults on women in the nearby town they had just passed through.

Reaper continued barking his orders. "Butterfly, Iceman, take the lead; that is, if Shortstop doesn't mind."

Shortstop bowed at his waist slightly and signaled the others onward with the outstretched arm of a gentleman. "Oh, it's my pleasure. Please proceed."

Beginning their trek to the farmhouse, the boys laughed at their buddy's well-placed and well-timed humor. Their mood improved further when the company medic, Doc, ran up to them. "Hey guys, wait for me. I'll be joining you on your mission. And ah, Hollywood's going to be OK. We were able to stop the bleeding, and he's being sent to the back of the lines. He's got a golden ticket for a trip back home."

A chorus of "thanks" and "alright Doc" was shared amongst the group as they continued their march. With Rocco taking the lead, the boys felt invincible again. Although Tommy Gun was dead, they all saw what Rocco did to those machine gun nests. If that wasn't heavenly intervention, then none had ever existed in all of human history. The angels were missing for a brief moment when Tommy Gun was mortally wounded, but they returned quickly and propelled Rocco to a fantastic feat. There was no reason that he should still be alive, save for the angels.

Meeting little resistance, the Rangers made their way along the access road. It was morning and the sun had just risen over the nearby hills. The sun's rays glistened off the morning dew and created an idyllic scene. For a split second, there was no indication that they were in the middle of a war zone. The boys stopped to enjoy the view and the sun's warmth before continuing their journey to the rally point.

Looking out over the horizon, Jimmy was awed by what he saw and turned to his friend. "Rocco, this is one beautiful place. It feels like paradise here. I can't believe there is so much misery and death to go with it."

"It is special, buddy. It's unexplainable. I wish we could enjoy the view longer, but we need to get moving. I think I see the farmhouse." Rocco pointed to a spot in the distance where the farmhouse stood and where his life would be forever changed. "Hey, wait a minute. Do you see that? There's someone stumbling up the road toward us. Looks like a civilian, an old man."

The squad approached the man carefully, unsure whether it was a trap. Rocco didn't think the man posed a threat and made a path straight to him.

Reaper yelled to his soldier. "Hey, be careful! You can't be sure whether he's friendly or not."

Rocco wasn't worried. "This guy's no threat, but it looks like he's been through the wringer."

The man appeared distraught and heavily bruised along his arms and face. While he was holding an old cane to help him walk, his staggered gait indicated an injury to his legs. Rocco reached out his hand gently and spoke to the elderly man in Italian. *"Signore, che e successo?* What happened?"

The elderly man's eyes lit up. Hearing someone speak to him in Italian raised his spirits. *"Parli Italiano?"*

"Si. Mi chiamo Rocco Farfalla. Come ti chiami? Yes. My name is Rocco Farfalla. What's your name?"

The man smiled as tears rolled down from his eyes. He was delivered into the arms of a friend, *un amico, un paesano. "Mi chiamo Ettore."* He proceeded to tell Rocco his story. "I was beaten by these animals that invaded my farmhouse. I was left for dead in my own field. I guess this old body is a little tough to kill."

"Yes, you are, my friend."

"When I woke up, I saw these animals taking two girls into the barn. Those vicious bastards were laughing, and the girls were screaming for help. I had to find help for them. I've been walking for a while, but I kept on falling because of the beating they gave me."

"You said two girls?"

"Yes, two girls I had never seen before."

Terrible thoughts raced through the young warrior's mind now. Could it have been Noemi and Bella? No, it couldn't be. God and His angels wouldn't allow that to happen. They were on his side, weren't they? Why would they have kept him alive through all the battles from North Africa, Sicily, and mainland Italy?

"And these girls had beautiful sweaters, one red and one blue." This piece of information sent a horrifying jolt through Rocco. He didn't detect a change in the elderly man's voice, which appeared to have a small hiss to it. Nor did he detect a slight grin form on the man's face.

Rocco stared resolutely at the distant farmhouse and then suddenly took off like a jackrabbit. Not understanding what the man had said, the other Rangers called for him to wait. They quickly chased after their buddy and hoped they didn't run into any enemy traps.

The elderly man continued his walk down the road but soon transitioned into a faster pace and whistled a comical tune. The trap had been laid, and the plan was executed flawlessly. He was being delivered like a birthday present wrapped with a giant red bow. The man was now out of sight of the sprinting Rangers. Before slowly disappearing into the morning mist, he whispered one last ominous musing. "Born in fire and shaped by death, welcome to the world, sweetheart." Chaos, the Whispering Demon, had completed a final task for Uncle Trick, but it wouldn't be the last time Rocco and Chaos would meet. An evil laughter punctuated the finality of a job well-done. Now, it was up to Rocco to complete his part and for the Beast to emerge from its cocoon.

Rocco tore across the field, the epitome of a man on a mission. Horrible thoughts raced through his mind faster than he could run. Torture, blood, and dear God no, rape! All these hideous possibilities ran through his mind and drove him to the precipice of madness. But a merciful Father wouldn't let that happen, would He? Still, the distraught young man ran and ran, through tall grass and over a trickling stream. There was no way he was going to stop. Exhaustion wasn't a word in his dictionary that day, nor were charity or mercy, for that matter.

The Rangers tried in vain to keep pace with Rocco, but it was impossible. There was something superhuman about him. Jimmy trailed closest behind him and yelled to his friend. "Rocco, please slow down! What's going on? What did the old man say? Hold up!"

Reaper caught up to Jimmy and kept pace. "Iceman, what the hell is going on? What set him off?"

"No idea. He's running toward the farmhouse. All I know is that guy said something that set him off. I'm wondering if it has anything to do with his family. The priest told him they were headed in this direction yesterday."

Reaper, now panting heavily, was able to stammer through a response. "Oh crap. I hope not. I've been hearing rumors about some bad things happening behind enemy lines, but I didn't think it was true. Seemed too crazy to be true."

"Me too. Can't be true." Jimmy struggled to catch his breath.

Rocco arrived at the farmhouse and stopped to survey his surroundings. He quickly noticed an open door to the house and ran in boldly without fear for his own personal safety. The kitchen was a mess of overturned furniture and broken glass and pottery. Next, he ran to the first of two outlying rooms and kicked in the closed door. He found nothing. His panic grew exponentially by the second.

Rocco ran to the second room where the door was partially open. An odd and uneasy feeling came to him making the young man pause for a second before entering. He slowly pushed the door open and saw the remnants of the butchered body of Mario, his old family friend. Bending over his mutilated corpse, Rocco's panic turned to anger. At this point, Jimmy and Reaper entered the room as well. Their feeling of disgust and shock was clearly visible.

Jimmy probed Rocco for information. "Hey, buddy, are you ok? Who is he? Is this the guy the priest told you about?"

Rocco jumped up and stared blankly at his friend. "The barn! The old man said they were taken to the barn."

"Who, Rocco, who?"

The young Ranger darted through the house, into the courtyard and over to the barn. It was here that the demon's artistry in concert with the diabolical actions of six malevolent men would be revealed. Rocco paused at the barn door, not wanting to have his greatest fear realized. "Is anyone in there?"

There was no response. Again, he asked. "Is there anyone inside?" Still, no response. "OK, I'm coming in."

Slowly, Rocco pushed open the door, and hell sucker-punched him in the gut. It was the sight of his beautiful mother hanging from a beam, with blood flowing from her mouth. Rocco fell to his knees and screamed the most awful cries anyone had ever heard. The Rangers, who had gathered in the courtyard to figure out what was happening, recoiled in terror. Rocco's prolonged wail reverberated across the valley, like a wolf mourning a devastating loss.

Gunslinger held his hands up to his ears and expressed what the others couldn't. "Dear God. It sounds almost inhuman." Such was the outcome Chaos and Uncle Trick were seeking. Like the butterfly that was proudly tattooed on Rocco's chest, they had their boy ready for his transformation, but there was another step he needed to take.

The Rangers ran into the barn to understand what happened. Entering it cautiously, they saw the cause of Rocco's wails. It didn't take a genius to know it was his mother hanging there.

Jimmy walked slowly to his friend and knelt beside him, while continuing his howling wail. The wolf was grieving, and the beast was winning. "I'm so sorry." Jimmy knew there was nothing that could be said that could alleviate the pain his buddy was experiencing.

Reaper dejectedly stated the obvious and seethed. "I guess the rumors were true. Those bastards." He couldn't stop staring up at her. He was in shock, but something needed to be done. "Alright boys let's bring her down slowly. Cowboy, grab the rope. Easy now, easy."

The Rangers lowered Valentina gently to the ground to the waiting embrace of her loving son. Rocco held her lifeless body close to his chest and quickly detected the injury to her mouth. That once and still beautiful face glowed under the bruises and blood. "They knocked her teeth out. Those bastards knocked her teeth out."

Without thinking, Cowboy innocently asked why they would knock her teeth out, but he caught himself part way through his sentence. "Oh, Oh my...my…." Tears streamed down from his eyes. He had seen a lot of war's barbarity firsthand, but the sight of Valentina's lifeless corpse was too much for this hardy cowboy.

Rocco continued to hold his mother and noticed she hadn't turned cold. "Oh God, she's still warm. She can't be dead more than an hour. What kind of cruelty is this? I was late by less than an hour! Less than an hour! Why?! Why?! It's all my fault. I should have never left them."

Rocco looked at Jimmy for some relief, but instead he saw the girls' sweaters hanging where the animals had placed them. Another gut punch pounded his wounded soul. He lowered his mother's body and jumped to his feet. In all his grief for his mother, Rocco momentarily forgot about his sisters. He cried out and frantically searched the stalls in the barn. "Noemi! Bella! Noemi! Bella! Where are you? It's your brother, Rocco." There was no response. The anger within him grew exponentially. He knew they were dead, given how their mother had died, alone hanging from a beam. From what he saw and after what these animals did, he wondered whether death was a better option than living. There was no other rational possibility. In utter mental turmoil, his thoughts wandered to another horrible prospect. Had Mama been left hanging to watch the mutilation and assault of her babies? In his mind, there was only one conclusion; the men — no, the animals — who committed this crime needed to be slaughtered. Rocco was ready to explode. The beast was bursting forcefully from its cocoon and there would be no stopping the transformation that day.

Hell's Fury

Another squad of Rangers, who had been supporting Rocco's team on the line's left flank, entered the barn. They had heard the intense and terrifying wails from a short distance away. His cries had reverberated around the countryside, frightening animals and humans alike. It was easy to consider that something was wrong, but like all good Rangers, they ran toward danger and not away from it.

Captain Rutledge, a strong and imposing veteran of two wars, addressed Reaper and the squad. "What happened here? Sergeant, is your team alright?" No one could respond, as each man had his hands to his face to hide the tears flowing from distressed and sorrowful eyes. The captain and the other soldiers with him surveyed the room. They saw the crumpled body of Valentina on the ground and Rocco standing stoically with his fists tightened and veins bulging from his head. "My God. Who did this?"

Reaper shook himself out of his shock. "Where are the mountain soldiers?"

"What? Why?"

Reaper's emotion became more intense. "Captain, where are those bastards?!"

The captain was troubled by the sergeant's tone and reaction. He spoke cautiously to keep an emerging volatile situation as calm as possible. "We just got word that they're at the base of the next hill. The whole area has been cleared of enemy troops. It was one heck of an operation."

Reaper groaned dismissively. "Yeah, one heck of an operation."

Jimmy's attempts to console his friend were futile. "Rocco, I'm so sorry. We'll find them and make them pay."

Rocco slowly came out of his paralytic state and muttered repetitively. His groans were at first incomprehensible but then slowly became intelligible with each repetition, rising in intensity and finally building into an eruption that stunned the other Rangers. "I should have been here. It's all my fault. I should have been here. It's all my fault. I should have been here. It's all my fault. I SHOULD HAVE BEEN HERE!!! IT'S ALL MY FAULT!!!"

Without warning, he grabbed his gear and ran toward the next hill. The butcher's bill was due for payment.

Captain Rutledge tried to control the situation and bellowed an order to rein in this volatile Ranger. "Soldier, where are you going? Sergeant, stop him! Don't let him leave!"

Reaper, his jaw clenched tightly, replied in a measured yet angry state, something akin to a smoking volcano about to explode. "Captain, there's going to be hell to pay today. The stories about those guys are true. They killed his mother and sisters. You can see their handiwork on his mother lying on the ground."

The captain was horrified. "What? They did this?"

Jimmy and his Ranger buddies chased after Rocco. "Wait, we'll come with you." It was no use in trying to keep up. Rocco ran like the devil.

With each step, Rocco entered deeper into Hell. His mind was dark, save for one objective. The bastards needed to be slaughtered, preferably without a gun. A knife would be the preferred tool for delivering judgment on these animals. They had to be slaughtered like animals, because no human would do the things that had been done to his mother and sisters. Dehumanizing these men would make his next task easier to justify. He needed to feel them die, up close and personal, using the strength of his hands.

During his race to find this evil gang of men, images of his family flashed and whirled in his mind like a summer carousel; first alive, then dead, alive, then dead. The torturous merry-go-round would not stop and pushed him further into madness.

Jimmy yelled. "Rocco, wait for us! We want to help you!" The squad kept running with their brother. They knew what was going to happen but were too angry to care. Their minds were also focused on vengeance that was going to be terrible and painful. There was a score to settle, and the punishment had to be medieval. The control switch sustaining their humanity had been turned off, but they never knew it. Anger blinded them in the pursuit of retribution. Their sudden transformation from men into a mob was complete. The sound of Rocco's wails still echoed in their minds. For these men, justice now equaled revenge. It was somewhat remarkable that they were in the vicinity of Vesuvius, whose eruption 2,000 years earlier had caused so much death and destruction. An eruption was near, but Rocco didn't want any help that day. He didn't want his buddies to be involved in something that would destructively impact the rest of their lives. "Stay back! This is my fight!"

The men who committed these heinous crimes would be dead soon and it didn't matter whether they surrendered or not. Murder would be met with murder. Rocco's innocence and uncontaminated soul were now placed on the dark altar as a sacrificial offering to Hell's Beast.

From a distant and dark perch, Uncle Trick was giddy with delight. From the start, he had always believed that his latest recruit would be one of his best. Now, all that was needed to complete Rocco's transformation was a little mayhem. Normally, Uncle Trick would do his recruiting after death, but Rocco was special. His innocence and love of family made his tragic story and soul extremely desirable. So much so, he took extra delight in the young man's descent. In Uncle Trick's words, he was "delicious."

Rocco arrived at the Gourmier camp and quickly noticed that they had another young woman with them. She was sitting by the campfire, shaking and sobbing. The men were laughing at her while they ate. The soldiers reflexively raised their guns once they saw Rocco and one especially jittery man asked for identification in a language foreign to him. Realizing that he was in danger, Rocco stopped immediately and raised his hands. He knew he had to gain the trust of his intended victims quickly. A jittery trigger finger would instantly end his mission in failure. "Friend. Friend. Ally. OK? Friend. OK?"

The soldiers slowly looked over the new guest to their camp, while several whispered faintly to one another. Finally, the leader approached Rocco and recognized the US Army uniform. He yelled back to his group to be at ease, as each man lowered his weapon and placed it on the ground. The leader, a sergeant, invited Rocco to sit by the fire and pointed to the coffee pot. "Coffee. Drink." The other Rangers were still far behind and puffing wind. They couldn't keep up.

Rocco walked straight to the young woman, as the soldiers sitting around the fire watched him closely. One offered a crude remark in broken English. "Well Yankee, now you want turn? Haha, haha." The camp erupted in laughter.

The young warrior whispered to her in Italian as he led her to a spot behind a large rock several feet away and laid her down gently out of sight in the guise of assaulting her. *"Non avere paura. Sono un amico.* Don't be afraid. I'm a friend." The distraught woman stared at her savior with a look of disbelief and relief. She grabbed his arms tightly, not wanting him to leave. Before she could speak, Rocco raised his finger to his mouth to keep her silent. *"Stai tranquillo. Va bene.* Be calm. Alright."

A soldier nearby heard him speak in Italian and became immediately alarmed. He approached Rocco cautiously and lowered his gun.

An eruption of violence ensued from Hell's new warrior. Rocco struck the soldier with a knife and planted it deeply into his chest. The blow caused the mortally wounded soldier to squeeze the trigger on his rifle and to accidentally shoot another Gourmier in the head. That was a lucky shot -- two down and four to go.

In a fraction of a second and in one swift motion, Rocco unholstered his pistol and shot the next two soldiers in their stomachs. He wanted them to endure the most painful death possible as punishment for their sins, and a gut shot would do the trick. This left two soldiers to be executed.

With the skill of a Series A Italian football star, Rocco kicked the fire and sent a burning log into the body of a soldier who was about to shoot him. The soldier screamed and cursed profusely as he attempted to put out the flames on his coat before he could be engulfed in the fire.

The last soldier, the sergeant, fumbled with his rifle and pulled out his revolver. It would have been a comedic sight if not for the circumstances. He was able to get a single shot off and hit Rocco in the hip, but the wound didn't stall his attack. The young warrior from Puglia jumped toward the sergeant and pushed away his gun, stabbing him in the stomach and slicing away at his gut until his intestines fell out. His mutilated body fell to the ground along with his bloody innards.

Rocco turned his attention to the soldier who had been dealing with his burning clothes. This final tally for the butcher's bill was able to fire a shot and hit the vengeful Ranger in the shoulder. Even with two wounds, Rocco could not be stopped. Falling to the ground, he rolled closer to the fire. As luck would have it, the soldier's rifle jammed. This gave Rocco time to grab another log with his good arm, drive it into the face of the screaming soldier, and shoot him in the head.

The whole episode took less than a minute. By this time, the other Rangers arrived at the campsite to see Rocco standing over the two soldiers who were previously stabbed but still breathing. He was cursing the soldiers for all they had done. "Listen, you animals, I am Vengeance. I am Death. For what you did to my family, you will burn in Hell. Each life is worth an eternity of pain and suffering. You will never know peace. You will never know happiness. You will only know regret for having done this. Remember my name when you see the Devil and tell him that Rocco Farfalla sent him six presents. Now tell me where you left the girls from the farmhouse. Where are their bodies?"

The soldiers smirked and died. He had wanted them to suffer longer, but unfortunately, they were not alive long enough to divulge the whereabouts of his sisters' bodies. Regardless, he could barely stand any longer. His wounds needed attention; otherwise, he would be joining these men in the afterlife. Seeing his Ranger squad running toward him, Rocco waved and flashed a sheepish grin.

Just as he was about to faint, Jimmy ran over and caught his buddy in his arms. Holding him tightly, he slowly lowered Rocco to the ground. "Hang on. Hang on. You're not dying today. You hear me? We gotta lot of crap to do back home still. We're gonna open a beach bar on the Cape, right? All those beautiful women are waiting for us. Why didn't you wait for us, you idiot? Why didn't you wait for me?" The emotions of the moment overwhelmed him.

Rocco struggled to smile at his concerned friend before falling unconscious. "Hey, ahh, it was my show, buddy. I had to do it alone. Hey, there's a girl behind the big rock over ...over...there. Make sure she's alright. I need to...."

A medic ran over to the fading Ranger to attend to his wounds. "Hey, Butterfly, wake up! Wake up! No going to sleep."

Rocco slowly opened his eyes and smiled. "Doc, yeah, I hear you. Do you mind toning it down? You're giving me a headache."

Jimmy begged the medic to help his best friend. "Doc, you gotta keep him alive. He can't die." He stared at the medic working on his friend intently for a moment and then remembered the girl. "Doc, I have to check on a civilian. We may need you after you're done fixing him up."

Jimmy rushed to the rock but didn't make any sudden movements so as to avoid scaring the girl. Seeing a distraught young woman cowering in fear, he noticed she had been physically assaulted. His stomach turned in disgust at the thought of what these animals did to her. War is a heartbreaking and grimy business, but this was too much for any good person to handle. Jimmy maintained his composure the best he could. "Hi, don't be afraid. You're safe now. Come with me." He stumbled through a few Italian words that Rocco taught him. "*Come, ahh, come you chiamo*? I'm no good at English. Forget about Italian. What's your name?"

The young woman rose to her feet, took Jimmy's hand and spoke the best English she could. "Stella. My name Stella." The two walked out slowly from behind the rock.

Stella saw the medic working on Rocco and ran to him. She knelt beside him and sobbed. *"Un angelo. Grazie. Grazie."*

Stone-faced and expressionless, Rocco looked to the clear sky above him. *"Non un angelo. Un diavolo.* Jimmy, please take care of her. Her family must be looking for her. Those bastards didn't tell me where my sisters' bodies are." His revenge complete, Rocco passed out.

"Doc, is he OK?" Jimmy wasn't sure if his buddy had been stabilized.

While Jimmy was looking after the young woman, the rest of the Rangers walked around the campsite silently, stopping only to inspect the bodies of the dead soldiers. The scene seemed surreal — beyond belief is a more accurate depiction — but it wasn't. It all happened, every nasty and filthy deed that led to this day. Any naivete or ignorance of the darker side of life each person may have had at the start of this day was now gone. The bodies of the Rangers might have been unscathed but not their innocence, a fatality that doesn't show up in the casualty reports.

Soon, main units of the advancing Allied armed forces drove into the campsite on trucks, completing the capture and occupation of the area surrounding Collina Verde. Several asked the Rangers what had happened. Was there a battle with Adolph's boys?

Reaper answered coldly. "Battle? It was an execution."

The soldiers backed away and did not press him further. They sensed a high degree of anger pervading the camp, and for each man, it was better not knowing what happened there that day.

Rocco was rushed to a field hospital for surgery. Everyone in his squad stood up for him in the days that followed when questioned about the events leading to and during the engagement. While some Allied officers debated bringing charges against him, they knew it would be better not to do so. These Allied 'shock troops' had injured the war effort enough with their barbaric actions. Charging a Ranger, a hero in the eyes of many for the deadly vengeance he had executed on these men would be another disastrous blow to final victory.

Ultimately, Rocco was shipped back home about a week later as soon as his vitals were stabilized. In fact, his division commander got him aboard a transport flight heading back to the US, after stops in Morocco and Greenland. This had the desired effect of removing the Ranger from further investigation and suspicion. Rocco's war was over, or so he thought.

It took the better part of two days to get Rocco back to Boston and then transported by ambulance to the Camp Edwards medical facility. Exhausted and still recuperating from a second surgery to clear his shoulder wound of an emerging infection, the young man slept for most of the journey. On the ride to the camp, he was given the 'hero treatment' by the ambulance drivers. They were told 'he had stopped some bad men from doing some bad things' but had no idea what that meant. Rumors of his heroism spread like wildfire from the field hospital to the plane to the ambulance, with each retelling becoming more fantastical. By the time the ambulance got to the hospital, it was believed that Rocco had defeated a whole enemy division singlehandedly.

It was during the ride to Camp Edwards that Rocco's descent into madness went into overdrive. When he was awake, his mind reflected on his actions back in Italy on that fateful day. At times, he would stare silently off into the distance, wide-eyed and still. At other times, Rocco would have a discussion with a family member. "Bella, where are you going? I told you to stay away from boys. Mama, what's for dinner? Is that fried eggplant I smell?" The void between reality and the world he was currently creating was growing larger each day. The young man couldn't bear the guilt and the grief of losing his entire family. His mind invented an alternate reality, one where they had survived and returned with him to the US.

Since his eyes were closed and he was speaking in Italian, the two ambulance attendants chalked this up to delirium brought on by the anesthesia and pain medication.

The attendant riding in the back of the ambulance with Rocco commented on the patient's state. "Wow, this guy has been through the wringer. The meds have got him loopy still."

"Yeah, I think you're right. I heard this guy killed two Nazi generals by himself."

"Yup, I heard the same thing, except it was three generals and a colonel. Remind me not to get on his bad side."

And so, these ramblings continued for the several hour ride south to Camp Edwards from Boston. Round and round went the merry-go-round, gaining speed with each rotation until the ambulance arrived at its destination. The first part of Rocco's story was complete. Its second part and conclusion; however, were going to be epic.

Home

Joe finished telling his story to Libby and sighed deeply while staring intently at the crucifix. "No man should have to go through what he went through. It makes you wonder if Heaven really does exist. His story can easily destroy a person's faith."

Libby remained motionless, mouth agape and struggling to speak. Tears flowed down her face and over her rosy cheeks to punctuate the sadness of Rocco's heartbreaking chronicle. "I never knew such horror existed in the world. Maybe I'm just naïve. We are fighting a war, I guess."

Joe's mood quickly changed as he turned his attention to the entrance to the chapel, paused for a moment and took a deep breath. "Angel, I have to go. Maybe, you should stay here and pray for Rocco for a few minutes before you leave." Joe hurried to the front of the chapel and exited through a door that was located behind the altar.

"That was odd. Par for the course today." Libby said a few prayers for the man she had come to love and rose to leave. As soon as she walked out, she stumbled into a man, knocking him to the ground. "Oh, I'm so sorry sir. Are you ok? Let me help you...." Libby's countenance suddenly changed when she saw the person's face. A cold shiver shot through her body, rendering her momentarily paralyzed with anxiety.

The fallen man rose to his feet. "Oh, sweetheart. I'm fine. Are you OK? It looks like you've seen a ghost."

"No, no. I'm, ahhh, alright."

The man leered at the young nurse. "OK, but do you know Joe, the fisherman? I'm a very close relative and I really need to speak with him. He's been a naughty boy. I see you've been praying. Was it for anyone special? Are the prayers working?"

Libby shuddered standing next to the man. She knew she had to get away from him. The man exuded a level of creepiness that she had never before experienced. "Sorry, I need to get back to work." Libby darted away from him as quickly as she could.

The man smiled and shouted to the scampering nurse. "Don't worry, love. I'll find him myself, but I'll be seeing you." Walking down the corridor in the opposite direction, he whistled an evil sounding tune. Unaware of who he really was, Libby was right to feel uneasy about the stranger. She couldn't have known that Uncle Trick, the Prince of Darkness, had come to Camp Edwards for a visit, and he was feeling devilish.

All things considered, Rocco was alive and healing, albeit physically but not spiritually. Uncle Trick, however, wasn't happy. He never considered the possibility that Rocco would have survived that day. His prized new recruit did not complete the planned transformation and join his legion of Pale Riders, which could only have come through death and rebirth. Overconfidence being one of his many flaws, Uncle Trick knew he would have to up his game and increase the intensity of his efforts. He could no longer afford to take Rocco's conversion for granted. The young man was standing at the cliff's edge and all that was needed was a little push, but Uncle Trick was impressed. In his words, the kid was "resilient."

Libby ran to the courtyard to bring Rocco inside for lunch, as she did every day without fail. The more time she could spend with the man she came to love the better. Entering the courtyard on another beautifully sunny summer day, she saw another nurse standing behind her beau and whispering into his ear. The roses that were blooming near them seemed exceptionally larger and brighter in the midday sun.

Rocco was sitting motionless on a bench, his eyelids clenched tightly and chin resting on his chest. This was the first day where he didn't need a wheelchair to get around. Apparently, his hip had begun to heal exceptionally fast. A single crutch was all that he needed. Additionally, Rocco had also been speaking about his family visits less frequently. It was apparent that his internal injuries were healing as quickly as his physical ones, and she welcomed it without giving it a second thought.

Libby walked faster toward them. "Hello, excuse me, nurse. Hello, excuse me." No response was returned.

The nurse raised her head, looked at Libby, and smiled. She then turned and walked in the opposite direction to avoid any possible confrontation, or suspicion for that matter. It wasn't time for a meeting yet. The nurse made her way into a ward where senior officers were convalescing and ducked out of sight.

Libby slowly bent her legs and crouched next to Rocco. "Who was that nurse? I've never seen her before." Remaining lost in his thoughts, her beau remained still. She placed her hand on his arm gently, hoping to get a reaction.

Her gesture had the desired effect as Rocco suddenly snapped out of his impassive state. "Hey, doll, where have you been? I'm starving."

"Rocco, who was that nurse talking to you?

"What nurse? You're my nurse, *cara mia*, but I wish…I wish…" Rocco stumbled in his attempt to express his deepest desire, one that he's had since the first day he met Libby. "I wish you were more than that." He smiled with one of his well-known boyish grins.

Libby was surprised to hear Rocco display such an open expression of tenderness or perhaps love. She knew he had survived a nightmare, and she always wondered if he could ever love her. Being called *cara* made her pulse quicken. She knew he wouldn't have said it lightly. "You…you…you called me *cara*?"

"Sure, why wouldn't I? You are the best thing that's ever happened to me. Without you, I would have rolled myself off that cliff over there a long time ago. I see you, inside and out. You make me want to be a better man, but I know you deserve better than me."

Libby smiled and held his hand. "Better than you, *caro mio*?" The young nurse had evidently been learning Italian in her free time.

A sparkle returned to the startled soldier's eyes that had been absent for far too long. "Libby, you've been studying! You said it perfectly too." Rocco wondered whether there was a real possibility for him to be loved or even to feel love, considering what he'd done and what had been done to him. He could feel his body stepping back spiritually from the cliff's edge.

"Well, I thought I'd surprise you after I learned a few more words and phrases. Do you really think I said it the right way?"

Rocco winked at his loving friend. "Without a doubt, but for a minute there I thought we were back in Puglia."

She patted his hand with a playful tap. "Oh, you're such a mischievous little boy at times."

Rocco laughed loudly for the first time in many weeks. "I had to work my way into your heart some way, didn't I?"

"Yes, you did, rascal. I've been hoping and praying for you to recognize me. You're not playing with me, are you?"

"Recognize you? Really? You hit me like a bolt of lightning the first time I met you. I can't describe it any better."

Libby caressed Rocco's hand tenderly and smiled. "Maybe, we were hit by the same lightning bolt. Nothing will ever change that. C'mon, let's go get some lunch. You must be starving."

"Yup, I could eat a horse, and I think it's on the menu today."

The sweethearts made their way to the hospital cafeteria like two giggling teenagers in love. They didn't need to say a word. The atmosphere surrounding them was full of love. They were so enamored with each other that they passed Nurse Maggie in the corridor without saying hello.

The old nurse raised her hands to her hips in mock irritation. "Well, that's a fine how d'ya do. I thought I was your girl, mister."

Neither Rocco nor Libby broke their stride. The mischievous boy didn't even bother to turn his head. "Sorry, babe, we're done. I've been swept off my feet — or my foot — I should say."

Nurse Maggie shook her head playfully and smiled. She was relieved to see life breathed back into the young man, for whom she felt a maternal fondness. "Always a rascal. Always a rascal. Enjoy lunch, you two."

The cafeteria food was especially bad that day. Some sort of slop that they called American Chop Suey was on the menu. Rocco stared at this alleged edible object on his fork. He wondered how and why the food could be so bad. "You know I was kidding when I said horse was on the menu. I think that they reused the leftovers from World War I. It must be part of their plan to get patients released faster. Here's the caption, 'Get well soon or else you've got to eat this food longer.' That has to be it."

Libby agreed wholeheartedly. "I think you're right. I heard it can cure cancer too."

Rocco was beaming now. "Libby, you kill me. That's the funniest thing I've ever heard."

For the rest of the lunch, it became readily apparent to the other diners that these two individuals were fast becoming one. Every hand movement and head nod exhibited their emerging love for all to see. Instead of eating, they passed the time with meaningless banter and gentle laughter, the kind that one would expect from two paramours who were unquestionably becoming bonded.

At the end of lunch, Rocco asked Libby to take him back to his bed. "I'm feeling a little worn out. I would like to go rest."

"Of course, Ranger. I'll walk you back."

"It feels like I was hit by a ton of bricks but in a good way. Maybe you can sit with me a little longer." A large grin was now displayed on his face to the delight of his new love. His smile was punctuated by a couple of raised eyebrows.

"OK, easy does it, cowboy. Let's get you to bed and maybe get a bucket of ice along the way to cool you down a bit."

"No way. This fire's not going out." The hobbling Casanova continued to work his charms even though he didn't need to do so. He had already won Libby's heart.

Libby escorted Rocco to the ward and helped her wounded warrior climb into his bed. "OK, I need to get back to work. I'll drop by before my shift ends. Would that be ok with you? Now, please get into bed and rest."

Rocco was quick to respond. "Any time I can get, *cara mia*. Any time."

The two parted and Libby continued her nursing duties while Rocco quickly fell asleep. She had never been happier.

At the end of her shift, the young nurse came by to check on her beloved. She kissed his forehead and whispered in his ear to say goodnight. "Still asleep? Good. Sweet dreams, *caro*." Words of love and devotion now flowed so easily from the young nurse's lips. It was only a short time ago that she had been tongue-tied whenever she was near the love of her life.

Soon after Libby walked away, Rocco started talking in his sleep for the first time since the ambulance to Camp Edwards when he had been heavily sedated. "*Tu sei il mio tesoro. Ti amo oggi e per sempre.* You are my treasure. I love you today and forever." Was Rocco turning a corner in his life to a brighter future? It certainly seemed that he was, but a curveball was about to be thrown at him.

He slowly woke from his deep slumber to see an eerily quiet and dark ward. All the other patients were still fast asleep. The pain of the past still weighed heavily on his heart and soul. He closed his eyes and reached out to the person who always had been the rock in his life and the man he most admired. "*Papa, dove stai? Prego per me.* Where are you? Pray for me."

"Calling for your father, are we?" Seemingly out of nowhere, a mysterious-looking nun appeared at the foot of Rocco's bed. A local religious order had been volunteering in the hospital and lending a helping hand to assist the nursing staff. An extra set of hands was always welcome when a patient had to be lifted or moved from a bed or wheelchair, but these sisters worked almost exclusively in the daytime. This nun was covered head to toe in a full religious habit, where only her face was visible. Rocco, like many Catholic boys of the day, referred to nuns dressed in this manner as penguins.

Rocco was startled. "Whoa sister, where did you come from? You almost scared lunch right out of me, and it didn't need any extra help."

"I heard you're the comedian on the floor. My name is Sister Lilith, I'm your new night nurse."

"Oh really? What happened to Lucy?"

The nun was standing at the foot of the bed, with her hands on its foot rails. "She's not feeling well. She's got some sort of bug."

"I hope she feels better soon. She's aces. But seriously, where did you come from? I didn't see or hear you walk up to the bed. And why are you here alone tonight? Shouldn't you be back at the convent for evening prayers or something?"

"Silly boy, I've been checking each patient for the last hour and you're my last one. I'm working a little extra overtime today since they're shorthanded. Anyway, my shoes don't squeak." The nun pointed to her feet as she demonstrated the silence of her footwear. "And we don't want to disturb the other patients now, do we?"

She lifted the patient chart that was hanging on a hook at the foot of the bed and flipped through the pages studiously. "Hmmm, I see you have been making a dramatic recovery lately. Well, physically anyway. Somebody must think you're special."

Sister Lilith continued to review Rocco's chart, commenting on his recovery and regurgitating various incomprehensible medical terms. Listening to her voice and analyzing her face, he became acutely aware that something about her seemed off. He had a strange feeling that he had met her before but struggled to recall where or when. While bewildered, Rocco had sufficient suspicion to conclude that she was an imposter. "There's something familiar about your voice. I can't place it, but I know we've met before."

"Well, I've heard that line before, soldier." Moving toward the head of the bed and leaning down, the nun whispered into his ear. "You're going to have to do better than that." She then lifted her head away from his ear and grinned.

Rocco's body froze in fright because he recognized that evil smile and those familiar facial features now. But how could this be? She was the soldier whispering into other people's ears in Italy, but her face was unmistakable, albeit somewhat altered or disguised. "I don't understand. Who, or what are you? I saw you in Italy. You were in uniform." A cold sweat ran down his face now to exacerbate his confused state.

Sister Lilith, who hadn't yet revealed her true name, sat on Rocco's bed and sensually stroked his hair. "You've seen me many times, my beautiful boy. You didn't think we were done with you, did you? What you did to those men was pure poetry. It was an honor, and absolutely exhilarating, to have watched your artistry in action. I devoured every morsel you fed me that day. He was right to have picked you."

"What do you mean? Who picked me? And for what?" Rocco's heart pounded ferociously against his chest. Panic and fright had overtaken his sanity. "I'm having a nightmare. That's it. I'm having a nightmare with a scary freaking nun. I just need to wake up."

"Oh, my beautiful boy, you ARE the nightmare. You are, however, right about one thing. You need to wake up. Do you really think that you judged all the men that could have been judged? There are many more out there waiting to experience the full effects of your talents. Mmmm, I can't wait for another feeding."

A door at the far end of the ward swung open and distracted the nun. "Well, that's enough for tonight. I'll be seeing you, beautiful. Now go back to sleep. That's it, sleep, sleep." Rocco fell back into a deep slumber with a simple touch of her index finger to his forehead, and off she went, walking away slowly to avoid suspicion.

Outside the hospital, the nun found Uncle Trick sitting on a bench and waiting impatiently for an appraisal of his new recruit. Sister Lilith walked over solemnly and reverently which contradicted her intentions with Rocco. Her gait was similar to one any reasonable person would expect of a reverend mother, slow and steady yet determined. She sat down next to the diabolical ruler of the underworld and gave him an update. "Well, it seems our boy has been getting special treatment."

Uncle Trick, the Morning Star, was not happy to say the least. "Chaos, tell me something I don't know. I can smell an Angel of Virtue's scent around here."   He rotated his head from side to side in jest, consuming the spiritual scent surrounding him. "I assume it's the Healing Muse; that's the only one who could've helped our boy. Raphael's probably been around too. My damn little brother!" He slammed his cane to the ground to emphasize his point.

"Our boy has made a miraculous recovery. It's definitely the Healing Muse, but I do sense your brother around too, probably to protect her."

Uncle Trick scowled angrily, although his minion had additional information that wouldn't improve his disposition. "There's another person we need to be worried about. Rocco has fallen in love with a nurse who is the epitome of - excuse me while I vomit - purity and innocence."

"Who is this nurse? And why didn't our friend tell us?"

"Her name is Libby, and she loves him too. You know she's a civilian, which does limit our possibilities. And one more thing, she's got some power that I'm not sure I can figure out yet. She's special, that's for sure."

"Power? Very interesting. Hmm, our friend the captain needs to start contributing more to this enterprise."   Uncle Trick turned a suspicious gaze to his minion. "Tell me how you didn't know about the Muse. Kind of odd, don't you think?"

"Ease up, boss. You're looking in the wrong direction. We've both been – pardon the expression – tricked."

Uncle Trick growled his disapproval. "Chaos, I tell the jokes not you. I want to know how they snuck in here under our noses. Find out!"

"Okay. Okay. But it's going to take a lot of work to figure out how they've kept themselves hidden from us and to turn this around. The Muse is doing something new. That's for sure."

"Well, get to it, and I'll see if Raphael's been hanging around our boy too. Tonight, I think our new recruit will benefit from a personal visit, maybe in a nightmare. He'll be a captive audience."

Chaos enthusiastically agreed and the two evil comrades went their separate ways.

Back inside the hospital building, Rocco and the other residents of the ward were in a deep slumber. Uncle Trick was standing outside and staring at a sleeping Rocco from a nearby window. He was falling into a trance to invade the dreams of a young man whom he desired to be the newest and most lethal member of his small legion of reapers.

"Hello, Buddy Boy, Hello."

Rocco was still sleeping but seemingly awake within his dream. "What is this? Who's calling me?"

Uncle Trick's slithering voice echoed across the dreamlike ether. "I'm glad to have finally met you?"

"Glad to meet me? Who are you and where am I? It's so dark here. Why can't I see anything?" Rocco remained in a deep REM sleep; however, his eyes were rolling frantically under his lids. The rest of his body was motionless and calm, which belied an unnerved, yet unconscious state.

"I'm a friend who admired your devotion to your family, and most of all, your artistry in Collina Verde. Your judgment was beautiful and honorable. No, it was righteous." The Morning Star wanted his recruit to accept that what he did was justice and not brutal revenge, but he was also fully prepared to use Rocco's overpowering feeling of guilt to seduce him to join his legion.

"Artistry? You said artistry. Why did you say that?"

"Because that's what it was. Your action was the work of an artist, like Michaelangelo painting the Sistine Chapel."

"Why can't I see you? Why are you hiding from me? Show yourself!"

"Are you ready to see me and accept your calling? You just need to step forward and take my hand."

"What do you mean? Who are you?" Rocco's screams reverberated across his dream world.

"There are other terrible people you left behind, inflicting the same trauma and destruction in your old home. You only took care of a small group. There are so many more from all parts of the world, in every city, town and village. They come in all shapes and sizes. Villains are everywhere. Let's not miss the forest for the trees."

"What do you mean? I don't understand. It can't be true."

"But it is true. How do you feel knowing you couldn't save your family? You've been pretending to see them every day, but you know they're not real. Your guilt has driven you to a world of make-believe, instead of one where the truth lives. See it, Buddy Boy, see it."

"Oh God, why?"

"God's not going to help you. Did He help your family? Is He helping all those young women who are being brutalized as we speak? There are so many more animals in this world that need to be put down."

Rocco repeated the words he heard. "There are animals in this world that need to be put down." Our hero was falling.

Twisting the dagger further into his prized recruit, Uncle Trick used all the tools in his kit. "What would your mama say? Wouldn't she want you to help those in need of assistance and to protect the innocent? Puglia is crying for you."

"Puglia is crying."

With a jolt, Rocco was awakened from his dream and catapulted from the darkness. Uncle Trick wasn't happy, which wasn't unusual lately. "Dammit, who woke him?"

Rocco's eyes popped wide open to see Libby standing over him with a concerned look on her face. She had a dream that he was in trouble and rushed over to the hospital before her shift started. "*Caro,* are you ok? Were you having a nightmare?"

Her radiant face was well received by a shaken Rocco. Although he tried to hide it, he did show a few tell-tale signs of trauma, including a quivering voice and a trembling hand. "Oh, oh, I guess I was. I dreamed of being in total darkness. It was bizarre, very bizarre, but seeing you washes away the nightmares."

Libby held her beloved's hand to help calm his nerves. "You were in total darkness? That does sound scary. I'm here now; everything's going to be OK. Just like your name, you're a rock that can't be broken."

Libby sat on the bed next to her beloved and caressed his face to help ease his pain. Rocco smiled at the woman who had become his rock.

Beaten, Uncle Trick stomped out of the courtyard angrily and disappeared into the morning mist. "This girl is trouble."

Descension or Dissension

At the local dock, Captain Joao, or Joe as Libby called him, was on board the Fisherlady preparing the boat for the day's run. His attention was completely preoccupied with detangling the nets and yelling at his reluctant crew.

"Hey, you two, get the knots out of this net! After almost a hundred years, you morons should know how to detangle a net by now. I have a bunch of idiots working for me, a bunch of idiots. Maybe, I should have left you behind to burn today or at the bottom of the Atlantic with that prized, harpooned whale you slaughtered." Captain was referring to the time and place where he first met these two souls he had judged. He had hoped that they would be more useful in death than they were in life. Unfortunately, this wasn't the case. "I never realized that you two murderous slugs knew nothing about sailing, only killing."

Captain's attention turned from these crew members to others to get the boat ready more quickly. The morning continued in this fashion with Captain barking orders and his crew reacting accordingly. It was a beautiful early summer morning. The sun radiated across the distant horizon and provided a welcomed warmth for a fleet of hardy New

England fishermen. It was the type of morning that most people would say was perfect. So, it came as a surprise, when Uncle Trick came walking down the dock, tapping his cane, and whistling his diabolical tune.

Stopping at the edge of the dock, Uncle Trick greeted his old friend in a tone that sounded equally pleasant and ominous at the same time. "Captain Joao, how are you my old friend? How are the fish biting? Must be good, because you've been fishing new places, haven't you?"

Captain, resigned to the fact that this wasn't going to be a pleasant social call, tried not to appear suspicious and responded with a half-hearted greeting. "Trick, what brings you around?" Regrettably, he knew why his boss had come. The time he had spent with Libby recently had made a positive impact on Trick's new recruit.

"Well, Buddy Boy, I was just at the hospital visiting our new member of the team, and you know what I saw?"

Captain shrugged and continued to work on his fishing gear. "No, what?"

"Ahhh, a most amazing thing! Our boy is healing miraculously, and he found love. Can you imagine that? Love!"

"Really? Well, you said he was special."

Uncle Trick bellowed his displeasure, cowering the crew into a frightened and supplicated position. "Do you think I'm a fool like your crew here? And stop playing with those damn nets!" The Evil One lowered the tone of his voice to avoid attention. "C'mon big fella, are you trying to double-cross me? *Me!* Have you forgotten who *I* am? Or have you spent too much time in the sun, and it's baked your brain?" The Great Deceiver leapt onto the deck to emphasize his anger. The crew scurried below deck, fearing they would also feel his wrath.

Captain waved his arms and claimed ignorance of the situation. "No way! How could I, or anyone, deceive you? I've gone to the hospital a couple of times. The last time I went there was a few days ago and everything looked fine. He was a lost boy, who needed a little more time to cook."

"Well, I guess it's been a remarkable couple of days, don't you think? He's not using a wheelchair anymore, and that cute little nurse has brought him out of his stupor. What's her name?"

"How would I know her name?" He didn't fall for Uncle Trick's trap. "He's out of his wheelchair? Must be a Virtue, the Healing Muse. You know they can conceal themselves pretty good."

Uncle Trick tapped his elongated index finger on his cane and hissed his irritation. "I could smell her scent. She's been there for sure. Chaos didn't detect her either. The Healer is a good hider, but she's been getting help too."

"Your brother?"

"Raphael, my little, do-gooder, sweet brother. It's too bad -- he's my favorite family member."

"Wow, is this your caring side? You almost sound, hmmm, familial; well, almost anyway." Captain's injection of humor was not well-received.

Uncle Trick growled at the old mariner. "Not funny, Buddy Boy, not funny. I want you back at the hospital later today to find out more about this nurse. Chaos is convinced she's got a spiritual power of some sort. She obviously has a strong bond with the Trinity. What is in balance must become imbalanced, and I think we only need one small push."

"Okay, boss. I'll get over there this afternoon."

"I want you to work on Rocco too. No more observing. You need to be an active participant now. Get him to see the light, or the darkness." Uncle Trick snickered at his little quip.

"Now who's telling jokes?"

"Just do what I tell you and you'll hear a few more jokes. Otherwise, well, you know what happens when I'm not happy."

Having made his point, Uncle Trick hopped onto the harbor's dock to make his exit. Mirroring his entrance, he walked down the dock, tapped his cane, and whistled his old diabolical tune again.

Meanwhile, at Camp Edwards, Libby was attending to her nursing duties, but there was a dark cloud hanging over the ward. Another nurse's patient had passed away earlier in the morning, and everyone felt the loss deeply. The patient was a young sailor from Maine wounded on a destroyer escorting merchant ships to Great Britain. A piece of metal shrapnel that had lodged in his chest had shifted and pierced his heart. The medical staff had been so careful in their efforts to save this young man, still a boy in reality, but ultimately the damage was just too great to repair. He was one of the last casualties of the enemy wolfpacks sinking cargo ships that were the Transatlantic lifeline for the Allied nations. Many ships were lost to this watery graveyard, but many more got through with the help of sailors from the US and Great Britain, like this young Mainer.

Libby felt the loss profoundly. She watched somberly as Maggie and another nurse packed the young sailor's personal effects. The sailor, who was just eighteen years old, reminded her of Mikey, her little brother who recently joined the Marines. The two shared a special bond. Growing up north of Boston in the pre-war years, Mikey would often refer to her as 'Mom' when her protective side would kick into overdrive. She would pester him about his schoolwork, washing up before dinner, wearing clean clothes and other things that would drive a boy crazy.

A doctor walked up to Libby and stood beside her. "These are always the saddest moments for me -- a boy, barely a man, lost before he could even begin to enjoy life."

Libby remained focused on the activity occurring in front of her. She whispered dejectedly without turning to look at the doctor. "So true. So true."

"I hope you don't let this wear on your spirit. You have a special light that can't be extinguished, and an empathy that can't be destroyed. The Trinity shines through you, child."

Libby whipped her head around, but no one was there. "What?" Confused, the young nurse scanned the ward to find whoever had spoken to her. No one was found. Everyone else was busy with normal daily tasks. The speaker's presence, while not visible, was detectable. The young nurse could feel a warmth surrounding her that offered her some comfort and serenity.

Since it was close to lunchtime, Libby walked to the courtyard to sit with Rocco for a few minutes. She wanted to make sure he was still handling the emotional toll of his nightmare. She found her beloved enjoying the midday sun, sitting with his eyes closed and head raised to soak in the warm rays. He sat in his normal spot next to the large and beautiful rose bush in the courtyard.

Libby was surprised that Rocco did not have a walking aid with him. "Well, you don't need your crutch anymore. You are making a fantastic recovery."

Rocco remained motionless, continuing to soak in the sun's warmth. "It's all because of you, *bellissima*."

"*Bellissima?* Another word I need to learn. I get the feeling you're being fresh."

While he was returning to his happy and jovial state, he was always genuine in anything involving Libby. He looked at his love and winked. "Not me, never."

"Is your nightmare still bothering you? Remember, it's not real."

"I know, but at the time it felt so real. It's over now. I've got the sun and you."

"Can I ask you a question that I've been afraid to ask? It's about your fam...."

Rocco stopped Libby halfway through her question. "Family visits? That's all done. Everyone probably thought I was nuts or something. I guess it was a strange way for me to cope, but I don't know if I'll ever get over the guilt. I should have been faster, better..."

"*Caro*, no, you're only human. We can't control the world. It's impossible." Libby leaned in closer to Rocco and smiled. "We can't even control whom we love."

Rocco held her tightly. "*Tu sei il mio tesoro. Ti amo oggi e per sempre.*"

The smitten and adoring nurse shed a tear because she knew these were words of love, even if she didn't understand their meaning. "You have a knack for always saying the right thing and knocking me off my feet. Let's go to lunch."

"Great, but please no more horse meat. If I have any more, I'll be running at Suffolk Downs."

The two sweethearts walked to the cafeteria, hand-in-hand and giggling like teenagers once again. No one existed in their world but them. Uncle Trick's shenanigans failed to push the Ranger over the edge. He was going to have to ratchet up the pressure. Otherwise, he risked losing him to the light forever. The Muse had done a miraculous job of healing his recruit, while Libby had mended his mind and soul.

From a distant point at the opposite end of the courtyard, the Healing Muse watched with great satisfaction as Rocco and Libby departed for lunch. "Love is so beautiful. Don't you think Joao? I know you're standing behind me. Please join me."

"One of these days I will be able to sneak up on you undetected."

"What do the kids say these days? Fat chance?"

"How are the two lovebirds doing?"

The Muse pointed to the giggling sweethearts. "See for yourself."

Captain smiled joyously, something he hadn't done in a long time. "That's wonderful, just perfect."

"I have to say it came as a surprise when you called on me to intervene on behalf of these two individuals. At first, I wondered if you were up to something despicable and perverse, but after meeting these captivating children, I knew they were special. Joao, my child, there is still a soft spot in my heart for you. I will never concede defeat in your redemption."

Captain bowed his head in reverent respect of the Muse. "Don't waste your time on me. I'm irredeemable and too far gone."

"Then why help these two? The bonds of the Trinity are under attack each day, especially from the anger and actions of my sister. What brought these children to you?"

"Oh, there are days when I think my humanity isn't completely gone. You've always said redemption is available to all of us, but I don't know. The world is an ugly and unforgiving place, one where malice trumps kindness constantly. I see it getting worse every day. This latest war is just the tip of Armageddon. These two offered me hope. After Uncle Trick instructed me to get involved in Rocco's recruitment, I watched him intensely to get an accurate measure of the man. What I found hit me hard. The character and innocence of this soldier and nurse were born of noble purity, the Trinity incarnate. I started to think there was hope again."

The Muse clasped her hand gently on Captain's arm. "Heaven will never surrender. It will never - how do the people describe it – throw up the towel."

Captain laughed. "You mean throw *in* the towel, but I get your point."

There was a twinkle in the Muse's eye now and warmth that extended to the old captain. "Joao, the Trinity is alive. It surrounds us all. One day, you will see it and embrace it again. I know it."

"Tell me how you can hide from your sister. You're her family but she can't see you. How's that possible?"

"When she fell, her bond with me broke but not my bond with her, if that makes sense. I know where she is every minute of every day. I often cry for her. One day, I know she'll return to us as well."

"I wish I had your confidence."

"You do. It's just hidden under the Morning Star's tricks and all that fish oil and scrambled eggs."

Captain laughed heartily. "Oh my God, you're telling jokes now? Armageddon isn't coming; it's already here."

"I've been practicing. What do you think? Can I make a movie career out of it?"

Captain enjoyed seeing the Healing Muse's fun side. "That's it. I've heard it all now. Maybe I should start calling you Amuse and not Muse?"

The Muse shook her head and smiled. "Now, that was terrible."

The two clandestine coworkers in Rocco's salvation parted company, happy and content in the knowledge that they had a good day.

The rest of the day proved uneventful for the residents and staff of Camp Edwards. Libby was done for the day. Before she left, she made sure her beloved was settled in for a good night's sleep. Her normal shift ended hours earlier, but she gladly put in overtime to help out, and more importantly it was an excuse to keep a watchful eye over Rocco. Sitting on his bed and caressing his hand, Libby stayed until Rocco fell asleep. Once convinced that her sweetheart had fallen into a deep sleep, she made her way quietly out of the ward.

Little did she know that he was faking. Rocco smiled at the necessary deception and thought to himself. "Looks like it worked. I don't want her around here if that creepy nun comes back."

"Creepy nun? Why do you think I'm creepy?"

After an initial shock, Rocco became still and focused on his nightly visitor. He would not be scared again and no longer play the part of prey. Remaining silent, he leered at the nun and did not speak. *Holy crap, it's her again. Where did she come from?*

"Through those doors, silly boy."

"How did you know what I was thinking? I'm afraid to ask what you are, but I think I know. In the old country, parents would tell their children about an evil spirit who torments people. It would tempt children to do bad things."

"Geez, I need a better publicist if you think that's me, beautiful. Humans don't need any help getting in trouble. They do just fine on their own."

"Well, whatever you are, I know you're evil. So, piss off. *Madonna, aiutami.* My Lady, help me."

"Please don't say her name. It gives me such a stomachache to hear it in that dialect too."

Rocco took delight in being the torturer rather than the tortured for once. "What, Madonna? Madonna. Madonna. Madonna. Ma—."

"Enough, boy!" Sister Lilith's eyes glowed red to showcase her displeasure as she hissed her measured, yet angry, response.

Rocco stopped poking the bear — or penguin — and listened to the nun. "I came here again today to free you and to show you a righteous path. I didn't come here to take part in your juvenile antics."

Rocco laid still, happy with the fact that he struck a nerve. "Please leave. You're not wanted here."

The nun sat on the bed alongside her prone patient. She moved closer and attempted to run her fingers through Rocco's hair, but he would have none of it. He slapped her hand away. "Back off lady. Back off."

Sister Lilith was flabbergasted at the slight, or so she wanted him to believe. "Who raised you? You must have been raised by a nanny goat, or a pig maybe."

Rocco's face turned beet red. "Don't you dare talk about my parents, my mother." He tried to sit up in bed but was prevented by the nun's well-placed hand on his chest. "Let me up."

"Shhhh, lie back down, beautiful. Do you mean the mother you let die at the hands of those animals? Well, it appears that I've struck a nerve. It's time you heard something that will open your eyes."

Rocco was unable to move and snapped back at his captor. "You have nothing to say that I want to hear. You're nothing, got it? Nothing."

"Oh beautiful, I'm so much more than nothing. I've been around since the beginning, watching humanity make a mess of this world and destroy all of its gifts. Nothing? That's laughable and so human for you to think that. Who am I? Don't you want to know?" She leaned forward to whisper into Rocco's ear and to emphasize her point. A slow, demonic murmur added a sprinkle of terror to her voice. "I am discord, depravity, hatred, and fear. I am the dark whispers in the night, thriving on intolerance and deceit. Humanity is an abomination to the Trinity. My name is Chaos, and I am Legion."

Rocco was speechless, because a part of him agreed with the demon's declaration. A spiritual door had been pushed open slightly, and the young man's soul was now at risk. For many years, an unrelenting thought had reverberated in his mind; specifically, mankind had always been a vicious pack of animals, and the vast majority were not redeemable. What else would account for the past three decades, three centuries or even three millennia? Libby's hold on Rocco was failing.

Humanity's growth in finding better and more efficient ways to inflict cruelty on their brothers and sisters was astounding. Often the voice of reason and compassion would win, but humanity's unrelenting Sisyphean labors generally seemed futile in the end. Invariably, the rock, nearing the mountain's top, would roll back down on the innocent, and misery would be the victor. Fear and indifference brought about the age of the dictator and provided Chaos a human feast.

"Ahh, beautiful boy, I think you're beginning to understand. Sleep now. I'll see you soon."

Once again, Chaos placed Rocco into a deep sleep and exited the ward. In the courtyard, Uncle Trick waited for his minion's update. "How's our boy? Is he ready for another visit tonight?"

"He's back on track, but I would leave him alone tonight. Let my visit sauté inside him for a bit, and you'll get better results. His mind is cracking."

Uncle Trick was delighted, perhaps even euphoric. He raised his arms in a sign of apparent victory. "Excellent, my girl, excellent. Now we have to keep that irritating nurse away from our boy. Get it done."

Chaos popped her head up in surprise. "But she's a civilian."

"I'm not telling you to kill her, or to cross any line. We all have our limits but I'm sure you can find a way. I'm counting on you."

Uncle Trick winked at his servant and walked out of the courtyard. He disappeared into the night, whistling his evil tune and leaving Chaos to reflect on his order. She looked back at Rocco through the window with a slightly pained and forlorn expression. Through all her dealings with Rocco, another door had apparently been opened. This door led to a place that she never thought could be rebuilt. Was it possible for

Chaos to show signs of internal chaos? Still in her nun's habit, the demon walked away and pondered the emerging disorder in herself. Have these two individuals made an undeniable impact that altered her essence? She speculated that it couldn't be true. "No way, it's just a minor and temporary illness, like the common cold. It'll pass soon, won't it? I think it will. My name is Chaos. Say it again. My name is Chaos. The spirit that once inhabited this body is an unwelcome apparition, a misbegotten reflection of an ancient time. Right?" Conviction was giving way to doubt and inner turmoil. Uncle Trick's hold on her was failing and the next couple of days were going to be eventful to say the least.

Misery Rules

Rocco's sleep was uninterrupted; however, it was far from peaceful. Images of death and destruction haunted him until morning. Misery, the Demon of Dreams, ruled Rocco's sleeping domain and there was no way to evict him. Uncle Trick wasn't leaving his future apprentice unattended, regardless of Chaos' recommendation. The Prince of Lies wanted him now, not later. He sent the demon to invade his sleeping victim's dreams and to push him decisively into his legion of reapers.

The demon's appearance made him altogether more terrifying than anything mankind could create or inflict upon itself. He had no horns, razor-sharp fingers or pointed shark teeth to impale a victim. He had no slithery skin or blazing eyes as would be expected of a serpent from Hell. Misery appeared as a pre-pubescent boy with rosy-red cheeks and dressed in an immaculate white suit. His appearance was an affront to the innocence of youth and the Sacrament of Communion. The demon took delight in impugning Christians, especially Catholics who used their many rituals to show reverence to God and the Trinity.

Misery would materialize in a dream first in his innocent visage to break down a victim's defensive barrier and to obtain his trust. In short, it was the best way of entering and reading a quarry's mind with the ultimate goal of subjugating him in a state of complete fear. Once in, the gloves came off and he receded into the background unseen. The demon would morph into a terrible visage and sit on his victim's chest as he had done to the people of Tranquillo. He would then summon all sorts of horror based on a person's particular fears.

For Rocco, it was guilt, pure and simple. His guilt of not saving his family weighed on him every moment of the day. Forgiving himself was never considered an option. Misery took hold of this and sent him into a tailspin faster than a bullet-riddled plane over Europe. The demon placed dreams of his mother and sisters being assaulted, images that Rocco tried to eliminate but could not. Through every rip, tear and blow, the violent assault continued throughout the night. He was unsuccessful in turning away from the visions. It was as if his head was held in a vice and his eyes were taped open. There was no escaping the horrible sight and sounds of the bodily invasion that devastated the three most precious women in his life.

He tried to scream but nothing came from a mouth opened as wide as physically possible, frozen in agony, with tears flowing from his bloodshot eyes. He watched in horror as Noemi and Bella stared directly at him while remaining expressionless and motionless. The vision of these two innocent sisters being humiliated and assaulted felt like a knife being driven deep into his heart only to be removed and reinserted with every deviant action of these animals.

A cocktail of guilt mixed with terror and pain was being served, and it was the only drink on the menu. His pain didn't matter because he needed to save his family.

Rocco continued to struggle with the invisible constraints holding him back. Anger and hate exploded within him. Rocco wanted the world to feel his wrath. "Noemi, Bella, close your eyes and leave your bodies! I'm coming for you! Please, hang on! Dear God, why won't you stop this? What kind of a God are you?"

Adding to the horror was the evil laughter that embodied the enjoyment expressed by these animals. Hearing one after another say 'your turn' sent Rocco spiraling deeper into Hell. In short order, his heart was pounding hard against his chest wall, and he was ready to kill again. "Mama, I'm so sorry. I should have been there to protect you. Noemi! Bella! Please, no more! You bastards, I'll rip all your hearts out with my bare hands."

Rocco fought hard against the nightmares and Misery took notice. "This boy is strong. You've got some support, but I'll break you down."

Rocco struggled mightily. "This can't be happening. Libby, where are you? The demons are attacking me, but I don't understand why. I'm trying to see your face. I see you now. I see you." The panic in his voice grew with each second.

Misery smiled with satisfaction in the deep dark recesses of his nightmare realm. The demon drooled with anticipation as he contemplated the next act of his evil production.

The attackers noticed Libby standing nearby in this manufactured dreamworld and stopped their assault. With evil intent, they stared at their innocent victim trembling in the corner and pleading to be spared. "Please don't hurt me," she cried. "Please stay away." Her pleas would not dissuade the soldiers from their objective, as they walked menacingly toward the woman who had become the love of Rocco's life.

This was the tipping point. Rocco couldn't stand the onslaught any longer. The world had ridden over him like a steamroller — flattening him, body and soul. He had already lost his family. Now this vision showed him how much more he stood to lose. Rocco was standing at a crossroads, and he needed to decide which turn to take. He chose the angels. The young man from Puglia screamed to the heavens for intercession. He remembered Jimmy's prayers before battle. "God, St. Michael, anyone, please help me!"

Then suddenly, Misery felt a tremor in Rocco's dreamworld. "What's that? Someone is waking him up."

Rocco opened his eyes and nearly jumped out of bed. Standing over him was a doctor that he had seen once or twice before but had never met. "What? What happened?"

"It looks like you were having a bad dream, Ranger. Take it easy now. That's it, nice and easy." The doctor comforted the distraught and confused patient. "I could hear you thirty feet away. It must have been one heck of a dream, but you're okay now my friend." While the doctor's attention was fixated on helping his patient, he also shot a concerned and annoyed glance at the far side of the ward. Perhaps, he could sense Misery hiding in a darkened corner, who would have been filled with anger watching his quarry being snatched from his clutches.

Rocco shook off the residue of sleep. "It was a dream. Was it really? Mother of Mercy, it felt so real." Perspiration soaked his pajamas through to the hospital bed sheets. "Geez, it feels like I wet the bed. I need to get up."

"We'll get those changed for you right away. Nurse, we need some help here! Rocco, have a seat here." The doctor helped him to a chair next to his bed.

"Certainly, Dr. Galen. I'll get some new sheets and pajamas from the linen closet. Nurse Chapel, can you help me?"

While the nurses were gathering the linens, Rocco stared intently at the doctor's face. There was something about him that he found odd, yet familiar. A confused and suspicious Rocco engaged with the good doctor and yearned for an answer. "Dr. Galen, if that's your real name, I feel like this isn't the first time we've met, but I can't recall when or where. There's something about you that's puzzling. Have you been watching over Libby and me?" His defenses were on full alert again, as he continued to inspect the rescuer from his nightmare.

Dr. Galen smiled. "What makes you think that's not my real name? And I watch over everyone, not just you and Libby."

"There have been too many odd things happening, the nun, the creepy guy. You name it. And it's all focused on me for some reason. Somebody wants me. It's like I'm being recruited to be something or someone else. I can see something different with you too."

"Well, Rocco, life is a mystery. The sunrise amazes me every morning and the sunset every evening. *La vita e bella, veramendi?*"

"You think life is beautiful? Sorry Doc, I don't see it. Life is a dog-eat-dog fight where only the strongest and cruelest survive. The defenseless and innocent people of the world are fodder for the meat grinder. Death can only be met with death."

"Do you really believe that everyone's destined for a cruel ending? Does Libby?"

Rocco remained silent and still for a moment, attempting to formulate a response to Dr. Galen's question without appearing rude or offensive. While angry at the world, he tried to act like a gentleman. His mother would want him to do so. "Libby? She is too pure for that line of thinking. She's the one that needs protection from the animals in this world. These bastards are like weeds; they grow everywhere and are ready to pounce on the good and virtuous, tear them apart and devour their souls. We're just meat puppets to them." Rocco paused to gather his final thoughts. "Who can say I'm not right? God? Where is He? Not here. That's for sure. What is He other than another absentee parent."

The caring doctor huddled closer to a good man in distress. "Anger and hatred have crept into your heart and blinded you to the world's beauty. Please don't become another casualty of this war. You are seeing life through only one lens." Unexpectedly, the doctor offered some spiritual advice. "Don't fall for the lies of the Beast. Like a dog on a bone, he'll prey on your fears and vulnerabilities."

Rocco stared intently at the doctor. "Who are you?"

The doctor rose from his crouching position and replied in a matter-of-fact manner. "I'm a healer. I'm your doctor."

The nurses returned to change the bed linens and Rocco's sweat-soaked pajamas. "Pardon us while we change the bed sheets."

The kind doctor excused himself. "Ranger, I'll see you again soon. Nurses, please take good care of our patient today. It looks like we are getting drenched with rain, so everyone will be inside. No day in the sunshine for the soldiers today."

"Yes, of course, doctor."

Dr. Galen departed the ward and smiled as he walked past the darkened corner that had raised his suspicion a few moments earlier. "Not today demon, not today. Go back to your lord, little man. I think it's time for your nap."

Misery was fuming because he knew the doctor's true identity right away. Generally speaking, a supernatural being can recognize another supernatural being. "The game's still on, old man. This fight is far from over, far from it."

Reflecting on what the doctor had said to him and unaware of the recent verbal volleys with the demon, Rocco was completely distracted and didn't even hear Dr. Galen leave. "Hey, I got a question."

One of the nurses helping Rocco change his pajamas looked at him. "Yes, what's your question?"

Rocco looked around the ward. "Sorry, I mean for Dr. Galen. Where is he?"

"Well, he just left. And you know what? I can't believe how much you've healed so far, even since yesterday. Your shoulder and hip are looking fantastic."

Rocco was stunned as well. He had been so focused on those earlier delusional visits with his family and forming a romantic bond with Libby that he forgot about his injuries. While he was able to move his wounded arm and hip, it was evident that there was still more healing to do. "Wow, they're a little sore but I feel good, really good."

The nurses gawked at the handsome young man, astonished at his progress. The younger one, whom Rocco knew as Libby's friend, quipped playfully, "Yup, too bad Libby can't be here today. She would want to see this. I can understand what Libby sees in him. Oh boy, hubba bubba."

Even with the playful banter, panic quickly returned to Rocco. "What do you mean? Where's Libby? Is she OK? Did someone hurt her?"

"Oh, no, lover-boy. Someone stole her bicycle overnight, so she asked us to take care of you until she was able to come in. She's probably down at the police station filling out a police report, but today might be tough. There's a heavy storm coming in and we may all have to hunker down until it passes."

Rocco wasn't happy. The news of the incoming storm amplified his fears to a whole new level. He wanted Libby close, not only for her protection but also for the support she provided when he was in distress. She was his rock, and he could feel a downward spiral coming. Without her, the young Ranger was unsure whether he would recover this time. The battle was intensifying, and Rocco's mind was leaning toward the darkness. The nightmare's images were implanted more deeply into his psyche than Dr. Galen had thought. Misery's words rang true, the fight was far from over.

Meanwhile, at the local police station, Libby was completing a report on her stolen bicycle. It was a fairly routine form but for some reason she had difficulty filling it out. It wasn't like the form had hard questions. Rather, her mind was elsewhere. Thoughts of Rocco reverberated incessantly through her mind, causing her to fill in responses that didn't have any semblance of accuracy. Was he OK? Did he have more nightmares? The questions kept on coming faster and faster, creating a degree of confusion that unsettled the young nurse. At least a half dozen forms ended up in the trash can. "Sorry, Chief, my mind is like fudge today."

The old police chief, who had been protecting the quaint Cape Cod town for over thirty years with a brief interruption due to the Great War, remained on the opposite side of the counter trying to help Libby. "Oh, don't you worry one tiny bit. You've got one heck of a tough job. Taking care of our boys battered by war can't be easy. We all appreciate the work you do up there." The chief winked and smiled cheerfully. "But we all know the nurses do all the tough work. Saw it in '18 and seeing it now in '44."

"Awww, Chief, you're making me blush."

"Don't worry about the form. I'm sure your bicycle will show up soon. They always do. Kids wanting a quick ride to the beach tend to find a bicycle lying around to borrow. I sent the deputy down to the beach to see if it was there. He should be back soon."

Libby was relieved at the prospect that her bike wasn't gone for good. "Thanks Chief, I really want to get to work soon."

As soon as Libby finished speaking, the deputy rushed into the station. "Is this your bike?"

"Yes, it is. Thank you so much!"

"Sorry to report that it has a flat. We've got a kit out back to fix it. Shouldn't take long," he said as he glanced up at the gathering dark clouds. "And I hope it doesn't because it looks like a bad storm is moving in. It's only been six years since the Hurricane of '38. Chief, remember all the damage around here."

"Yup, it was the worst I ever saw. The deaths and property damage have to be the most that the Cape had ever experienced. I know you've got a nose for storms. What are you smellin' today?"

"One's coming soon. The skies are getting really dark. Chief, I think everyone should hunker down until it blows over."

"I agree. Let's hit the stores on Main Street and the beaches to get everyone sheltered until the storm passes. The weather forecast did say a storm was coming but it didn't sound too worrisome. These Atlantic storms can be tricky, I guess. Sorry, Libby, the bike repair is going to take a little while longer. You're better off waiting the storm out here."

Libby was stunned. "But I need to get to the hospital."

The deputy offered her comforting advice. "The hospital was built to withstand storms. They'll be fine. You on the other can't be on a bicycle in the middle of a hurricane."

Libby ran to the window to form her own opinion of the weather. "Hurricane? I thought we were just getting a little rain. Whoa, the skies got dark really fast. It looks like dusk out there."

The nurse dashed to the phone to call the hospital. She prayed that the storm wasn't going to produce anything more than bad weather for the Cape. A loud and destructive hurricane could bring back bad memories for these wounded warriors. She had seen the effect of a small summer thunderstorm on the patients, but a hurricane ratchets up the memories of trauma a few levels and decibels. Libby was now alone in the station, anxiously waiting for the nursing desk to answer her call.

"Dear God, please watch over Rocco and the boys. They've been through enough the last few years."

"Good morning, Camp Edwards. Can I help you?"

"Rosie, is that you?"

"Yes, it is. Libby, is that you? Did you find your bike?"

"Yeah, I guess some kids took it for a ride to the beach. I have to learn to lock it up. How are things there?"

"Everything's good, and yes, including your Valentino. It's too bad he doesn't have a brother." Rudolf Valentino was a major heartthrob of the silent movie era, and the nurses all thought it was an appropriate nickname for Rocco.

Rosie's comedic response eased Libby's anxiety. Both had a good laugh on the phone. "Rosie, I told you he's better looking than Valentino, and yuck, he'd be an old man now."

"Doesn't matter. Handsome is handsome in my book, girlfriend. Anyway, I checked on him today. His recovery is amazing. It looks like he's almost fully healed. Doctors can't explain or believe it, so they want to keep him around just in case they are missing something."

Libby was relieved. "That's great to hear."

"But there is one thing." Rosie paused to collect her thoughts. She wanted to give her friend an appropriate update without creating additional anxiety. "He did have another nightmare. It must have been a wild one because he sweat right through his pajamas. But don't worry, he was alright when he woke up. Dr. Galen was there too."

"Dr. Galen was there? Interesting. He's been popping up more and more lately around Rocco."

"Yes, he was. What time are you getting your derrière in here today?"

"That's another reason for the call. The chief wants me to wait out the storm at the station. He doesn't like the look of the sky. He said it reminds him of the '38 hurricane. They're shutting down the shops on Main Street and clearing the beach. You should talk to the boss about locking things down there too."

"Now that you mention it, the sky did get dark rather quickly. OK, stay where you are. Everything's fine here. I'll go talk to Nurse Maggie."

"Good idea. And Rosie, thanks for this morning."

"Anytime, girlfriend. Anyway, we didn't mind changing him out of those wet PJs." Rosie interjected additional humor into the conversation to lessen any anxiety Libby may have been feeling.

It worked. Libby appreciated what her friend was trying to do and laughed. "Hey, hands off."

"OK, OK. Can't blame a girl for trying. I'll see you right after the storm. Stay safe."

"And you too." Libby hung up the phone feeling more at ease knowing that Rocco was in good hands. How could she have known of the pending supernatural battle to be fought for Rocco's soul and destiny? The next few hours would be extraordinarily intense, more so than any battle fought by the Rangers. The keystone underpinning Uncle Trick's scheme and Rocco's future was about to fall into place.

The hurricane arrived on cue. The locals would later say it had been fiercer than the one in '38. Powerful bolts of lighting and booming rolls of thunder punctuated the force of the storm. For some peculiar reason, the path and eye of the storm drove directly over Camp Edwards.

The chief and his deputy came back to the station just when the rain started to fall. Shaking the rain from his coat, the chief expressed relief at getting the warning out when they did. "My goodness, that came out of nowhere. This one's gonna be a doozy for sure." A crash of lightning accentuated his declaration. "Yikes, that was loud! Looks like the storm's headed toward the camp. Libby, did you call them like I asked?"

Libby approached the chief, trembling and anxious. "Yes, I did chief, but do you think they'll get hit hard?"

The deputy chimed in. "Oh, don't you worry. That's the safest place on the Cape, besides the police station. Tell me, is Rosie working today?"

"Yes, Adam, she is. Still sweet on her, I see."

Adam was a strong and handsome local Cape Codder, who had served with the Marines through many of their island-hopping engagements since the early days of the war. He had fought at Guadalcanal and had been wounded at the Battle of Cape Gloucester in January. He returned home through Camp Edwards for his final medical discharge. Adam had performed his duty well for his country during his two years with the 1st Marine Regiment. Now, he was back to protect the homefront. Adam and Rosie developed a strong connection over the past few months. At first, the fledgling romance was uncertain. Rosie had made him work hard to win her, but he never gave up. After all, he was — and will always be — a Marine. Sheer will and determination are indelible parts of their constitution, in love and war.

"Awww, Libby, you know it."

"Yes, I do, Marine."

Both of these young sweethearts peered out the window in the direction of the hospital. They focused their thoughts on the safety of their loved ones.

The chief walked up behind them in a now eerily quiet police station. "Will you two lovebirds stop worrying and get away from the windows! The hurricane shudders broke last year, so let's not have any broken glass ruining your pretty faces, especially the deputy's."

Adam signaled Libby away from the windows to a more secure location to wait out the storm's fury. "Very funny, Chief, very funny. OK, let's move you over to behind the counter. It'll be safer there."

Fury

The hurricane wasn't a typical one, as it actually gathered intensity upon making landfall. Trees were uprooted and propelled into houses, causing millions of dollars of damage. Cars were tossed aside as if the Cape were a stand-in for a Hollywood movie set. For the patients at Camp Edwards, the storm offered a harsh memory of the far-off battles waged so ferociously. A group was sitting with Rocco in the game room staring in wild wonder at the sight and sound of Mother Nature in action.

A Navy veteran, recovering from burns received in battle, stared at his bandaged arms and offered his thoughts. "Reminds me of the boiler exploding on my ship. I'll never forget that."

Others joined in as well. "Reminds me of an air raid over London."

"No, it sounds more like we're being bombarded by a battalion of 88s. Rocco, what do you think?"

Rocco, standing at a door that led to the courtyard, didn't move an inch. His eyes were fixated at the oncoming stormfront. His response was succinct and emotionless. "Hell's coming."

The other patients looking on nodded their heads in agreement. Rocco had hit the proverbial nail on the head. The hurricane's intensity had all the components of a modern battle, flashes of light followed by powerful explosions and massive destruction. Whether man-made or natural, confusion, turmoil and fear ruled the day.

A sudden flash of lightning startled the group. The storm was getting closer to its target, and Rocco believed deeply in his heart that it was coming for him. It occurred to him that weather and wars were geographically described in similar terms like *front*, where battles were raged, and people were at risk. In his eyes, the hurricane was a mere reflection of the disorder common to mankind and the natural world. The supernatural and natural worlds were two allied forces complicit in creating hell on earth.

Rocco and the other patients watched the storm silently from the game room. He never noticed the medical staff calling the soldiers to move back to the ward for safety. Slowly, the men made their way back to the ward and left Rocco standing alone in the room.

The whispers started again. "Hello, beautiful. Enjoying the sight?"

Responding in a dismissive manner, Rocco was in no mood to hear the demon's enticements. "Chaos, can't you find another rock to crawl back under? I've told you, whatever you are, to leave. You're just an invention of my screwed-up brain."

"Oh, beautiful, you're the only rock I want to crawl under. Would you prefer I look like this?" Instantaneously, Chaos transformed into a duplicate of Libby. "Would you chase me away now?"

Rocco grew anxious and confused. "What the hell? Libby, is that you?"

Chaos stroked Rocco's hair playfully. "Yes, I'm here lover. I've always been here waiting for you."

Distraught and on the verge of becoming overwhelmed with fear, he stepped back and questioned the reality of the situation. "Has it always been you creeping into my mind, making me feel good about myself, only to twist me into knots? Was any of it real? *Cara*, were you real?"

"Oh, beautiful boy, I'm as real as it gets, but I need protection too. The world is evil. There are vile and disgusting individuals out there right now harming innocent people like me without reprisal. Who is going to protect us from these despicable animals in the world? Uncle Trick wants to show you the way. God has no answers because He is an absentee parent who cares for none of us. Maybe, He enjoys watching all the terror in the world, because He could stop it at any time. You know that's true, don't you?"

"I don't know what's true anymore except that I feel like I'm a puppet on a string." Rocco's sanity was fracturing, and his spirit was showing signs of distress, so much so that he whispered Chaos' wicked words repetitively. "The world is evil. The world is evil. The world is evil. God is evil." On and on, the carousel turned. Chaos was winning.

"All those lies that the doctor fed you earlier today were designed to trip you up from your destiny, defender of the defenseless. If not you, then who, *Caro*?"

Rocco was seemingly falling into a trancelike state. Hearing Chaos disguised as Libby and calling him *Caro* hit him hard. "If not me, then who? If not.... who?"

"Heaven thinks mankind is worthy of the benefits of creation, but all they're good for is mayhem and destruction to the Trinity, the bonds of life itself. God knows this. Who is the real Prince of Lies? Why do you resist? Think of your family."

Rocco struggled to find the mental acuity to speak to his faux sweetheart. "Libby, I don't understand. What do you want from me? Just come out and say it. Who is this guy called Uncle Trick?"

"It's not what I want from you. It's what you want. Can you see your destiny? Look into the storm and see through its eye."

Rocco stared into the storm and saw visions that turned his stomach. He saw death and devastation across the world. There was slaughter, rape, children crying next to murdered parents, children lying in mass graves, and the destruction of families. Accompanying these visions was a sinister laugh taking delight in all the horror being thrust upon the innocent. The horror continued unabated and cycled through all parts of the globe. A father beating his wife in front of crying children was followed by a family dying by an arsonist's hand. He could see Rangers being killed in France, ambushed by the enemy. Horror came in all forms and creeds. The direst vision was one of people being herded into showers to be gassed and then thrown into mass graves.

Rocco closed his eyes tightly, shaking his head from side-to-side and begging for all the violence to stop. "No, stop! Please stop! Why is this happening? Libby!" Outwardly, Rocco appeared still and silent, but inwardly he was a whirlpool of pain and suffering. Chaos had entered his mind only. The final battle for his soul was internal and out of sight from the others in the hospital.

Dr. Galen's hold on him was failing. It was questionable whether he had truly made a formidable impact on him at all. Perhaps, it was just an illusion fabricated by Rocco to placate the good doctor. Regardless, D-Day for the Ranger was here, and his battle continued. With each passing second, he stepped further and further away from the Trinity's light.

"Libby, what is this? Who are these people?"

Chaos whispered into her quarry's ear to continue her lies. "These are all the people in the world suffering and dying now. They are the ones who want to destroy the Trinity, and they need to be judged, one-by-one. The Trinity needs you. Let Uncle Trick show you the way."

Rocco's voice trembled upon hearing the demon's revelation. "The Trinity? What do you mean? What does all this mean? I want to know who Uncle Trick is, but I'm afraid to ask. He is the Devil, isn't he?"

"Oh, beautiful boy, he's much more than that. He is truth. He is the way. No one else can show you the reality of life, but you need to choose. Free will, a gift not worthy of mankind, is the only thing standing between you and your destiny. If you don't believe me, why don't you ask your mother?"

Chaos stepped back into the darkness of Rocco's mind and transformed once again, this time into Mama. "*Il mio bambino.* My baby boy. The world has done so much damage to our family. *Bello,* just look at me and what those animals did to me....to Noemi and Bella." Chaos stood in front of Rocco in a visage of a beaten and toothless mother and roared. "*Guardami!* Look at me!" Her cry echoed through his mind.

Rocco's heart crumbled and rendered him helpless to the demon's supernatural strength. "Mama, I'm so sorry! I tried! I tried!" Soon, his voice quivered, as he fell further into despondency. "What did those animals do to you and the girls? I never even found their bodies to give them a decent burial. Were their bodies blessed? Did anyone say a prayer when they put them in the ground, or were they just tossed into a pit?"

"Why don't you ask God? Or did you already ask, and He didn't answer? Typical, an absentee father letting mankind run cruelly over His creation. Do you think they can be redeemed, that free will can lead them to harmony within the Trinity?" Morphing into her original form, Chaos' voice shuddered as she spoke, her emotions on the current state of the world were clearly evident. Could she have been a casualty of all the hate and violence too? "Look what's happening. In less than fifty years, mankind has created the most efficient methods of killing each other. Where's the remorse? Where's the regret for not stopping it?"

Rocco stared at Chaos dumbfounded at her form. She appeared more angelic now than demonic. Her skin had a dignified pewter tone that seemingly ebbed and flowed with her emotions, sullen but with a hint of a shimmering glow trying to break out. Her long and flowing raven hair draped across a gentle form that belied the evil deeds she had performed to date. "What's this? You can't be the one who has been tormenting me?"

"This is who I am, who I'm supposed to be, but the world has ruined me. I am the first victim of mankind's malice. Creation was once happy and blissful. The Trinity was in balance, but humanity exchanged benevolence for malevolence. The gift of free will drove them to choose greed and hate over charity and love. Progress and evolution were to be sought at all costs, not for advancement but for domination. Look what they've done to me and the world."

Rocco remained motionless as he listened to Chaos' shocking revelation, his rage slowly coming to a turbulent boil. Finally, he had reached his tipping point.

Unseen in the corner of the game room, Uncle Trick and Captain Joao looked on. Uncle Trick was in a particularly good mood at the development and whispered his approval. "Chaos worked her magic today. I didn't see that last act in the script. We have him now."

Captain Joao remained quiet, standing next to his employer. His stoic, indifferent exterior belied the inner turmoil he was feeling. There was something about Rocco that awakened a dormant part of his soul that he thought had long since died. Never had Uncle Trick recruited someone while they were still alive. Having such a direct impact on a person's life violated a basic rule that kept the Trinity in balance. Free will could not be forcibly surrendered, neither could a person's soul, for that remained a part of the mysteries of life. In situations where Uncle Trick did overstep, an equal and opposite response would be provided by Heaven. In this situation, two of God's healing angels, the Muse and Raphael, were sent to provide a troubled young man a different yet healthier outlook on life.

Still, free will remained in the purview of the individual. It's similar to the old English proverb; "You can bring a horse to water, but you can't make him drink." This supernatural battle has been waged for millennia and for as long as man has existed. Lately, Uncle Trick's side has been winning. The occurrence of two world wars in less than half a century was proof of his recent winning streak.

Captain whispered to his boss. "Why is this man so special? I have never seen you recruit the living before."

"Well, Buddy Boy, let's just say it happens from time to time. When I smell a soul so pure that is going to receive the kind of terror he did, I know he is going to be an exceptional reaper. Sometimes, old Uncle Trick can be tempted too." A sinister laugh slithered from the mouth of the King of Serpents. "That boy is absolutely delicious."

Back at the police station, Adam and Libby waited impatiently for the slow-moving storm to pass. The slower the storm moved, the greater their anxiety and concern grew. The decibel level of ordinary sounds increased tenfold. The station's old grandmother clock's hourly bell sounded like a hammer hitting an anvil. The door to the office bathroom creaked like a vampire's coffin opening slowly on a dark and dreary Transylvanian night. The door's slow and measured movement made its old hinges squeak incrementally louder and louder. It was a maddening and torturous sound that frayed the nerves of the two distraught sweethearts.

Libby squirmed as she sat in the chair next to the deputy's desk. "I can't take this anymore. Why is this storm moving so slowly?"

The chief shook his head and approached the young nurse and deputy. "Ohhh, c'mon kids. Everything's going to be fine. The hospital is in good shape where it is. After all, it's on high ground and built sturdy, ain't it? Deputy, you've been through worse in the Pacific. This should be like eating strawberry ice cream at Casey's."

"I know, I know. But this time it's not me I'm worried about. This hurricane's got a mind of its own. It looks like it's stuck over Camp."

"That's just the way these storms work; however, Mother Nature can be unpredictable at times." The chief made a sudden movement toward Libby. "Like now!"

"Yikes! Darn it, Chief, you scared the wits out of me."

"Sorry, a bad attempt to lighten the mood, but like I said there's nothing to worry about."

Suddenly, the station's front doors blew open from the force of the hurricane's winds. Behind it, a nurse ran in. It was the same nurse that Libby noticed in the courtyard with Rocco. "Whew, what a storm! A girl could get knocked into Rhode Island in one shot."

The chief and deputy ran to secure the doors. The deputy was incredulous at how the nurse was able to make it through the storm. "Where did you come from, Miss? This is no time to be out in a storm. Good thing you had the sense to wear rain gear."

The nurse shook the rain off her coat and smiled at the inhabitants of the police station. "Well, hello to you too, deputy. It's raining cats and dogs out there. I was on my way to Camp Edwards. My name is Melissa Healey. I'm one of the new nurses."

The chief stared at his deputy for his transgression. "Apologies for my deputy. His head isn't screwed on tightly today."

The embarrassed deputy smiled sheepishly. "OK, OK, I'm sorry. The storm's got me on edge a little bit."

"That's quite alright, Marine."

"How did you know I…"

Nurse Healey quickly turned her attention to Libby. "I know you. Aren't you Libby Endicott?"

"Yes, I am. Come on in and let's get that wet jacket off of you."

"You're a lifesaver. This storm came out of nowhere. I was walking along and then wham, a bucket of water slams into me. Well, that's what it felt like to me, anyway. Did you get caught in the rain too?"

Libby took the nurse's wet jacket and hung it on a rack to dry, while the chief and deputy went about other police business at the station. "I came here to report my stolen bicycle. I guess some kids borrowed it for a quick ride to the beach, not that it's a good beach day."

Melissa shook her head. "No, it's not."

Libby and Melissa walked back to the window to check on the hurricane's progress. Peering out into the carnage of overturned signs and damaged buildings, Libby had one of her uneasy feelings. "Melissa, right?"

"Yes, it's Melissa."

"Tell me, Melissa, didn't I see you in the courtyard recently with Rocco?"

The new nurse smiled. "Could have been me. I've been busy getting to know each patient. Don't tell me you're jealous."

"No, but what were you talking about? Rocco seemed to react so well to whatever you were saying." Sensing something odd about this nurse, Libby paused for a moment to collect her thoughts and to cast an inquisitive eye. Unknown to her at the time, this feeling was similar to the one Rocco experienced in his interaction with Dr. Galen.

"And….and, there's something about you that makes me feel …. feel …. feel warm and protected. You must think I'm nuts."

Melissa moved closer to Libby and transformed her voice to a more comforting tone. "Oh child, you are perfectly sane, although I hear that love can make you nuts."

Libby continued to survey her new associate with a suspicious eye; however, she was comforted by Melissa's words. The chief and deputy were oblivious to the nurses' conversation and continued to work at their desks. It was as if they didn't notice the two young women in the station.

"Libby, you have a purity about you that the world needs these days. You are a strong and vibrant warrior for healing people. I should know."

"What do you mean? Why is your voice different? I can't turn around to see you either."

"You don't need to see me. I'm here to whisper encouragement and inspiration into mankind's ears….to give them hope that they can be healed….to give them assurance that they are valued. I am the Muse, and we have to go. Rocco needs you. The ancient trickster is tempting him, hitting his vulnerable spots and trying to get him to reject Heaven. Will you fight for him?"

Libby responded quickly and firmly. "Yes, of course, I will fight for him." A tear flowed over Libby's cheek as she thought of her *Caro*.

"The eye of the storm is over us now and the hospital is only a mile away. But wait a moment while I arrange a ride for you."

The Muse moved to the deputy's desk and whispered in his ear. Libby was able to turn her head slightly to gaze on the Muse speaking softly in Adam's ear. She was a vision to behold.

Suddenly, Adam jumped up, grabbed the car keys and ran to Libby. "We have to go to Camp. Don't ask me why. We just have to go."

The chief stood up from his desk, dumbfounded. "Where the heck are you two going?"

"Sorry, the nurse said we have to go."

"What nurse? Libby?"

"No, the other nurse."

"What other nurse? Are you crazy?" Bewildered, the chief looked around the station for this invisible person.

Apparently, the appearance of Nurse Healey was a dream to the inhabitants of the station, but only Libby and Adam could remember her.   Adam and Libby were off to Camp Edwards and their appointment with destiny.

"Chief, you spoke to her when she came in from the storm."

"What? I was at my desk for the last half hour, and no one came in. No one."

"Libby, we need to leave now. Let's take the Jeep. It's already covered, and it'll be easier to get over any obstacles." Several years earlier, Jeeps had been given to police departments along the Cape Cod coast to help with monitoring the shoreline and bays for German submarine activity.

The deputy sped down Main Street, circumventing the carrion of downed powerlines and trees. Because they were in the eye of the storm, the scene was eerily quiet now. "Libby, you did see another nurse, right?"

"I saw something, that's for sure. It's odd the chief didn't."

The Jeep screeched to a halt at the hospital's main entrance, and the two worried travelers sprinted inside. Adam and Libby found Rosie running frantically down the hall to the front desk. "Hey, what are you two doing here? I was just about to call the station. Libby, it's Rocco. Something happened and we don't know what."

Libby grabbed Rosie's hands frantically and pleaded for more information. "What do you mean? Where is he?"

"C'mon. He was standing in the game room then all of a sudden he walked outside and into the storm. None of the orderlies could stop him. The doors closed behind him, and we can't open them now. The hurricane is causing a lot of damage out there. We're all running around like chickens with our heads cut off. The orderlies are trying to get to him but it's too dangerous out there. There is so much debris blowing around, and the wind and rain just picked up again after a quick lull."

Libby was distraught. She ran to the game room and frantically banged on the doors to the courtyard. "Rocco, what are you doing?! Please come in! Rocco! Adam, can you help me open these doors."

The deputy struggled mightily to unjam the doors. He couldn't even push the doors open, which was odd for a strong Marine Corps veteran. "They won't budge. Wait a minute. It looks like something's wedged into the outside handles. Let's go to another door."

Libby was frantically pulling at the door handles. "Oh my God! There's no time. He's walking toward the bluff."

The wind and rain howled with increasing intensity, which only served to fuel the young nurse's anxiety to an alarming level. She continued to beg for help, but none was forthcoming, until she caught sight of something running toward her from the courtyard. "Oh my God! Is that a wolf?"

"Yes, it is. Libby, stand away from the door. That's the biggest wolf I've ever seen."

Adam stood in front of Libby unsure of what the wolf's intentions were. His arms were extended behind him, since it was the only way he could think to protect her. A lot of good that would do when you're up against the fangs of a ravenous wolf.

"Adam, what is it doing?"

"I think it's trying to open the doors."

The wolf was clawing at the piece of metal that was obstructing the door. After two swipes, the door blew open. Panting menacingly and with red eyes glowing, the wolf stood in the doorway motionless and stared at Libby. The intimidating animal raised its head and let out a tremendous howl that echoed across the courtyard. It was so loud that locals would later attribute it to the hurricane's ferocity. They would have no knowledge of the supernatural events of that day.

The wolf backed away from the doorway and quickly ran into the nearby woods. After she had taken a second to compose herself and gather her thoughts, Libby walked out from behind Adam's protective shield and sprinted out the door and toward the bluffs. There was no time to waste. Adam followed close behind and yelled for her to wait for him. "Libby, watch out! I don't know where that wolf is. Wait for me."

The young nurse would not stop because she had a mission to achieve; namely, to get to her beloved and save him from going over the edge of the bluff. The wind and rain continued to fall with intensity, but her determination to reach him could not be suppressed.

Unseen by the sprinting duo, Uncle Trick, Captain Joao, and the demon Chaos were standing next to a huge boulder near the edge of the bluff. They utilized their supernatural powers to remain invisible while the climatic events unfolded in front of them. They had heard the wolf's howl and quickly dismissed it as a wail for a lost cause.

Uncle Trick smiled grotesquely and danced a happy jig. "The wolf is crying. The wolf is crying. I beat the wolf. I beat the wolf."

Captain shook his head. "Are you going to pay attention?"

Uncle Trick leered at his old friend. "Geez, look at the fun killer. Or are you sad that the wolf lost too?" He still had his reservations about Captain's loyalty regarding Rocco's recruitment.

Rocco approached the edge and began tearing off his hospital clothing, first his shirt and then his pajama bottoms until he was as naked as the day he was born. It was only fitting to leave this world the same way he entered it.

Uncle Trick, on the other hand, saw Rocco's actions differently and gleefully hissed his perspective on the moment. "Look at my boy getting ready for his baptism and transformation all at once! He is absolutely delicious."

Captain Joao remained emotionless, staring at the sight with an air of indifference to the entire situation. Underneath his stoic exterior, however, a different battle waged, one in which Rocco would not succumb to the Dark Prince's enticements. He saw a young man who deserved better than the fate that awaited him. He closed his eyes and thought of his own family. Perhaps, even a miracle was possible.

Chaos, dressed in her nun's habit, looked back across the field leading to the bluff. "Well, well, looks who's coming. How did she get here?"

Uncle Trick was beside himself with anger, fixated on the young nurse running to save the love of her life. He had tried to maintain his ordinary-man persona as a way to slither into people's lives, but it always contradicted his true threatening nature. Today, his true essence revealed itself. His face grew pale and beast-like, with his eyes separating and glowing blood red. This was the look of the Fallen One who had not felt grace's warmth for so long. He growled to Captain Joao and Chaos. "How did she get here? I thought we had her bottled up. It couldn't have been that damn wolf, could it? Buddy Boy, are you hiding something from me?"

Captain shrugged his shoulders proclaiming innocence, even though he wished for this to happen. "No way, I'm surprised too."

"You'd better not be hiding anything from me, if you know what's good for you. You've been acting a little weird lately."

Chaos continued to look at the oncoming Libby, at first with a degree of bewilderment and then with growing admiration. She saw someone pure and strong, a force of nature. "The girl's fearless. Why doesn't she give up? She has to know it's pointless."

Uncle Trick's scorn for Libby and humanity had no bounds. "Fearless? Hah! Don't be absurd. She's just another meat puppet to be used and abused."

Uncle Trick's response didn't sit well with Chaos. She had developed a fondness for Libby and her sweetheart Rocco. Her own heart was softening. Her reaction was decidedly scornful. "Seriously, tell me how you really feel."

Libby approached a screaming Rocco, standing at the edge of the cliff and cursing the heavens. His arms were raised to summon God to face him. "Where are You? Come and face me! Don't be afraid of me. I'll take it easy on You!"

Rocco's taunts were followed by a roll of thunder and a crack of lightning a short distance away. The rain fell harder as Rocco called upon God for a fight. Pounding the sky in anger to fight a God who wouldn't fight back, his blasphemous taunts intensified with each passing second and crack of thunder. "Is that all you got? You're nothing! Nothing! You're an absentee Father, that's all! I'm right here. Come and take your anger out on me. Maybe you don't exist at all and I'm talking to the wind." Rocco continued to scream his taunts and threats to the heavens to the delight of Uncle Trick. "Face me, you son of a....!"

A thunderous and ear-piercing lightning bolt struck closer to the bluff, startling even the supernatural pack watching the events transpire. "Woah, that was close! I guess Pop's a little upset at my boy. He is absolutely everything that I've ever wanted." The Beast's hunger for the special young man's soul had always been clear; however, it appears that even the Devil has desires.

Rocco wouldn't budge. He had hit his tipping point, and in his mind, there was no going back. Only one person could rescue him from his terrible fate. Libby had to convince him of the power he had to save himself. He controlled his own destiny.

Libby stopped several feet away from her beloved and yelled into the harsh elements that were battering her body. "Rocco, what are you doing? Please stop this. Please step away from the edge."

"Libby, is that really you? What are you doing here? Please go back. This fight is between me and God, no one else. He let my family die! He let those bastards do those evil…. oh, oh…those evil things to them. Why, damn Him, why?!" Rocco stared at his love, his arms outstretched and eyes begging for an answer that would make sense. No parent would allow this, least of all one who is supposed to be father to all creation. He couldn't bear the thought that life was random and at times chaotic. Disorder had become the world's order. Harmony and tranquility were a state of mind, basic elements for maintaining one's sanity when dealing with the instability of existence. What the young man didn't comprehend at the time was that the beauty of life was in its randomness. Sometimes, however, this randomness came crashing down on the heads of the innocent in the most tragic and horrific ways. Although an undesirable outcome, the horror that was inflicted on the Farfallas was just one of these countless incidents throughout history. His family's tragedy weighed on our hero as he inched closer to the edge.

Libby approached him carefully, slowly inching closer to avoid escalating the situation. "Rocco, there is no good answer for what happened to your family. The only answer is that there are bad people in this world, and we have to be better than them. God wants us all to be better. We just have to open ourselves to facing a whole big, beautiful, crazy world and all of its challenges, while growing, learning and loving each day."

Rocco glared with steely-eyed determination over the bluff. "The world is evil. That's the answer, the only real answer. Heaven is a far-away dream, and Hell is closer than you think. It's right here. Someone, something is calling me to take a step over the edge and into the darkness, but I think it's more like I'm stepping into the light. Everything's becoming clearer to me, who I am and who I need to be."

Distraught, Libby pleaded with the man she loved more than life itself. "Rocco, if you take this step, well then, I'm going to have to take it with you. Do you really think you can leave me like this? You want to abandon me? I thought you loved me."

Libby's provocation had the desired effect on the man she loved. His mind and soul were vaulted back into some semblance of sanity. He screamed, "What…what did you say?"

"I said if you take that step, then I will be there with you. If you are going to leave me, then I'll go too."

"No, don't say that. You're everything to me." Rocco dropped to his knees and cried. "I can't let this happen to you. My heart would burst. No, not you. Not you. God, where are You?! Why won't You face me?!" Rocco continued his pleadings until his anger turned to sorrow. "Why won't You face me?! Why won't You face me?! Please, why won't You face me?"

Libby reached out and held Rocco's hand tightly. "He's all around us. We can see Him if we just open our eyes. He is in a beautiful sunrise and sunset. He is in a dirty-faced, impish child."

Rocco stared at his *amore* — his true love — with eyes equally full of sorrow and tenderness. "Do you honestly believe that?"

The young nurse was smiling softly now, happy that she was getting through to her beloved. Her smiles turned quickly to tears of joy when a still naked Rocco fell into her arms and cried. "I'm so sorry. I failed you and everyone close to me. You deserve better. They deserved better. Why didn't you let me go? You'd be better off without me."

Libby's voice maintained a firm yet comforting tone. "Never, do you hear me, never. What you did to those men, you did as judge, jury and executioner. What those men did was monstrous. You thought killing them would make up for what they did to you, but all these events wounded your heart and soul. Revenge didn't replace the damage these men inflicted. You will carry it forever, but I'll be there to carry it with you. It'll be no one else's burden but ours. Forgive yourself, *caro*, forgive yourself."

"I can't ask you to bear this burden with me. It's not right."

"Ask me? Are you kidding? I'm not going anywhere. *Caro*, you need to stop beating yourself up."

"It's all my fault. I wasn't strong enough, fast enough, good enough, to save my family." Rocco was finally able to express the guilt and regret that weighed on him so heavily.

"You didn't cause their deaths. You're not to blame. Everyone knows it but you. Don't let the demons of doubt infect your soul. You can't control life, and life can't control you."

"I was so angry at life and at me that I just wanted to kill and destroy everything in my way, including me."

"The war's over for you, Ranger. You can't let hate and guilt consume you. They leave no room in your heart for anything else. It's time to heal and live a long life with me. *Caro, ti amo.*"

Rocco nodded his head and reclaimed his will to live. Libby's words had the effect of a 1,000-pound weight being lifted off his shoulders. "You are the strongest person in the world, my queen. *Anche io ti amo, amore mio.*"

The young nurse laughed softly and caressed her beloved's hair. "You'd better believe it, buddy. C'mon, let's go."

Libby rose and extended her hand to lead her beloved away from the bluff. Now in a calm and peaceful state, Rocco wanted to stand up but realized he was unclothed. Always a gentleman, Rocco's modesty would not allow him to stand up in his current state. Adam, who had been standing a safe distance away to give his nursing friend some space, jumped forward and covered the naked Ranger with his raincoat. "Here you go buddy. Are you OK?"

Rocco responded quickly and positively to ensure his state of mind, as well as his state of being, was clear. "Yes, we are."

Soon, the three were walking back to the hospital. Remaining invisible to them, the three supernatural comrades studied the developments closely. Uncle Trick looked on in disgust, his anger exploding at the thought of losing the prize he so intensely desired. "Chaos, get out there and do something. I will not be beaten by some sort of woman meat puppet." His contemptible disrespect for the female gender was clearly on display.

Chaos flashed a surprised and angry look at her boss. She wanted to fight back against the offensive and repugnant Dark One, but she remained passive. She figured it wouldn't have resulted in anything positive, regardless of her effort. Her mind was far too jaded at this point in her existence.

Seeing her reaction, Uncle Trick thought it better if he were seen in his unthreatening visage. Although this didn't prevent him from furrowing his brow condescendingly and further expressing his loathsome disposition. "Oh, c'mon, don't start with me, precious. Get out there now!"

Reluctantly, Chaos stepped forward but was immediately stopped by a hand beside her. It was the Muse who had come to watch over Libby and Rocco. "Where are you going, sister?"

A startled Chaos jumped back and gazed on her visage of perfect pewter skin and brilliantly flowing hair. "What? Grace, what are you doing here?"

"Oh, I'm just here for the view. And you, sister?" The Muse, whose true name was Grace, could always be counted on to add a little levity to even the most serious situations.

Uncle Trick was equally shocked at the Muse's unexpected appearance. He had no forewarning of her lurking presence or imminent arrival. "Muse, where did you come? You've been learning new tricks to hide from me, haven't you? Well, you're not wanted here. Go back to Father and mind your business. The kid's mine. Do you hear me? Mine."

Uncle Trick stepped toward Grace but was immediately stopped by Raphael, who had been watching the events from the storm's eye. "Brother, what do you think you're going to do? You've lost."

The Dark One jumped back in surprise and spoke in a tone dripping with contempt. "You? He had to send you. I must be off my game. I didn't see the both of you lurking around. Well, don't think for a minute that I'll let you stand in my way either, brother or not." Uncle Trick made a threatening move toward the archangel.

Raphael warned him of the repercussions if he were to continue. "Do you want to see our big brother? He's itching to come down and knock some sense into you, but I told him there wouldn't be a problem." Standing in front of his fallen sibling, the archangel maintained a gentle and loving posture. After all, he was the Healer, not the Warrior.

"Do you really think I'd hurt you, most of all?" The Dark One stopped and looked upon the brother he had always held dearest. I guess even the Devil could have love in his heart, albeit the size of a pea.

"No, but this needs to stop. Chaos, hear me, please. Your sister cries for you. All of your sisters are crying for you."

Grace held out her hands to reassure her sister of the love she still felt for her. She called Chaos by her real name to plead for reconciliation. "Harmony, it's been too long. Your grudge against humanity has to end. If today's events don't convince you of their capabilities and capacity to see the beauty in life, then please tell me what will?"

Chaos doubted her sister's optimistic and confident outlook on humanity. "I can't believe it. I just can't. Look at what they've done over the last thirty years alone. Do you really think there's hope for them? They're an infestation to the Trinity." The sadness in her voice became evident to her sister.

"I do, and there's a piece inside of you that does too. I can see it. Libby and Rocco gave us renewed hope that humanity is growing and learning from its errors every day. While celebrating their successes, they just can't seem to stop judging themselves for every part of their lives, be it the past or present. A life of constant criticism bends their perception of reality and ultimately results in harm, but I have hope. Please take my hand. Sister, please take my hand."

Chaos unloaded all her repressed feelings and thoughts. "I don't know if I can. It's been so long since I've felt Father's warmth. It just feels like Heaven is too far away from me. He won't understand. Look at my blasphemous image! How could He forgive me?"

Grace approached her wayward sibling to reassure her. "Sister, He will. Father's been waiting for you with open arms."

Slowly, and at first reluctantly, Chaos reached to take hold of the Muse's hand. Instantly, her visage changed from a nun to her angelic state, a near mirror image of her sister. Holding each other, their skin glistened and sparkled in the emerging sun's rays. A magnificent rainbow shot across the bluff and into the sea. As quickly as the storm had started, it ended in glorious fashion.

Harmony bowed her head and rested it on her sister's shoulder. Chaos was gone. "Can I really be forgiven? Father is so angry that I let Him down."

"Never, that's not who He is. That's not what the Trinity is. Why don't you ask Him? His embrace will show you how He feels."

"But I've been bad for so long, I'm not sure I can remember how to be good."

"Bad. Good. Forget the past. Look to the future. You are needed. I need you, sister. You fell for the Dark One's lies, but the beauty of life is that forgiveness and redemption are open to everyone, even a misguided angel. Humanity's war is going to end soon, and this world needs healing and harmony. They need us. There will be difficult days ahead, but the future may surprise you."

"I'm so sorry. Please forgive me. I've missed you so much, sister." With Harmony's plea for forgiveness, the two Angels of Virtue hugged each other tightly. The rainbow's radiance shone more brilliantly across the horizon, signifying that the happiness of the moment could not be undone.

Raphael noted the beauty and warmth of the rainbow's glow. "Stunning, absolutely stunning."

Uncle Trick was in no mood for pleasantries and groaned a response. "I'm going to vomit. I almost had him, my beautiful boy."

Raphael laughed at Uncle Trick's naivete. "Oh, brother, you still don't realize you were after the wrong person."

The Fallen One growled and stared at his lost prize being led away. "What do you mean? It couldn't have been…. that girl."

Raphael smiled, concealing the answer from a brother who yearned to know. "Farewell, brother, time for you to go."

Uncle Trick continued to stare angrily at Libby and Rocco making their way back to the hospital with Adam. He smacked his cane against the rock until it shattered into several pieces. He shouted like a rabid madman cursing to himself and pausing to speak each word in rhythm with every strike of the cane.   "This …is … sickening … and … I … lost … Chaos … back…to … the … Virtues."

Uncle Trick let out a tremendous howl that shook the trees bordering the bluff. The Beast was not happy. He didn't enjoy losing, especially to those so-called meat puppets. His eyes blazed red with anger and saliva dripped from his hideously shaped mouth until he was able to regain his composure. "Alright, that's enough of that. Buddy Boy, let's get out of here. I don't want to be around for any more surprises with these meat puppets today. We need to keep on searching for new reapers. Our legion is dwindling." Both Uncle Trick and Captain leaped over the bluff and flew off to an unknown destination to regroup.

Flying with his defeated boss, Captain was puzzled as to what other surprises were in store for Rocco and Libby. He had no clue as to the meaning of Uncle Trick's mysterious statement. For that reason, he decided to keep a clandestine eye over the two during the coming days.

With their exit, Raphael bolted into the sky and disappeared into the heavens. The Virtue sisters quickly followed. It was a good day for healing to start.

Warrior

As the weeks passed, a slight hint of Autumn became evident in the air. While the calendar still read summertime, the hurricane had quickly cleared the humid and damp conditions from the Cape. The news from the Pacific and European Fronts continued to report gains in the Allied war effort. There was a genuine hope that the war could be over by Christmas, although ending a war proved to be a far more difficult task than starting one. The world would have to wait until 1945.

Rocco's condition continued to improve. The doctors wanted to keep him close to monitor his mental health. Believing Camp Edwards was the best place for him to heal, they elected not to ship him to Pilgrim, even as a last resort. Libby maintained a daily vigil to help nurture and guide Rocco's path back to full health. The warrior in her would not accept any other result.

Daily, Rocco would meet with the Camp's psychiatrist to talk through all that he had experienced. He didn't shy away from discussing that terrible day when he lost his family and turned into a vengeful executioner. As was expected, he'd have good days and bad days, but the good would far outnumber the bad. During his last week in the hospital, the doctors became satisfied that his worst days were becoming a distant memory and that he had conquered his demons of guilt. He was ready to rejoin the world.

Dr. Galen gave Libby the news that Rocco was going to be released in a couple of days, on Saturday, to be specific. Libby was elated at the news but wondered about the delay. "Dr. Galen, that's great news, but why can't he leave today."

"Oh, you know, the top brass always has us filling out so many forms on patients. Paperwork, paperwork, paperwork. It doesn't matter who he loves or not." Dr. Galen winked at the young nurse.

"I'm sorry for being impatient. I appreciate all that you've done for him and for making a difference that can't be measured. I thank God each night for sending us an angel."

"Oh, let's not go overboard. I'm a simple doctor who loves his job. Anyway, I think you and Rocco want to be here on Saturday."

Confused, Libby tilted her head and tried to understand the doctor's cryptic statement. "What do you mean? Is something going to happen?"

Doctor Galen grinned mischievously, "In a way, in a way. You're going to have to wait. Also, I'm moving on to a new assignment. You won't be seeing me again, well, not for a long time anyway."

Libby hugged the good doctor tightly. "Thanks for everything. I know there is something different about you, but I don't think I should ask. Take care, doctor."

"Be well, Libby. You and Rocco have a happy life waiting in the wings. Enjoy and cherish it."

Libby ran off to tell Rocco the good news. Finally, he would be able to move on with his life, and they could start their new life together.

She couldn't contain her joy as she raced past patients and hospital workers.

A hospital orderly jumped out of her way. "Libby, slow down. Where are you going?"

Nurse Maggie, who was walking with the orderly, smiled. "Looks like she got good news. That girl can run faster than a jackrabbit."

Passing each person and dodging every obstacle standing in her path to her beloved, Libby would offer her apology. "Sorry, sorry. I need to get to…oops, sorry."

Dr. Galen stared at the sprinting nurse with delight. "Slow down, Libby, slow down. You're going to break your ankle." The doctor smiled and shook his head, reveling in the joy of the moment. Suddenly, he turned his head to the side and spoke to someone behind him. "Captain Joao, nice to see you again."

Captain had been walking down the hallway toward the doctor and Libby. He had been in stealth mode all week, looking in on Rocco and trying to ascertain what the mysterious surprise was. To this point, his clandestine pursuit had succeeded. "Well, Raphael, still got eyes in the back of your head?"

The doctor answered the captain with a tone suggestive of a bored child visiting his grandparents. "No, but I can smell all those eggs you've been eating. You must be up to two or three dozen a day."

Captain enjoyed the levity, even coming from an archangel. "Not quite, but close. How are the kids?"

"They're doing exceptionally well, but why are you here? You must be interested in knowing something. I guess even reapers hate surprises." The angel offered a smug smirk to the old reaper.

Captain gave an impassioned response. "Ohhh, c'mon, you have a secret and it's killing me. I don't understand why I can't see what's coming this way. And by the way, I prefer being called wraith and not reaper."

Raphael laughed at hearing Captain's sensitivity to not knowing the forthcoming surprise and his preference for being called a wraith and not a reaper. "Poor baby, I'm not sure which one to pick on first."

"How about we start with the surprise? Would that be acceptable to you, your majesty?"

"Listen, what does your boss call you? It's Buddy Boy, isn't it? You're going to have to wait. Gossip is for the newspapers."

Captain ran his fingers repeatedly through his hair, frustrated at the angel's lack of cooperation. "Are you kidding me?"

"Rocco has been through enough pain and suffering. Libby saved him like I knew she could. She is a true warrior."

Captain paused for a moment and looked at the docile angel standing next to him. "Libby, a true warrior? How did you hide her from your brother?"

"When she was born, like all children, an angel gave her a gentle kiss on her forehead as a blessing from the Trinity. I was there when Libby came into this world. When I kissed her, she looked at me and smiled. I had never had that happen to me before, so I kissed her again to hide her from evil. Her spirit was the purest I had ever seen. Rocco is special but not like her."

Captain smiled. Hearing the angel's sentiments about the two sweethearts softened his hardened heart. "And Uncle Trick will never have them or any of their line. They belong to the Trinity."

"Absolutely. And one last thing. We haven't given up on you, old man. One day, one day, you will see through the lies too."

"Well, on that note, I'll be leaving before I get a cavity from all the sugar being fed to me." Captain departed, walking slowly down the hall and thinking about continuing his clandestine pursuit. He needed to find out the surprise; after all, it was killing him.

Libby ran to Rocco's bed but found it empty. "Rosie, Rosie, where is he?"

Her friend smiled and pretended not to understand Libby's question. "Who? Can you be more specific?

"Oh, c'mon, you know who I mean."

"Loverboy just went out to the courtyard for a little afternoon sun."

Libby rushed immediately to the courtyard to find her sweetheart. There, she found Rocco sitting on a bench with his face turned up to the sun. The young nurse yelled to the suntanning Ranger loud enough to capture the attention of the entire yard. "Rocco! Rocco!"

Her startled young beau rose quickly to his feet. "*Cara*, what's gotten into you?"

Libby jumped into Rocco's waiting embrace. "You're going to be released on Saturday. Did you hear me? Saturday, in two days." The nurse and patient kissed in celebration.

Others in the courtyard clapped and cheered their approval of the young lovers. Claps and cheers of "alright" and "woo-hoo" echoed across the yard to the mortification of the kissing and blushing duo. A new patient walking with the support of another nurse raised his eyebrows. "Wow, this sure is a friendly place."

Saturday couldn't arrive fast enough. Rocco was making plans to start his new life once he got released. One of these plans included asking Libby to marry him. He had saved a lot of his military and battlefield pay — in hopes of using it for his family. Since they were dead and gone, this money now had a different purpose; namely, a wedding ring and a down payment on a house nearby. Rocco had grown to love the Cape but not nearly as much as he loved Libby. Rocco asked Adam and Rosie for advice on the best place to get an engagement ring, one that Libby deserved. An ordinary ring wouldn't pass muster for this Ranger. They recommended a local shop that specialized in collectibles and unique jewelry.

Unbeknownst to Libby, Adam brought Rocco to the store on Friday to pick out a ring. There, he found a vintage Victorian era ring that exemplified Libby's timeless beauty and character. When the shop's proprietor showed Rocco the ring, after a countless number of other rings that the young suitor considered inferior, a smile burst instantaneously on his face. "Holy Moly, that's the one!"

"Good choice, young man. She's a real beauty. I'm sure, just like your girl."

"Yes sir, just like my girl."

Rocco couldn't wait to propose to Libby. He was ready to burst with excitement at the prospect of giving her the ring. On the ride back to Camp, Adam asked whether he had worked out a time or place for the proposal. "Have you thought how you're going to do it?"

Rocco appeared stunned. "You know, I haven't even thought about it. I was just going to give it to her."

"Woah, are you kidding me?! Do you want to start this marriage off on the wrong foot or what?"

"You mean how I ask her is going to make a difference?"

"For a girl, heck yah. You'd better think about how you can make it special. Maybe wait until tomorrow."

"Good idea. I need to think about it. Thanks, buddy."

For the remainder of the short ride back to the hospital, Rocco leaned his head out of the window and tilted his face to the sky. A warm breeze generated by the moving car flowed through his hair and created a serene moment for the young Ranger. He pondered how his life had changed over the last few months from hitting the lowest of lows to the highest of highs. Were his experiences just a subplot in the universe's theatrical production about the meaning of life? Or was he being tested? No, the latter couldn't be true. That would be too cruel even for today's often surreal world. Ultimately, he decided to stop overthinking life's meaning. Rather, he would just accept being happy each day going forward. One thing he did understand was that true happiness came from living in the present and looking toward the future but never dwelling in the past. Libby had shown him the path and he was firmly tied to it.

Rocco arrived back at Camp before Libby noticed he was gone. He knew Libby had a second sight, a superpower *per se*, for discerning fact from fiction, especially from him. Trying to fabricate a reason for his absence would go down faster than a Stuka dive bomber, so he had to play it cool. His plan was to avoid her as much as possible on Friday while he formulated a plan to surprise her with a proposal. He composed a plan that included her hospital friends to be part of the ruse.

Rocco decided to have all the nurses stand in two rows like a military honor guard with him at the end of the line and in front of the large blooming rose bush. Rosie was to lead an unsuspecting and blindfolded Libby out to the courtyard, where she would then remove the blindfold.

It was going to be perfect, although Libby did have a whiff of something brewing. During Rocco and Libby's last dinner in the cafeteria before his release, the supposedly unsuspecting nurse found her beloved's mannerisms and disposition slightly off. Libby got right to the point. "What are you up to? You're up to something. I know it."

Rocco tried to be nonchalant, but it was no use. She had the scent of a bloodhound on the hunt. "I have no idea what you're talking about."

Libby laughed tenderly. "No, huh, you can't even look at me. Look me in the eyes and say that again." The last part was her true lie detector because she knew he wouldn't be able to keep a straight face.

Rocco had to think quickly to get her off the scent. Luckily, Rosie had just walked into the cafeteria and caught the worried suitor's eye. "Hey, Rosie, no date with Adam tonight?"

A startled Rosie saw the look of dread in his eyes and walked over. "Hey guys, enjoying one of the cafeteria's luxury dinners I see."

Rocco nervously stood up and pulled out a chair for Rosie to join them. "Please have a seat."

"Sorry, I can only stay for a minute or two. I have to get home to get ready for my date with lover boy."

Libby transferred her focus to her friend, although it was only for a moment. "How's it going with Adam? I have to say I always pictured you with a Marine."

"Yup, he had me sold once he put on his dress blues."

"Well, on the other hand, this one is up to something, and he won't give it up."

"Libby, you're inventing things now. You know soldiers, and this one in particular, are poor at keeping secrets."

Rocco stuffed his face with food to keep him from saying anything suspicious. He was able to mumble a response. "Yup, that's me."

Rosie stood up and begged their pardon, because she really did have to get ready for a date with her beau. "Have fun you two. I can't keep a Marine waiting." Once out of Libby's view, the nurse gave a subtle wink to Rocco.

"So, she's in on it too?" Libby's powers were amazing.

"No, what? No!" A befuddled Rocco didn't know what else to say as his mouth failed him.

The nurse laughed at her panicked beau. "Oh, don't worry. I won't press you any longer …. well, not today, anyway. I'll take you back to your bunk. Tomorrow's a big day and you'll need your rest."

Rocco heaved a sigh of relief. "Yes, it is."

Saturday morning arrived with a brilliant sunrise, bringing with it the prospect of a bright future. Rocco put on his dress uniform for the occasion, knowing that it would add a level of elegance to the proposal. Libby had been distracted by Rosie and was busy in a ward at the opposite end of the hospital.

Everything worked to perfection. Rocco waited in the courtyard and in front of the rose bush. The nurses lined up in parallel and four to a side. Inside the hospital, Rosie was able to convince Libby to wear a blindfold for a surprise coming her way. "Libby, we have a little surprise worked up for you. I need you to put this on."

"I knew you two were up to something."

"Turn around, please. And we'll get this party started."

Libby smiled nervously. "What are you up to?"

Rosie laughed and led her friend by the hand to the crowd waiting outside. "Just follow me and all will be revealed."

At one side of the courtyard, Captain Joao stood in an alcove waiting patiently for Rocco's surprise to be unveiled. Earlier, he had heard several nurses secretly discussing the day's planned events and telling each other how Libby hit a home run with Rocco, although one of them noted her concern. "I was worried the night of the storm when Rocco had that … that … I don't know what to call it. I think the doctors described it as an episode or something. But Libby really got through to him and he's been a doll ever since."

Another nurse replied and shook her head. "You're telling me! He scared the heck out of me that night. It was like he was talking to the storm, and it was talking back to him. Libby, though, she is a warrior, absolutely fearless."

Captain beamed, remembering the nurses' conversation had brought a little warmth to an otherwise ice-cold heart. He was delighted for the two young sweethearts, and the fact that Uncle Trick was still miserably unhappy about losing Rocco made the day that much more enjoyable in his eyes.

Led by Rosie, Libby arrived in the courtyard, blindfolded and apprehensive about what was happening. "Okay, can I take this off now?"

"Almost, almost, you Nervous Nellie. Okay, one more step and we're here." Rosie removed the blindfold to reveal a clapping and cheering crowd. Libby shrieked at the sights and sounds, not fully understanding what was happening. Turning her head slightly toward the rose bush, she finally saw the reason for all the subterfuge, Rocco on bended knee holding a bouquet of roses freshly cut from the bush. Libby clutched her hands to her chest and began walking through the gauntlet of clapping nurses.

Standing in front of her beloved, she made note of her surprise. "*Caro*, you got me good, didn't you? I don't know what to say."

"Libby, you are the most precious person in my life. I can't explain why I deserve you. It's a mystery to me, but without you I'd be lost. You are my heart, my soul and my future. For as long as there's air in my lungs, I will love and cherish you, my queen and angel. If you can find it in your heart to stick with an unworthy but no longer broken Ranger for the next fifty or sixty years, then you'll make me the happiest man in the world." Rocco presented the ring. "*Cara*, you are the love of my life. I will love you forever. Will you marry me?"

Libby was overcome with emotion. She leaped into her beloved's arms and knocked him to the ground. In between kisses, she was able to provide a response to his proposal, to the resounding cheers of the crowded courtyard. "Of course, I will."

Adam, who also attended the festivities, walked over to the sprawling bride and groom. "Congratulations! This is fantastic, but we need to pick you up off the ground before you get both of your uniforms dirty. C'mon, Rosie, give me a hand."

The joy of the moment was such that it even elicited a clap and cheer from Captain. He approved of this surprise and the happy ending for two genuinely good people. "Well, what do you know, I guess happy endings are still possible."

As Captain turned to leave, satisfied with the day's outcome, the real surprise walked into the courtyard. It was Jimmy and Cowboy. Their tour of duty completed, and their military obligations satisfied, they were sent back home as part of the Army's plan to help train future Rangers. But why were they here?

Jimmy pulled one of the nurses aside. "Excuse me, do you know where we can find a patient, Rocco Farfalla. We heard he's been recovering here."

The nurse giggled with delight. "Are you kidding? That's him in the middle of the crowd over there. He and Libby just got engaged."

Cowboy was incredulous, staring at the two sweethearts holding each other tightly. "What?! You're kidding?! And boy, did he wrangle a cute one."

Staring cheerfully at the sight, Jimmy was no less at a loss for words. His heart skipped a few beats because he realized his friend's life had turned 180 degrees since Monte Cassino. "The kid's a firecracker."

"He sure is, but I wonder what he's going to say when he sees us. I hope he got your letters."

From the edge of the crowd, Jimmy yelled to his best friend he had ever known. "Rocco! Hey! Hey!"

Rocco scanned the crowd. "I know that voice. Jimmy, is that you? Oh my God, it's Cowboy too!" The three Rangers rushed toward one another. Jimmy and Cowboy gave their friend the biggest bear hug they could without hurting him.

Jimmy screamed, "You're okay! Thank God, you're okay!"

"Yes, buddy, I am, but what are you doing here?"

"Did you get my letters? They explained everything."

Rocco shook his head. "No, I didn't. Military efficiency rears its head once again."

Jimmy and Cowboy took a step back, looking at each other and then Rocco. The two Rangers smiled from ear to ear.

"What are you two dogs smiling about? You look like that cartoon cat."

Jimmy and Cowboy parted and revealed their surprise. Noemi and Bella had survived. In unison, the two sisters screamed for their brother. "Rocco!"

The young Ranger let out a scream. Unlike the one on that fateful day on the bluff, it was one of resplendent happiness. "Noemi! Bella! Are you real? Tell me you're not ghosts!" Sisters and brother ran to one another for an embrace that none wanted to release. This truly had been the happiest day of his life. "I can't believe it! I thought you were dead. I thought you were dead. Your sweaters were in the barn and Mama…." Rocco cried tears of joy and sadness; however, joy won the day. Sadness was now gone from his life. "I will never let you go again, never. Do you hear me, never!"

An astonished Libby stood at his side, piecing together what was happening. She tenderly touched his back. "Rocco, why don't you introduce me to your family?"

"Yes, yes." Rocco released his loving embrace of his long-lost sisters and held out a hand for his future bride. "Girls, this is Libby, the love of my life and soon to be wife. She is the reason my heart still beats."

Noemi and Bella jumped up and down at hearing the news, their happiness skyrocketing to the stratosphere and beyond. Jimmy had told them of the trauma Rocco went through in his search and the things that he had done near Monte Cassino. So, they knew that only someone of pure spirit could have saved him. The sisters held their arms out to the new family member for a Pugliese-sized embrace. Noemi, who had begun learning some English from the Red Cross, formed the best words to describe the development. "Sister, new."

Libby responded, and her elation was clearly evident. "Yes, sister. *Sorella*."

Rocco couldn't stop staring at the happiest women in his life celebrating a new bond. His heart was beating like it never had before. While the girls hugged, Rocco asked his friends how this reunion came about. "Jimmy, Cowboy, how did this happen? How did you find them? How did you get them here?"

Jimmy placed his hand on Cowboy's shoulder. "It's the oddest thing I had ever seen. We had one of your strange feelings that day and this guy was incredible."

Noemi stepped toward Cowboy and held his hand. She slowly repeated Jimmy's last word. "In-cre-di-ble."

Bella walked over to Jimmy and repeated her sister's affectionate gestures. "In-cre-di-ble." Apparently, Rocco's previous tutelage of the girls' lessons in English combined with those from the Red Cross had helped Bella as well.

Rocco was dumbfounded, his mouth opened wide and lips moving without any words coming out. Finally, and with significant resolve, he was able to get two words out. "What the...."

Cowboy flashed a giant grin at his friend. "Don't worry. You're not the only ones getting hitched. Looks like we hit a triple."

"What the...."

Jimmy jumped into the conversation. "My friend, let me tell you what happened. Cowboy obviously jumped to the end, but yes, we found your sisters and fell right away for them. It was like.... like.... magic."

Rocco's reactions now became comical, eliciting laughter from his old battlefield brothers. "What the...."

"You had been in the field hospital for nearly a week, and our unit had just been taken off the line to prepare for a new mission. You were stable enough to be sent home and we wanted to see you off. Do you remember that day?"

"Yes, I do."

"Well, we were being sent deeper into an area leading up to Rome for one final push. The General Staff wanted the city captured quickly and without damage. In their eyes, it should have been taken already. Just outside Rome, a German unit was dug in and there we saw some civilians stuck in no-man's land between us and them. Your sisters were there."

Rocco was anxious to know more. "How did they get there?"

"Hold on. We'll get to that part soon. The troops were dug in deep. Cowboy, what did you say? 'They were dug in deeper than a fat tick on a lazy dog.'"

"Yup."

"Well, after a day of back-and-forth volleys, Reaper decided we couldn't wait anymore. The civilians had been pushed out of their hiding spots by a stray shell, killing a couple of them. They were now about to wander in between the two lines. As soon as Reaper gave the order to work a maneuver to out-flank them, a horse suddenly came into camp. The German Army still used horses and carts heavily to get to the frontlines, which is kind of ridiculous when you think about it. Who brings a horse to a gunfight? This was precisely what Cowboy had been waiting for this whole damn war."

Cowboy grinned. "Yup." He was a man of few words.

"So, he sees the horse has a saddle, and he decides it's movie time. Cowboy leaps on the saddle and yells to us. 'C'mon boys. Let's end this now.'"

"Yup, it was weird. It was like someone was whispering to me, pushing me to get going and telling me to be fearless. It was a soft and comforting voice."

Jimmy continued the story. "Cowboy takes off right at the German lines hootin' and hollerin'. It was like a scene from a movie. Not one bullet hit him. Bullets were flying past him, and hand grenades were missing him by inches. It was amazing. The enemy troops were so freaked out that they ran off in different directions when Cowboy jumped over their foxholes. Even Gunslinger said that was the craziest sight he had ever seen on a horse. We captured some of their men including a colonel. All he could say was 'Hollywood Cowboys.' After securing the area, we approached the civilians to put them at ease. It was then that I saw these two beautiful girls trembling in fear and holding each other. Cowboy sees them too and rides up."

Cowboy was still holding Noemi's hand and looking deeply into her eyes. "I asked them if they needed a ride. Now, I didn't know her name yet, but Noemi puts the other girl, Bella, behind her to protect her from us. She said, '*Che vuoi?* What you want from us? We not bad girls.' While a little broken, I was amazed at how good her English was. Then again some say mine ain't so good neither. I told her to relax and that we are here to help. We kept on chatting about their health, if any were injured. Most of the civilians couldn't speak any English except the girls."

Jimmy jumps in. "At that point, one of the guys made a comment about wishing that you were here. It was something like 'too bad Butterfly wasn't around; we could use him to talk to these locals.' Hearing the word butterfly perked up Bella and Noemi immediately. I guess you taught them what your name meant in English during one of your visits. Bella stepped toward me. She was filthy and covered with mud, but boy, she was still beautiful."

Jimmy smiled and pulled Bella into a tight embrace against his chest. "She spoke slowly to me as she tapped her chest. 'My name.... English.... butterfly.' My jaw dropped. We were all stunned. I thought that there was no way that this could be true and that this was just an odd coincidence. She stepped closer to me and spoke again, 'Farfalla.... English.... butterfly?' That's when we knew it was them. I trembled and asked a question that would have seemed outrageous five minutes earlier. 'Bella and Noemi?' Both of them were as equally shocked as we were. They looked at each other and then back to me, replying 'Si' in unison. Over the next hour or so, Cowboy and I told them your story. How you were trying to find them. Discovering and burying your mother's body and then what you did to those animals.

A short time later we rode into Rome. Our fears about the enemy blowing it up were never realized. I guess they didn't have the heart to destroy that old, beautiful city. When I got to Rome, I wrote you a couple of letters about finding them. That was nearly three months ago. Anyway, Cowboy and I made sure they were looked after by the Red Cross."

"But how did you get them here?"

"Well, let's just say the General pulled some strings. He couldn't leave the family of a Medal of Honor winner behind."

Rocco was evidently confused, since he hadn't been awarded any medal. "Medal of what?"

Jimmy pulled out a piece of paper from the Secretary of the Army and read its contents out loud. "The President of the United States.... blah blah blah .... conspicuous and meritorious service with disregard for the loss of his life .... blah blah blah .... at Collina Verde. You can read the rest on your own but you're going to the White House to meet FDR. A courier gave this to me yesterday as soon as we landed. Congratulations, you knucklehead."

Rocco didn't say a word. Libby grabbed hold of his hand tightly. It was a clear reminder of the horror of war and that he could have been killed. "Rocco, you must be proud. You're a hero."

"It's nothing. The real heroes aren't coming home." Rocco bowed his head and thought of the boys who weren't coming home and the ones that did come back, but in pieces. All the people in the courtyard followed Rocco's example and bowed their heads in memory of the fathers, sons, brothers, and husbands lost on the battlefields thousands of miles away from home in places like Guadalcanal, Normandy, and Anzio, far-off places Americans had never heard of but would now never forget.

With a heavy sigh, Rocco broke the silence enveloping the courtyard and asked a question to his sisters, the anguish in his voice clearly evident to all. "How did you get away from those men? When I found them sitting around the campfire that night, they had another young woman. I thought you were dead. I'll never forget their laughter, that evil laughter." Libby gave his forearm a comforting rub to remind him he wasn't alone.

Noemi told her brother that it was pure luck. "Germans attack these.... these.... men. No time to do bad things to us. They push us out to be like a shield."

Rocco heaved a sigh of relief. The knowledge that his sisters were not violated was an energizing jolt to his heart, a tonic for a healing soul.

"We run fast, fast, fast, but no shot. We run for long time. We meet other …. what's word…. ref-u-gees. The Holy Mother protect us."

Rocco found it odd that these young women maintained their faith through all the hell thrown at them. He admired these young warriors, for their strength, their perseverance and their hearts. "Jimmy, Cowboy, can you explain how you guys got together? This is just… I don't know what."

Always the storyteller, Jimmy was glad to tell his part. "Well, it started that day we met. It was a beautiful day."

Rocco cut him off. Jimmy was a meandering storyteller. He could start one of his yarns and two hours later the listener would forget what the point of the story was. "No, no. You're not going to tell one of your rambling stories. The sun's going to set in eight hours, and we don't have enough time. Let's get out of here for today. We have three weddings to plan, and I have two sisters to walk down the aisle."

It was a good — no — it was a *great* day to be alive.

Fisherlady

"So that's it? That's how the story ends?" Jo-Jo raised his arms up in the air in faux surrender. "I give up. You're a worse storyteller than Captain and that guy Jimmy. You said this would be a fantastic story of death, guilt, love and redemption, while Captain napped. But the ending wasn't finished."

Michael laughed at the young acolyte, who had progressed quite a great deal during the past year. For some reason, the angel enjoyed playing with his head as much as Jo-Jo enjoyed irritating him, as a teenager does with an adult authority figure. "The story has an ending, but you will see it for yourself. Captain Joao will be waking up soon and the both of you have a place to be. All will be revealed soon. In fact, I hear him waking up now. Jo-Jo, even though you are still a royal pain in the ass, we are proud of you. 'Till the next time we meet." The angel then flew off the deck and into the heavens faster than a rocket. In a few seconds, he was gone.

"Great, he left the ending to the old windbag. I am in Purgatory." Jo-Jo screamed in Michael's direction. "Thanks! Thanks a lot!"

A groggy Captain stumbled onto the deck. "Who were you talking to? God, I must have been asleep for a couple of hours."

An irritated Jo-Jo responded. "It was longer than that, much longer."

Captain peered around the deck. "Oh no. Michael was here, wasn't he?"

"Yup, and he told me a story about our next destination and said that you're going to clue me in on the ending. Why you've been so secretive about this is a mystery to me. You've been telling me about an old friend that you have to visit. You never said why or who it was."

"Michael has a big mouth. I was going to tell you everything."

Jo-Jo waved his arms swiftly back and forth at the idea of Captain telling one of his stories. "No way. If you told the story, we'd only be a quarter of the way through it." Jo-Jo looked up to the sky and yelled. "Thank you, Tiny, for taking pity on me!"

Captain laughed heartily and shook his head. Their bond had developed so strongly over the past year that it closely resembled one of a father and son. "OK, OK, you big baby."

"It looks like we're headed to the Cape. What's down there?"

"Where did Michael end the story?"

"Something about a soldier named Rocco finding out his sisters were still alive and that there were going to be three weddings."

"Did he really end there? Well, no matter, all will be revealed soon."

A frustrated Jo-Jo responded and raised his arms up in the air again in faux surrender. "That's what he said! I swear the two of you have teamed up for the sole purpose of aggravating me. I should call you the PITA crew — because you're both pains in the ass."

"Hey, we're here. Get the boat ready for docking." Captain smiled all the way into the boatyard dock for two clear and distinct reasons.

First, he did enjoy bugging Jo-Jo. Second, he was going to see an old friend.

Jo-Jo yelled over to Captain. "What are you smiling at, you old fart?!" The young wraith clamored around the deck to prepare the Fisherlady for docking. "I swear the guy's gone senile. What else could explain not telling me where we're going or why? I'll just pick up the bumpers throw them over the side and move things around the deck like I always do. Why? Why not? I'm cheap labor, that's why. He's never had it so good. And where are the knuckleheads? Not here. That's where. And now he's got me talking to myself." Crash! The metal gear fell on Jo-Jo's foot eliciting a painful scream. Hopping up and down on one leg while grabbing the other, he looked more like a cartoon character than an avenging specter. "Ouch! That didn't tickle. I can feel you laughing at me. Please stop."

Captain stood and laughed with delight at his irritated friend. He didn't have to say a word. Jo-Jo said it all.

After pulling the Fisherlady into its berth, the two mariners began the short journey to a nearby home. There would be no need to fly. Captain wanted to continue Rocco and Libby's story at a slow and deliberate pace. "C'mon, let's take a walk. I'll fill in all the gaps and details for you."

"That'll be nice. So, why are these people so special to you? From Tiny's account, they seemed to have had an effect on you."

"They did, my friend, they did." A contemplative Captain remained laser-focused on their destination and barely glanced at his walking companion. "Rocco and Libby got married soon after where Michael's story ended. The others got married too. Each union was happy and unique in its own way.

Rocco and Libby had three beautiful girls. Libby remained a nurse all of her life, helping the injured coming back from war, and later she, ran a maternity ward for over thirty years. A tender and fearless warrior -- that's the best way I can describe her."

Jo-Jo was stunned. He immediately noticed that the tone of Captain's voice reflected a certain level of respect and emotional connection. The countenance on his face had a certain softness and peace about it as well. "She really made an impact on you. I've never seen you like this before, except maybe when you talk about your wife and family. Did you love her?"

Captain didn't respond. He continued walking and looking along the road ahead. "The girls were special, just like their mama. They all chose a path in life that reflected their personality. All became doctors. From time to time, I'd look in on them, just to make sure no one was causing them trouble or aggravation, especially when they were teenagers. You know how much of a pain a teenage boy can be." Captain finally smiled.

"Rocco had good days and bad days, but the good days far outnumbered the bad ones. Libby was always there to catch him. She was his rock. Rocco and Jimmy, one of the other guys that Michael should have told you about, opened a construction business that helped a lot of folks improve their lives. They gave back to their community before it became fashionable. Later, they realized their dream and opened a beach bar, calling it 2 Brothers on the Beach. It was paradise.

Jimmy and Bella, Rocco's sister, had a happy life with three boys with big, strong bodies and even bigger hearts. You know about the guy named Cowboy?"

"Yes."

"Well, he became famous throughout all of New England as Cowboy Cody on local TV. For many years, he taught children all about horse riding and the thrill of being a modern-day cowboy. Noemi was his co-star along with their three boys. Noemi was a pistol of a lady.

She was his wife in real life and played his wife on TV. It was a corny show, but I loved it."

The two travelers arrived at the front of the house which was their apparent destination. "Jo-Jo, we're here."

Jo-Jo stood on the sidewalk inspecting the outside of the house, trying to get a clue, or any small indication for that matter, why they were there. "What's going on? Whose house is this?"

Captain, hands on his hips, let out an extended sigh. "This is Libby's house. She's ready to move on."

Standing on the sidewalk in front of the house next to Captain, Jo-Jo waited to speak as he saw the deep emotional impact this visit had on his friend. "Libby? She must be over 100 years old." Jo-Jo spoke with a tone of admiration about the person he was about to meet. "She's a tough old girl, huh."

"Yes, she is. Rocco passed about fifteen years ago. It's now her time to join him. Let's go in 'shadowed' for everyone but Libby." Captain used the word 'shadowed' to describe a wraith's invisibility powers.

There was no need to use their other powers. The two wraiths made their way through the front door that had been left open to catch a cool sea breeze. Passing through the house, they appreciated the multitude of hanging pictures that showed a happy and beautiful family. One would never have known of the trauma that Rocco and his sisters had endured. Jo-Jo stopped for a moment and admired the warmth of a strong family. He pointed at several pictures in particular. "Look at them. So happy. There's no hint of tragedy. These ones must be Jimmy and Bella. Cowboy and Noemi must be in this picture." The young wraith reflected on his family and how much he missed them.

Captain saw an opening to inject some humor back at his acolyte. "What gave it away, Einstein? The cowboy hats?"

"Alright, you got me. That shot was a layup. Laugh it up, ancient mariner."

"Ohh, poor baby." Captain enjoyed a good laugh at Jo-Jo's expense, but his attention quickly turned to the destination of their journey. "Hey, let's go. She's close to the end."

In a bedroom in the rear of the house, Libby lay in bed surrounded by three generations of the Farfalla clan, children, grandchildren, great-grandchildren, nephews, nieces, spouses and more.

Jo-Jo commented on the number of people in the room. "Wow, look at how many people are here. She really had an impact on people's lives, didn't she?"

"Yes, she did." Captain walked over to someone standing at the foot of the bed.

"Captain, who is that person at the foot of the bed? He's not human."

"That's Michael's brother. Hello, Raphael, it's been a long time."

The angel maintained his focus on Libby and didn't turn his head to greet him. "Joao, I'm glad you could come today. And I see you brought your new friend. Jo-Jo, or do you prefer Isaac, it's nice to finally meet you. By the way, I like your nickname for my brother; Tiny is perfect."

"Hi, it's nice to meet you. Captain has told me a little about you. Are you here to take her?"

"Yes, I am." Raphael continued to maintain his focus on the woman he was to escort.

Suddenly, Libby raised her head slightly. "Dr. Galen? Joe? Is that you?"

The mourning family were puzzled and looked around the room to see to whom she was speaking. They assumed she was close to the end, believing their matriarch was now hallucinating. Seeing her like this made their sobs grow louder and sadder.

Raphael leaned forward and over the foot of the bed. "No, Libby. My name is Raphael and I'm here to take you onward. You have led a remarkable life. It's time to come home."

"Home?"

Captain leaned forward as well. "We've been watching over you for a long time. I've never forgotten our time together at Camp Edwards. You were and have always been an angel on Earth. I needed to be here to say goodbye to you, because your spirit stirred something inside of me that I thought was dead and gone. You've impacted people's lives more than I could ever accurately describe."

Libby struggled to speak. "I don't understand. Dead and gone? Both of you haven't aged a day in eighty years."

Captain and Raphael looked at this once vibrant individual who was now about to take another step in her existence. The angel nodded to Captain. "I'll take it from here." Raphael spoke in a soft and reverent tone. "Libby, we are from Heaven. Father would very much like to meet you, child. And let's not forget someone else who's been waiting patiently." The angel beckoned a soul standing in the corner of the room to come over.

A startled Libby smiled. "Rocco, is that you? *Caro*, my love."

Rocco stepped forward and held his hands out to call for Libby to join him.

Libby smiled at her family gathered in the room. "I have to go. I love you all." These were her last words as she took hold of her beloved's hands, and with one last gasp, she passed.

The sobs from the crowd of mourners became more audible. Her eldest daughter whispered what they all had on their minds but couldn't say. "Mama, it's time to be with Dad. Heaven is shining a lot brighter today."

No matter how old she was, or how full of a life she had led, the loss still hurt. Libby and Rocco stared lovingly into each other's eyes and walked to the bedroom door with Raphael escorting the loving couple. Their appearance was like that of their wedding day: young, beautiful and happy.

Captain and Jo-Jo watched Raphael and the two souls depart into a brilliant white light. Soon thereafter, the two wraiths were walking back to the Fisherlady. "Captain, thanks for sharing that moment with me, but can you tell me how you felt about her? Did you love her?"

"Not the way you think."

"Well, that's good because that would have been really creepy, you old goat."

Exasperated, Captain shook his head. "What's wrong with you?! Are you ever going to grow up?!"

Jo-Jo responded in a matter-of-fact manner that personified the youth of the day. "Nope, and you're stuck with me, old man."

Captain rubbed his forehead and begrudgingly accepted the truth of Jo-Jo's statement. "Greaaaaat. Let's grab a bite. I'm starving."

"Sure, there must be a rabbit food store around here. I mean now that you're a vegan, or is it that you're a *began* because you're trying to be one? I get confused where you are, mentally speaking. It's still morning, and a nice big breakfast will hit the spot. I would love some steak and eggs. Oh yeah."

"You're such a wise ass. I know a place that should have enough food to stuff your face. Would that be acceptable to your Highness?"

Jo-Jo clapped his hands together and rubbed them back and forth to express his profound pleasure at the prospect of a real breakfast.

"Finally, a real meal today. I need to pinch myself to make sure I'm not dreaming."

"Such a wise ass. I need an aspirin."

The Journey Continues

Acknowledgments

To all my friends and family who continue to support my love of writing.

A graduate of Boston College and Suffolk University, writing a novel has been a personal goal my entire life. The recent pandemic provided me an opportunity to unplug my brain from working in the volatile and high-pressure world of financial services for the past 30 years and to foster the latent creative side of my being. Additionally, I have shown a commitment to my community and its youth for most of my life. A one-time board member of a local Boys & Girls Club and a former President/coach of a youth softball league, I have come to appreciate the impact an individual can have on others. My life is joyfully shared with my wife Melissa, daughter Olivia and her husband Jimmy, and our precious dogs Tres and Rocco. Recently, we welcomed our beautiful granddaughter Siena into the world.